THE LOST ENDEAVOUR

GEORGINA MAKALANI

This is a work of fiction. Names, characters, events and incidents are the products of the author's imagination. Any resemblance to actual persons, living or dead, or actual events is purely coincidental.

ISBN: 978-0-6450346-2-2

Also by Georgina Makalani

The Last Dragon Skin Chronicles:
The Empty Crown
The Lost Endeavour
Shadows Awaken

The Magics of Rei-Een:
The Hidden Princess
Hidden Promises
The Hidden Phoenix

The Raven Crown Series:
Raven's Dawn
The Caged Raven
Raven's Edge

The Legend of Iski Flare (Novella series):
The Legend Begins
Red Wolves
The Riddle of Daralis
The Last Child
The Tree Maiden
Reflections
The Beast
Circus of Wonders

Other Stories:
The Mark of Oldra
The Heart of Oldra

Short Stories:
Stuffed Frogs and Spinning Teacups
Searcher
The Silence (in Glimpses)

1

Salima stood by the bars and looked over the witch lying in the small cell. The solid ice walls kept the entire space freezing, and the continuous bars gave no indication of a way in. The woman lay too still, her dark hair covering her face, her black dress shining silver with frost; and her hands were blue. Salima glanced around the space behind her, but there was no one else. Similar cage-like cells backed against the icy wall, with the same thick steel bars as the one the witch was locked in that ran from ceiling to floor and gave no hint of an opening.

She squinted into the too-bright light, failing to find its source. It was likely that the mage had conjured something to create it, as he had with the cells. It was his private domain, after all, and she hadn't seen any torches. She wondered if they might not survive in the freezing temperature.

The witch murmured something as she curled tighter in on herself, her body shivering. Although she didn't understand why or how, Salima knew she was the only one who could help this woman. Papa would kill her himself, if he knew where she was or that she had even managed to find such a place.

Finding Ed was more important than her safety. Whether she was a witch or a mage or something else entirely, this woman was the only one who had stood up for him. She had demanded, in front of everyone of importance in the kingdom, that the regent step down and allow Ed to rule.

He was a man, she had asserted, not a boy. Salima wondered, as she tried to find a way through the bars, if Ed would be forever known as the boy king whether he made it back to the capital or not. She blew out a long breath and rubbed her hands together. She could sense the cold, and yet she couldn't feel it as keenly as the witch appeared to. She leaned in closer, trying to see if there was any hint the woman still lived.

"I can't just refer to you as a witch," she whispered. "Ana," she called softly, but the woman didn't react. Salima glanced around again, half expecting a guard to appear at any moment. "Ana," she called more loudly, and the woman half opened her eyes. "Thank the gods," Salima murmured, squatting down and placing her hand on a bar to steady herself. "Are you alive?"

A smile split Ana's face, and her lip, and she winced. "Dragon," she murmured.

"What? No. I've come to get you out."

"They will find you," she wheezed, still unmoving.

"I could find someone to help. Papa won't let anyone hurt me."

Ana opened amazing green eyes that held Salima captive. "He doesn't know you are here," she croaked. She tried to push herself up from the floor, but her arm failed and she slipped back with a sharp exhale.

"Not exactly," Salima admitted. "But after what you said about Ed, he will help. I'm sure."

"Get me out then, little princess." Ana stared at her as though willing her to do it—or was she daring her?

"Is now the time to be smart?" Salima asked. "And I hoped you could get yourself out," she added weakly.

Ana's eyes fluttered closed. Every breath fogged before her, although Salima noted that they were small, shallow breaths. She blew out herself and felt a queasy uneasiness when her own breath didn't do the same.

Salima was sure that Ana was going to die, and if she didn't find some way to get her out, she was going to watch it happen. She ran her hands over the cold steel, but it gave no hint at an opening. "There is no way I can get you out," she murmured, desperation taking over as the woman before her curled in on herself again and her eyes remained closed.

"Fire," Ana breathed, the fog carrying the barely audible words up to Salima. "Use your fire."

Salima looked around her. *What fire?* There wasn't even a torch, despite the bright light. Was there a different form of fire she wasn't aware of?

"There isn't any," she hissed, running her hands over more of the bars, trying to feel for anything that would indicate an opening. There had to be a mechanism or the like to help her. There must be a way for soldiers to get prisoners in and out of these cells.

"You are f..." Ana's voice trailed off, and the shivering stopped.

Salima squatted down again, desperation fogging her thoughts. There was no way in. The witch, the one with the power, was slipping away. Salima didn't want to think too much, hoping she had only lost consciousness. Ana couldn't be dead. She was the only one who could help her reach Ed.

"I am what?" Salima asked, her hands tight around the bar. "Ana? What do you think I can do?"

A lone tear rolled down her cheek, and she was surprised when it didn't freeze on her skin. It dropped onto the icy flagstones and sizzled. A small puff of steam rose from the ground.

"I am fire," Salima whispered. She looked at the woman in the cage, motionless and quiet, curled on the ice before her. She had never thought she would need anyone other than her father, but she needed this woman to survive. "I am fire," she said more confidently, although the voice that flowed from her seemed unknown. The bars in her hands not only warmed, but moved.

She fell back from the cage in surprise, pulling the soft metal with her, and then she pushed it away from her as she moved to her knees. It was a small opening, but it was enough for her to crawl through and tug the woman towards her. She was heavier than she appeared. Salima grunted as she jostled over Ana's too-still body to get a better hold and hooked her hands under the woman's arms.

She pulled again, desperation running through her veins and causing her heart to race. Someone would find them; someone would know she had saved Ana. She tugged again, and then they were sitting outside the cell. She pulled Ana into her arms, the woman breathing out slowly before snuggling further into Salima's body. Salima looked up from Ana to the bars and shivered.

Reluctantly, she lay Ana down and crawled back to the bars she had twisted. She put her hands on them and willed them back into position. Nothing happened. "Come on," she grunted, pushing them harder. She sat back, wondering if she had really moved them or if Ana had somehow managed to help her. She closed her eyes, put her hands back on the still-warm metal and blew out a soft breath. "I am fire," she whispered, imagining herself as a ball of fire. She felt it burn through her, warming the world around her, and the bars slipped back into position.

As she opened her eyes, the frosty world around her melted. Water ran in small rivulets down the walls, and a mist of steam rose from the floor. She turned back to Ana, who sat behind her, rubbing her hands together and then wrapping her arms around herself.

"I think we should leave now," Salima said.

Ana nodded. Salima helped her to her feet and supported her weight as they headed for the door.

"Where are we?" Ana wheezed.

"Below the castle," Salima said, struggling with the weight of the woman. She appeared so slender, but she was far heavier and harder to manoeuvre than Salima had expected. The stairwell was pitch black compared to the bright room they had left behind. The steps were narrow and slippery.

"Can you help?" Ana asked.

"I am helping," Salima snapped, instantly regretting her outburst as her voice bounced off the walls above them. They both staggered. Ana slipped from her hold and landed heavily on the stone. "Sorry," Salima murmured, trying to find a purchase to lift Ana up again without groping her.

"You could dry this out."

"I don't know…"

"I saw…"

"You were unconscious and unable to see anything," Salima said curtly, cutting off Ana's words. Silence followed as Ana allowed Salima to pull her to her feet.

She had taken too long to get Ana out. She had only found the entrance by accident. She had followed the regent around for too long, trying to discover what he might know of Ed, when he had entered an area of the castle no king or regent would go. And then she had found the secret door.

Salima wasn't sure if they would come back sometime soon. She had waited in the shadows as he had disappeared inside and then returned not long after followed by the mage. She had watched the door for hours, well into the night, to ensure there were no guards and that they wouldn't return.

She had taken too long, she thought as she worked her way too slowly up the narrow steps. Ana had been lying on the floor in the cold, for how long she didn't know. When Salima had reached her, there was no one around, but that didn't mean no one would come.

She pushed on the door, and they were finally in the dimly lit cellar. She took a deep breath and lowered Ana to the floor. They might have made it out of the cells unseen, but there was nothing but open courtyard beyond. It might have been the middle of the night, but there was still the risk of being discovered.

"I should go for help," Salima said.

Ana grabbed her hand. "Don't leave me."

"Only going a little way to find…" She had no idea where she was going, or who would help.

"Forest," Ana whispered, leaning her head back against the wall.

"I'm Salima Forest," she said in return. "Oh no, Papa won't like this," she added quickly.

Ana hugged her arms around herself. The shivering continued, and Salima was sure she could hear her teeth chatter.

"Maybe," she murmured, awkwardly lifting Ana back to her feet. She tried not to grunt as she made her way through the cellar, trying not to fall over any of the boxes while listening carefully in case anyone was coming.

At the edge of the courtyard, she leaned into the shadows. She had snuck out often enough to know it was easy to make it through the courtyard without entering the torchlight, but doing so while holding up this woman was a different matter. She closed her eyes, listening for soldiers, and then heaved Ana forward and started for the practice halls. She only hoped they were unlocked. Papa never locked them of a day, but she had never tried to enter in the middle of the night.

2

Ed moved cautiously through the forest, searching between the dimly lit trees ahead of him. The thick canopy overhead hid the sky above and kept them in a state of perpetual twilight. He only knew it was night when it grew darker. Otherwise, he had no idea how long they had been walking.

Ende flinched at his side. Ed understood how eager the man was to be out of the trees. He had tried several times to lead them towards where he was sure they were close to the edges of the Near Forest. Each time something pushed them closer to its centre. A couple of times he had rolled his shoulders and appeared to brace for a leap, but no matter how big he became, Ed doubted he would be able to make it through the canopy.

Ed sighed, tt was starting to get darker, and although they followed someone else's path, he would soon suggest they stop for the night. He could hear Phillip Poales wheezing a little further back. The long days of walking had been harder on the older man. But they couldn't slow. Captain Drayton Sterling had kept pace with Phillip, and several times when Ed had looked back, he'd thought Dray held the man upright or was readying to carry him if necessary. Ed knew the soldier was just as determined to reach the capital and find Ana as he was.

He tried not to groan as Belle's grip tightened. It dragged at him. She too was tiring from the journey. She would never admit it, and she never let him go. Not since that first morning when she had woken to find the bodies hanging from the trees around them. As beautiful and as bright as she was, he was struggling with her weight dragging on him and slowing him down.

"We'll stop," he said, unable to carry the weight of the group any further. Not that they were a burden. But his focus was elsewhere.

He was trying to make it through the Near Forest with a dragon, a soldier, a farmer and his daughter, and a very strong feeling that the inhabitants of the forest didn't want him going anywhere but where they wanted him to go.

"Do you think they will allow us through?" he wondered aloud as the group started to unroll blankets and prepare the fire.

"Who knows what the Near Folk want," Ende murmured, starting the fire with ease.

Ed wondered just how he did that, and how Phillip and Belle hadn't worked out what he was. Ed had only been told because Ana and Dray had thought he should know just who it was he had travelled all that way to find. And his mother had known. He watched the old man poke more branches into the flames, sighing with relief as he held his hands to the heat.

His bent body, tattered clothes and long grey beard gave him the appearance of a hermit from the mountains. Before he had found Ana and Dray on one side of the Edge Mountains and Ed on the other, it appeared that was just how he had lived. But at some stage in his past, he had been Ed's mother's dearest friend.

The old dragon glanced at Ed as he continued to stare, but his perfect teeth seemed out of place when he smiled. He wasn't what he appeared to be; Ed knew that. He could become the dragon at any time. Which form had his mother known? Ed had almost asked the old man several times.

Dray was at his side, and Ed struggled to drag his mind to the present and focus on what the soldier was saying. "Sorry," he murmured, "say that again."

"I'd like to look for rabbit or deer."

Ed looked around. They had seen very little in the way of animals during their travels through the forest, but the idea that the Near Folk shadowed their movements made him more nervous than the lack of animals. He shook his head. The large man groaned and then bowed his head.

"I understand," Ed said. "I could do with something other than dry meat and biscuit myself, but we don't know what is out there." He held up his hand before the man could retort. "I know you can look after yourself, and you have done a wonderful job of keeping us all safe, but I can't risk you."

Dray bowed his head again and moved to the fire and Ende. Ed wondered for a moment if they would gang up and overrule him, but they continued in quiet conversation, making no move to run through the trees.

"Your Majesty." Belle patted the blanket beside her, some dried meat and biscuits spread out before her. "Would you like something to eat?"

"Ed," he murmured, still watching the others.

"I am not…"

Ed rounded on her. "Don't say that you are not comfortable to call me by name," he snapped. "You are comfortable enough to hold my hand or arm or shirt all day long." He instantly regretted it. Her face creased, and she looked down silently at the food before her, subtly trying to wipe the backs of her fingers over her cheek.

Ed looked up at the faces staring at him. He turned and walked into the trees, leaving them behind. If they called after him, he didn't hear it.

It was darker beyond the reach of the fire, and the trees closed in on him as he pressed forward. Ed was unsure why he couldn't face the others and frustrated with himself that he had hurt Belle's feelings. She had volunteered to join them, and she wanted to find Ana as much as he did. Sometimes she even smiled when she looked at him. In some ways, he missed the sharp-tongued girl he had first met in this very forest. She had helped him, he thought, putting his hand to his shoulder. Only not as well as Ana had.

He sighed, unsure where he was in relation to the others. He looked behind him, but there was no hint of the light of the fire. He stopped for a moment, wondering if the forest was protecting them from him, or if it was separating them.

He sat down with his back to a tree and shivered in the cool night air. Nothing moved except the leaves in the wind; nothing appeared to live out here. He wondered if they would wander aimlessly through these trees forever, hoping they were close to freedom, close to finding a way to Ana.

"Is this about her?" he asked the night air. "Do you not want us to find Ana?"

Silence answered.

"Do you think I can't be King?"

"What do you think?" the wind whispered back, and he shot to his feet. He looked around, but there was no sign of anyone.

"I don't know," he answered honestly, although he was sure his voice shook.

"Is it not what you were meant to be?"

"I suppose," he admitted, still unsure as to what he wanted or who had spoken. "I want to help Ana."

"By becoming King?"

He shook his head.

Icy fingers slipped across his cheek. He still couldn't see anyone. Nothing to indicate that there was anyone there. He had no idea what the Near Folk looked like or what they could do.

"What do you want from me?" he asked the darkness.

The sensation disappeared, and the wind died down in the leaves above him.

A small orange light glowed in the distance like a candle's flame. Ed took a step forward as it lit up the space around it. It rose into the air, moved closer and then darted away between some trees. Ed raced after it, tripping over fallen branches and raised roots. He rested his hand against a tree, and the light reappeared, closer now. Then it circled a tree, flickered and darted away again.

Ed gave chase, unsure what it might be and where it would lead him. Then he was standing in a small clearing, a blazing fire and his companions staring at him.

"Are you alright?" Belle stepped forward, concern clear on her face.

He nodded once and gave her a small smile. "Are you?"

She smiled and bowed her head.

"I'm sorry," he said, then looked around the group. "To all of you. I haven't been very patient."

"What did you find?" Ende asked, not moving from the flames.

"I don't know. Nothing, something, the wind."

"You found your way back to us," Dray said.

"I think I was led."

"What do they want from us?" Belle asked, her voice hushed as though they could hear her. Ed wondered just what they did know.

He shook his head, sat down on the blanket and picked up a biscuit.

The group watched him, and he tried not to focus on their stares. Even Belle didn't sit back beside him.

"What do you want from them?" Ende asked.

Ed stopped mid-chew and looked up at him. He gulped down the biscuit, thumping at his chest as it stuck in his throat. "What could I want from the Near Folk?" he asked.

"What did you want from me?" The flames of the blazing fire reflected in his dark eyes.

"My mother told me to come to you."

"When? She has been gone a long time, and you have lived in your uncle's shadow for almost as long. Why did you come to find me?"

Ed sucked in a deep breath and shrugged. He had no idea. It seemed to make sense at the time, but he wasn't sure what he could gain. "A place to hide," he murmured.

"Really?" Belle asked. He expected disappointment when he looked into her face, but it was something else. Pity, maybe.

"My mother told me in her dying breath that if it all got too hard then I was to find her dearest friend."

He thought Ende might have wiped at a tear, but the movement was quick. And even if he cried for another, the man surely would never allow them to see it.

"It got too hard," Ed admitted. "My uncle was never going to let me out of that room. I had a routine, a simple life, and I suppose I could have survived much longer with it. But there was nothing of substance, only classes and more classes, reading and my little room. The sword master was the only one who seemed to show any interest in whether I could actually be what I was thought to be." He looked back at the biscuit in his hand and hoped his voice hadn't cracked. "I don't know that I wanted to be King. That was what I was supposed to be learning to be, but I knew no one around me ever expected me to actually use the skills they were teaching. No one thought I would sit on the throne. They were probably right. My uncle knew more of what was needed, and the kingdom survives. I just needed to be somewhere else, be someone else. And I thought my mother's friend would be the person to help do that. She made it sound as though you would help if I needed it."

He looked up then, but Ende had turned back to the flames. Belle rested her hand on his arm. More pity.

"I want to help Ana," he said firmly. "I don't have to be King to do that."

Belle's hand tightened around his arm. "Salima?" she asked softly.

He shook his head. Salima was too hard to explain. She had

been raised so differently. "It is better she remains hidden," he said. "She mourns a different mother, knows a different father. How could I explain to her who she really is? And the knowledge would only put her in more danger."

"What if she wasn't…?" Ende asked, his voice barely audible over the sound of the crackling fire.

Ed looked up at him, his hands clenched at his sides. Ende looked uncomfortable, uncertain, and it was unnerving as he hadn't seen him that way before.

"Nobody knows who she is," Ed repeated. "She is safer that way."

Ende nodded once, and Belle's hand gripped tighter around Ed's arm again as she let out a small squeak of surprise. He looked from her to the direction she was focused.

A tall, broad man with a bare chest, tanned skin, flowing dark hair and a very long spear stood in the shadows of the trees. Ed clambered to his feet. The rest of the group was silent, although Ed noted that Dray's hand rested on his sword.

The man's focus was on Ed, and as Ed stood, the man dropped to a knee. His head bowed forward, and the movement of his hair revealed strange pointed ears.

"It is ok," Ed whispered to Belle.

"Your Majesty," the man said, his voice both deep and light at the same time, like the wind.

3

Ana watched the sword master pace back and forth as she hugged her arms tighter around herself and tried not to shiver. She was so cold, as though it had seeped into her bones, and no matter what she tried, she couldn't warm. She glanced at the girl sitting on the box to her side, who had so far appeared as warm as Ende. She longed to snuggle with the girl.

The sword master had stopped. As she looked at him, he glared at her. His eyes flicked to the girl and then back. Ana sighed. Rubbed her numb fingers together and wondered if the ache inside her would ever stop.

"This is dangerous," he growled, pacing again in the small storeroom. Ana wasn't sure where they were, only that they were somewhere in the castle. The girl had dragged her out into the courtyard, and then just as quickly they'd been inside again. Although they had entered a large space, Salima had pulled her forward into the smaller room. "What possessed you to think this was a good idea?"

"I couldn't leave her there," she whispered.

Ana was sure they'd had this conversation over and over since he had found them huddled in the dark. And she was very sure he blamed Ana for putting his daughter in such a position.

"I…"

"I don't want to hear it," he snapped, cutting Ana off.

She nodded, pulled her legs in closer, dropped her chin to her knees and closed her eyes. The shivering took over again at the silenced conversation, and she resented her dress. For such fine material, it had remained damp for so long.

"She'll die," Salima insisted.

"Your father is right," Ana murmured, her eyes still closed. The cold wall at her back pushed against her body's effort to try and warm itself. "He will hunt me out. Tell him you found me." She looked up at the sword master. "You might be rewarded."

"He'll never believe you got out on your own."

"I'm a witch," Ana murmured. Maybe if she rested, her body would have time to heal.

"Don't sleep," the girl snapped. She dropped beside Ana, who leaned into the heat of her. All she wanted was those warm arms wrapped around her, but instead the girl took her by the shoulders and shook her awake.

She reluctantly opened her eyes. "Let me go," she murmured.

"You are our only link to Ed," Salima said, the tears flowing. "You have to help us get him back."

"Well I'm glad you didn't risk yourself for me," Ana said, hurt suddenly that the girl had only saved her for Ed. "He's safer without me." She pulled back from the girl's hold and used the wall to slowly rise to her feet. The shaking became more uncontrollable, and she stumbled.

Despite his obvious mistrust of her and anger at her putting his daughter at risk, the sword master caught her easily. Instead of pushing her away, as she expected, he pulled her closer, his arms tight around her. "Find a blanket," he said.

"I'm so tired," Ana admitted, leaning into him. He wasn't nearly as warm as the little dragon, but he was far more comfortable than the wall.

"You're sick," he said, wrapping an arm around her shoulders and then guiding her back to the floor.

"I'm just cold," she said. "It was so cold."

At his silence, she looked up, and he shook his head slowly. "Damn him," he muttered. "We can't keep you here."

"I know this isn't safe for you." Ana wanted to climb back to her feet, but he held up a hand. She was grateful, as she didn't think she had the strength to stand again.

"There are many parts of this castle no one visits; we just have to get you there. And I fear if we wait until dark, it might be too late."

The door squealed open, letting in far more light than Ana expected. Was it daytime already? A slender figure was silhouetted in the doorway.

"Master?" a young man's voice called tentatively.

"I'm just trying to find something," the sword master said, resting his hand on Ana's shoulder. "I'll be right out."

He reached past Ana and lifted a long pole away from the wall. "Where is the other one?" he muttered.

"Is he ready for those?" Salima asked.

Ana could sense the glare, although she couldn't see it. But his voice was soft when he answered her. "I need some excuse. And you can't be seen coming and going all day. Go and find somewhere we can move her to. I don't like that fever," he murmured, as though Ana weren't sitting close enough to hear every word. "Find Cleric Peck."

"Yes, Papa," Salima answered quickly.

"Don't return until my students are gone."

The door opened again, and Ana squinted into the light.

"I'm sorry, Father," Salima said as they left the storeroom. "I was sure I put them where you told me to."

"It isn't that big a space to lose long sticks in," he said, as though the conversation had been started in the room before they'd left it. Ana wondered what else these two managed to hide from those around them.

And then it was dark, and she wondered if they would ever come back. Master Forest was correct; it was too dangerous for them if she was found. She pulled the blanket around herself and lay down on the wooden floor. It was cool, but not as cold as the cell had been. She closed her eyes as she slowly started to feel like she wasn't freezing to death.

A loud clack startled her, swiftly followed by another and then a yelp. She sat up, then tried to shuffle as silently as she could behind the box. It would be out of the immediate view of the doorway if someone were to open it and look in.

"Come now," Master Forest tutted. "You can do better than that."

"I don't think we have tried this before, Master," the young man returned, his voice hesitant.

Ana relaxed a little, and the noise began anew. She blew out a long breath, shivered again and pulled the blanket tight around her. Pulling her legs in close, she curled into a ball. The continuous noise on the other side of the door was somewhat comforting, and the rhythmic noise soon lulled her to sleep.

Salima stood in the small room for too long, watching the sun move slowly towards the horizon. She flexed her hand, wondering just how she had managed to pull those bars apart and how Ana had known she had such fire within her. If Ana had sensed it, could someone else sense it also? Like the mage. The idea made her shiver. Someone walked past the door, their loud heels on the wooden floorboards making her jump. But they didn't slow or pause by the door, and she squeezed her hand around the key.

She was in one of the many vacant rooms near the royal suite. It was as though the regent didn't want anyone close. Salima thought it was because he feared they might discover what he was. Or try to oust him. Her father had told stories from years ago of many visitors to the capital and the castle itself, of how Ed's parents had entertained and held meetings. The lords had even visited, but no more. Now the spacious visitor rooms stood empty—until the tribute of women arrived, and then Salima thought they wouldn't take up too much room.

The large four-poster bed stood out from one wall. Thick curtains, dusty from years of neglect, were tied close to the posts. Salima wondered if this was ideal for Ana. She looked back at the fireplace stacked with kindling, firewood piled nearby as though waiting for a guest who had never arrived. Two comfortable chairs sat before it. At least she knew the wood would be dry.

A washstand contained a basin and jug, but no water. She hoped she was the only one with the key as she moved back to the door and listened. In all the time she had been in the room, she had only heard a couple people move by. The rooms on either side were empty as well, which meant they shouldn't be heard. The chimneys all seemed to come together somewhere above her, so lighting the fire shouldn't give them away.

As she moved back to the wood, it almost called for her to push her flames on it. She took a step back, unsure why she hadn't sensed such a thing before. Was she really something made of fire, or had Ana allowed her to think so as she found her own way out? Thinking back to the woman in the cell, she doubted it.

No matter how she looked at it or felt about her own skills, the room needed to be warm for Ana. She looked about for something to start it. The room was empty of anything useful, and in the end she squatted before it and glared at the wood, daring it to start. After a moment she started to laugh. She couldn't play with a fire all afternoon; she needed to find the cleric.

She reached her hand towards the fireplace, and a spark flashed between her outstretched fingers and the wood. It not only caught, but it blazed to life. She sat back, bewildered by what had happened. If she really did have fire, she hoped Ana had a way to help her use it. As the kindling crackled, she found her feet and fed a couple logs into the flames. Without waiting to be sure they caught, she headed out into the hallway and locked the door behind her.

Cleric Peck was just where she hoped he would be, in the

library. Usually around dusk he moved into the quiet space to research something or other, and she had found him there before. Otherwise he would still have been working in the main workroom the clerics shared, where she didn't want to be seen calling for him.

He glanced up from the pages as she approached, concern creasing his brow. She usually raced for him when any of her father's students injured themselves or each other. She bowed her head and cleared her throat.

"I wonder if I could interrupt your study?" she asked quietly.

"Another one?" he asked.

She paused too long before nodding, and although he closed the book he'd been reading, he stared at her unmoving. Salima chewed on her lip. She could only hope her father was right and this man could be trusted with Ana.

"We need your help," she said, trying her best to plead with her eyes and not sound too desperate in case there was someone around.

He pushed up from the table, his old frame creaking as he did so, although she wondered if it was the chair. She had seen him move fast enough when it was needed. She wondered about the old man sometimes, that he might be more loyal to the laws of the kingdom than them if something were to go wrong. But her father would shake his head when she suggested it. Cleric Gilroy Peck had been there when Queen Ter-essa died, and her father assured her he looked after the crown first.

She only hoped that the witch, a friend of Ed's, would be classed as close enough to the crown to warrant saving. They walked in silence towards the practice halls. With the sky darkening above them, a servant moved slowly around the courtyard lighting the torches as they moved through it. Salima thought of Ana again, and how she had first seen her in that courtyard talking with Papa, how she had dragged Salima across the kingdom with a tight grip on her arm.

They entered the halls just as the last student left. He slowed to bow to the cleric, but he didn't acknowledge Salima at all. Generally, she didn't mind, but in the shadow of Ana, the beautiful witch and the woman who had Ed's attention, she felt somewhat disappointed.

Her father nodded as they entered the hall, and she dropped the bolt across the door. Cleric Peck turned to look at it and then at her before he turned back to Papa.

"What has happened?" he asked seriously. "Is it the king?"

"No," Papa said, and although he stood straight, Salima could sense the uncertainty. "A friend of his needs our help, so that she can help him."

"The witch," the old man said. Salima tried to find something in his voice to indicate what the man might think of her.

Papa cleared his throat. "She is gifted, but I don't think she is a witch."

"A mage?" Salima asked.

"She is Mariela's daughter."

The cleric stepped forward. "Truly?"

Papa nodded, already on his way to the storeroom. He opened the door and gestured inside. "If she has survived the day, we will need your help."

The old man strode quickly towards the door, but Salima was unable to move. What if Ana had died? How would they find Ed?

4

Dray thought it had been a very bad idea to follow the strange man though the forest. Although the young king was sure it was safe, Dray got the idea that Ende was just as conflicted as he was. In fact, the dragon appeared even more uncomfortable the deeper into the forest they travelled.

The world Dray now found himself in was very different from what he had expected. Although to be honest, he wasn't sure what that might be. He had watched in horror as the king had disappeared before him through the trees. Yet as he drew his sword, the king had reappeared almost as quickly, looking like a man who had been running.

Now they travelled as a group between two trees, no different from any other trees, and yet Dray felt something cold across his skin. A very different world opened up before them. Green-grey buildings that would have disappeared into the trees lined a worn street. It was too wide to be a path, and the trees were suspiciously absent. The large village sat in a clearing that appeared to have been carved into the forest. Surely someone would have mentioned such a place.

"The Seat…" he started to ask. Although he wasn't quite sure what he was asking.

"Not the Seat," the man said, barely glancing over his shoulder at Dray. The girl shivered, then clenched and unclenched her hands. She had been holding on to the king for so long she didn't appear to know what to do now that she wasn't. Dray was sure the king himself was relieved of the burden.

Ende continued to stare at the back of the man they followed. Although the sky had opened up around them, Dray was starting to feel as hemmed in as Ende appeared to be. As they moved along the street, more men appeared in doorways and between buildings. They were similarly dressed, and he didn't notice any weapons. Small faces, children, leaned back from the windows. He was sure they wanted to look, but parents might not want them too close.

At the end of the road, the path branched into two large forks. The building nestled in the middle was larger than any of the others they had passed. It was the same green-grey colour, yet somehow brighter. The roof was thatched with grass, and he glanced behind him at the other homes, realising they were similar. They didn't appear to be made from the trees, despite their colour.

He looked back and the door opened. The man leading them walked straight in, and Ed followed without hesitation. Ende opted to wait outside, and Dray ushered Belle and Phillip after the king before he followed them himself, giving Ende a nod as he passed him.

The room itself was dark. It took a moment for Dray to adjust to the light, and as he did it grew lighter and lighter. Small stars lit up the ceiling above them, and Belle let out a murmur of wonder.

"Welcome," a deep voice rumbled, and Dray sensed the wind through the leaves at the same time, as though the forest itself was talking to him. He looked at the older man seated at the end of a long table, wondering if he had been there the whole time. Similar in build and features to the man who had led them in, his silver hair was the only difference. He smiled at Dray as though he agreed with his idea of the forest talking to them.

The man indicated the table, and the king sat to one side. Belle moved quickly to sit beside him. Her father looked about before sitting opposite them. Dray remained at the end of the table, standing.

"You have sought our help."

The king nodded to Dray, and he sat by Phillip on the long bench, his hand resting on the solid wood of the table. The other rested on his sword.

"That was you I heard in the forest," the king said quickly.

"It was me," the man said, not taking his eyes from the king, "and it was all of us."

Belle glared, but the older man laughed, the soft sound making the stars twinkle brighter. Dray's hand closed around the handle of his sword.

"What do you want with the king?" Dray asked.

The man studied him for a time before he spoke. "What do you want with the king, Captain?"

Dray waited.

"You went north with one man, and now south with another."

"We are going to find Ana," the king said by way of explanation. It sounded flimsy, unrealistic to Dray's ears. He wondered what these forest men really thought of them.

The older man turned back to the king. "That is not all you seek, boy." It wasn't a question.

"He is not a boy," Belle said quickly, the anger clear in her voice. "He is the king."

"Is he?" the older man asked, looking at him closely. "Is that what you want?"

"I don't know," the king admitted under the unwavering stare. "I don't know what I would need from you."

The man sighed and looked towards the door. "He will not come in."

"He finds the space confining," Dray answered for Ende, although it hadn't been a question. He was certain that the man at the table, whatever he might be, knew very well what Ende was. "Can I ask who we have the honour of speaking with?" Dray lowered his head a little in respect, although he didn't know if such a gesture had meaning here.

"You might know us as the Near Folk," he said, glancing back at the king. "We have many names. It does not matter what you call us."

"What do you call yourselves?" Belle asked.

A whisper like the wind through the trees filled the room and then died out instantly. "It is not easy to pronounce."

Belle smiled then, appearing to relax somewhat. "Can you help him?" She indicated the king with a tip of her head.

"Is he worthy of our help?"

"Yes," she said simply, although the boy king looked at the table. Dray wondered if he was ready to be King.

"Leave him with us. We will decide."

"For how long?" she asked, the uncertainty returning.

"How long does it take to create a king?"

"He is already King," Dray said, standing. "We do not wish to trouble you."

Ed waved him down, but he stayed where he was. "Ana," he mouthed across the table.

"The girl can look after herself," the older man said, his voice sharp. Then he closed his eyes as though listening to the whispers of the forest. "At least she has help already." He looked beyond Dray at that point, towards the door. "A forest looks after its own."

The king opened his mouth and then closed it.

The old man smiled again. "She will not hurt the girl, no matter what she thinks she may be able to give her. They have a common goal."

The king looked towards the door and then back.

"You," the man whispered.

Dray wasn't sure if he felt more secure in the knowledge or more concerned. What did Ana want with the king's sister, and why was he so worried about what Ana might do to her? She was just a girl. She wouldn't hurt anyone.

"They will stay," the old man said to the man beside him as he waved a hand over the table, indicating the group.

The other man bowed and then turned to face them. He indicated that they rise, and the king bowed his head to the older man still seated at the end of the table. The younger man who had led them in turned towards the door. Dray waited until they had all moved beyond him and then looked back to the man at the table, his face unreadable as he nodded once.

Their guide led the way around the building they had exited and followed one of the branches of the road that led away from it. He moved quickly. As Dray jogged to keep up, he realised that Ende was no longer part of the group. He looked around and then back to the group moving ahead of him. As he caught them up, he noted that the road branched again and again. On the outskirts of the village, two small huts sat side by side, the forest behind them.

"Do not wander into the trees," their guide cautioned. "We will talk in the morning."

The night sky seemed to tease them from above. He hoped Ende wasn't too far away. The other three stood before the two small huts. Then Phillip stepped forward and glanced inside one of them. He moved to the other and opened the door.

"Beds and food," he said. Then, as Belle took a step towards the king, he added, "We will take this one."

She looked down before she nodded and followed her father inside. Dray wondered just what she wanted from the king. He didn't seem to seek her attention, and after his outburst earlier, it appeared that he found her frustrating. She was hard to read, but brighter than he had thought when he first met her.

He held the door for the other hut open for the king. They found two cots separated by a small table. A fire burned in the corner, and the table was covered with bowls of food. A lantern glowed like the stars on the ceiling of the house they had just visited. Dray wished they had been able to get some information from the Near Folk; a name or position of the man they had met would have been helpful.

He pushed a bowl filled with bread towards the king and waited. His own stomach was tired of dry meat, but he wasn't sure if the bread and fruit before him would satisfy him any more than the meat.

The king bit into a roll, and Dray took one too.

"What do you think these men can do for you?" Dray asked.

"I don't know, but they seem to know that I need help, and that Ana is safe."

"Is he only telling you what he thinks you want to hear?"

"Perhaps," the king said, looking up at Dray, concern creasing his features. "Do you think she isn't safe?"

"I don't know," Dray admitted, putting the bread down. He had lost any appetite he might have had. "We best sleep, and we can start fresh in the morning."

"You don't think one of us should keep watch?"

"If they were going to kill us, they would have. If they were planning to, they wouldn't have fed us."

Ed looked at the roll in his hand and then put it back on the small table. He fumbled for a moment with his boots and then slipped them off. He crawled back along the cot and lay down. Dray wondered how long it had been since he had properly washed and eaten. And he wondered how long they would be staying in the forest.

5

Salima stood at the bottom of the bed, her hands held tight before her. Papa stood to one side of the bed and the cleric to the other. Finally, Ana appeared to have stopped shivering. But that may have been due to the number of blankets that covered her and the fact that Salima could barely see her.

She was far from restful. When the cleric placed his hand on her forehead, she had murmured Ed's name, among others, and growled something unintelligible. The cleric had seemed a little nervous initially, but the longer he stood by her side, the more he focused on his work and not who she was. Salima thought there would be far more to this woman than she expected. It appeared that her father knew something of her past; the cleric didn't ask, but she was sure he knew more than he was saying as well.

"Is she going to survive?" Salima asked.

Neither of them looked towards her, but the cleric nodded. Then Ana sat bolt upright, the blankets falling away, and the two men stepped back. "Don't let me fall," she whispered, then fell back to the bed.

Papa rubbed his hand across his forehead and sighed.

"Hush, child," the cleric soothed. "You are safe now."

She clutched at his hand. The rapid movement startled Salima, but it didn't appear to startle him. "Dray?"

She appeared to focus on him for a moment, and Salima could hear her drag in a sob.

"Do you hope I am him? Or do you ask after him?"

She shook her head, and as Salima stepped closer she saw the woman's tears roll away.

"He will find you," the cleric said, his voice soft and calming. Salima was reminded of the soldier with Ed.

"But should he?" Ana asked.

Salima looked from Ana to Papa and noticed he was staring at her. She tried to give him a smile, but she was sure it appeared more a grimace than reassuring.

"Will he look after Ed?" Salima asked.

Ana nodded, although the strength appeared to have gone from her.

"Ed?" the cleric asked, looking across the bed to Papa.

Ana was staring up at him, and for a moment Salima feared what she might do. Then Ana looked more afraid of what the old cleric might do. She eased herself up again, and although the cleric reached out a hand to reassure her, she pulled away from him. She turned angry eyes to Papa. "How could you do this?"

He did take a step back. And Salima wondered if she could protect him from this woman if needed.

"Ana," the cleric said, his voice calm and low, "we only want to help you."

She shook her head as though she didn't believe him, her eyes darting around the room. But as the cleric sat carefully on the edge of the bed and pulled her hand towards him, she focused only on him.

"I..." she started, but Salima had no idea where the conversation was going.

"Tell me of Dray," the cleric said.

"Drayton Sterling?" Papa asked.

Ana nodded.

"How did you meet him?" the cleric asked. "He is not a soldier likely to…"

"Take up with a maid?" Ana finished, her voice a little lighter but her eyes still wary. "He saved me."

The cleric looked up at Papa on the other side of the bed.

"He didn't know why. I made him, in a way. I called out and he… It is my fault he is in the mess he is."

The cleric reached forward and brushed the hair that had fallen across her face, behind her ear. "He is a strong man. I'm sure he is where he is needed."

She nodded.

"Has he watched over you?"

She nodded again, and Salima thought Ana was much younger than she had first thought, perhaps closer to her own age, closer to Ed's age. When she was being scary, she seemed so much older.

"I don't know what to do?" Ana whispered. A shiver crossed her frame, and the cleric had her sliding back down into the bed as he covered her over.

"You need to get well first." He ran a hand over her brow again, then pressed his fingers gently to her neck. He shook his head slowly. "I will find some broth. Maybe you could walk with me," he said across the bed.

Papa looked to Salima rather than answer.

"I can watch her," Salima offered quickly.

Papa pursed his lips and then nodded once. "Keep the fire stoked."

Salima nodded, and the cleric rested his hand on her shoulder as he moved past her and towards the door. Her father paused to look over Ana and then at Salima before he left with the cleric. She was sure she heard the key in the lock and wondered if it was a good idea to lock them in. As long as they were quiet, there shouldn't be any chance of them being found.

She put another log on the fire, the wood knocking against those burning beneath it, and the coals shifted. Maybe they would be found. She had found them a place right by the regent. It wasn't a good idea. Ana murmured, and Salima moved quickly to the bed. Ana was still, but murmured again. Salima sat slowly on the edge of the bed and Ana shivered.

Maybe she could use her fire to warm her. She lay down beside the woman, on the outside of the blankets, and put an arm over her. Ana sighed and tried to move closer. Salima watched her for a moment and then sat up. Ana started to shiver again. Salima removed her shoes and lifted the blankets, sliding against the faint warmth of the woman and put her arms around her again.

Ana shivered as she shifted against Salima's body. She sighed, and after a few moments the shivering ceased. Salima worried at first that she had sucked the warmth from Ana and she was dying in her arms. But she had settled into a comfortable sleep, and although Salima could sense the cold in her, she could feel the fever as well. A hand moved from the space between them and over her side.

She wasn't sure what Papa would say about this, but at least Ana was warm.

Ana could feel the wind pulling at her as she glanced down at the endless drop beneath her. She couldn't make out the sea or feel the cold. It was as though she was wrapped in a blanket of warmth. She tore her gaze from the nothingness beneath her to the circular opening. Every detail of the stonework was clear before her, but those beyond it were blurry. Was she on the Walk again? Was Ende there to save her?

The wind pulled at her, firmer and more determined to drag her from the Walk. A hand was tight in hers, and she squeezed her eyes closed. It wasn't Dray; it wasn't his large, weathered hand that felt both firm and safe, but slick with blood. It was small and fragile, yet stronger than any other that had held hers. And hot.

She couldn't look, couldn't see who else she had dragged into danger with her. She squeezed tighter around the hand, and then they were falling. Tumbling through nothing as though the clouds surrounded them. But the warm blanket still surrounded her; the hand remained in hers.

She woke with a gasp and pulled from the warm hold around her. Someone murmured and rolled away from her. She carefully lifted the blankets, regretting leaving the warmth of the bed, and slipped out the other side. She took a moment to steady herself before looking at the silent figure standing by the fire.

"You know what she is?" Ana whispered.

"I know who she is," the cleric said.

"She doesn't," Ana said.

He indicated the chair by the fire, and she sat, holding her hands to the flames. She was much warmer, but her bones still ached. And being away from the girl, she felt the lack of heat.

He handed her a small bowl, and she cupped it in her hands, feeling the warmth radiate through her again. She looked into it and slowly lifted it to her lips.

"How did you know who she was?" he asked.

"I could sense Ed in her."

"You are… close?"

She looked up then, unsure how she could explain their connection, and she wondered what he imagined it might be. By his look of concern, she had an idea.

"Did King Barric know what she was?" she asked instead.

"He thought someone had tried to kill his queen and child, and that the only way to protect his daughter was to hide her."

Ana wasn't sure if he had avoided what she asked, or if the king had truly believed the child his. She took another slow sip of the broth, and it warmed her as it travelled down her throat. Maybe he had no reason to consider Ende the child's father or suspect his relationship with his queen. Ana wondered at it herself. The old man would have been younger then, but not by so much that a young queen would have been swayed by him. He still would have been in his sixties or so. She looked up at the man watching her and then back to the bed.

The sword master had been surprised by her calling Ende an old man. Maybe there was more to the dragon than she realised. More than she had allowed herself to see. She had been too trusting. She was still too trusting.

"Did you know my mother?" she asked the old man before her with his white hair and beard and bent fingers; yet there was strength to this man. He had held her so tightly before, as though for a moment she had needed him to hold her together. She was reminded of Dray and his very different hands.

When he didn't speak, she looked into his face and he sat slowly in the other chair. "Many years ago, when she was training before she met your father."

"You knew they married?"

"I guessed at it, when they ran and she was with child. Your father was a good man. He would have ensured you were both safe."

She looked back at the little bowl and took another sip, although it was harder to swallow.

"What happened to her?" His voice was gentle and coaxing, and she was reminded of Dray again.

She shook her head. "I was only a baby," she murmured.

"Your father raised you?"

She nodded again, focused on the bowl. Did he wonder if her father still lived, if he would come after the daughter trapped in the capital? Did this man truly want to help her?

"Who are you?" she asked, although the question sounded harsher than she intended.

"Cleric Peck," he said, bowing his head. "Do you have questions? Did your parents talk of me?"

"I have many questions, not all of which I think you can help me with, and my father died when I was a child. Telling me very little of his life here."

He leaned forward and reached a hand for her knee. "Who

raised you?"

"I did," she said, leaning away from his reach. "I worked in the Seat of the Lord as a maid."

"She didn't care for you?"

"Not in any sense," Ana said, wanting the broth yet unable to swallow any more. "I didn't know who she was until the day she tried to give me away."

He waited, and she looked into his expectant features.

"The day the mage came with Dray to take me away. But then he didn't want me, and they tried to throw me from the Walk."

"Why did he no longer want you?"

"I think he saw something that scared him. And then…" She couldn't relive the Walk again. It appeared to plague her sleeping and awake.

"Yet he brought you here."

"I think once they realised Ed was missing, they thought we would not be a danger together."

"Where is the boy?"

"I don't know," she said loudly as the door clicked and she jumped up, the bowl still tight in her hands.

The sword master moved quietly into the room, closed the door behind him and then looked from them by the fire to the bed. His eyes hardened.

"She was trying to keep me warm," Ana said quickly. "I wouldn't hurt her," she added. She had used the girl, but she understood what she was to Ed.

"I want to trust you," the man said, stepping further into the room, "for her sake, and the king's. Only I don't know what you are. Or why the mage would go to such lengths to bring you here and then lock you away to die."

"I won't do what he wants me to do." Ana wasn't surprised that he didn't trust her. She barely trusted herself. But he had helped her, saved her. "Maybe you should have let me die." She sat back slowly in the chair.

"What did he want of you?" the cleric asked.

"To put the regent on the throne."

"He is there already. And the boy doesn't want to be King."

"But he is the king, whether he wants it or not. He has no confidence," she added slowly. "He doesn't think he can be the king his father was."

The cleric made a *tsk*-ing noise, as though he didn't believe her.

"He was locked away as a boy, no experience in being a king, no one to show him how it was done; no one included him in decisions for the kingdom or talked to him of how the world worked. He knows less of the kingdom than the boys I grew up with."

The cleric blinked at her in surprise and then glanced at the sword master, who gave a small shrug.

"Prince Thom already sits on the throne," he said matter-of-factly.

"But it is not his. He only keeps it warm. He would have it for himself."

The sword master nodded slowly.

"You said that the regent had a plan for a wife or heir," Ana said.

The cleric turned to him quickly, and Ana wondered if he had shared such ideas with anyone else.

"I thought his plan was you," the sword master said, taking a step further into the room. "I thought he would use your power to keep him where he was."

She shook her head slowly. She doubted he was right. The regent wanted her power sure enough, but not her as a wife. Certainly not when she scared him as she did, although that hadn't been until more recently. He really thought she would do as he wanted her to.

She looked around as the morning light peeked through the curtains. She stood, sat the bowl down on the small table and went to the window. Pulling the curtains back, she squinted into the sun.

She wasn't sure what she had expected. She had heard so many differing stories, and she had no idea how they had found her such a room or where she might be hidden away. A very different world stretched out before her. Stone and brick buildings covered the world as far as she could see. They were much higher from the ground than she had expected, perhaps somewhere in the castle. She had memories of similar yet very different points of view from the castle on Sheer Rock.

A green world had stretched before her there. Here, she could see no green at all. People and horses moved through the streets between the buildings. She felt hemmed in, as though all of this stood between her and Ed. Or Ed and his crown. Could he walk through this? How had he made it out in the first place? Surely someone would have recognised their king. Even this early in the day, there was so much movement, so many people. The height and thickness of the walls prevented her hearing any of it, yet she imagined it would be busy and loud, like market day but more so.

She allowed the curtains to close, any excitement she had previously felt about the capital evaporated. She shivered.

"Mistress Merrin?" Cleric Peck said, too close behind her.

"I'll find my way out when it is dark. It is too dangerous for you to be here."

"I thought you would stop the regent," Salima whispered from the bed.

"I can't," Ana said, trying to hold herself up when all she wanted to do was sit. Her legs gave way before she could convince them otherwise.

6

Ed stood at the doorway of the small hut and took in the morning light over the village before him. He could hear some chatter and movement of people, but he had yet to see anyone. He wasn't sure if they should wait for their guide to reappear or if they were safe to explore on their own. But then, he also wasn't sure what was expected of him. Or what he was expecting from these people.

The Near Folk were a myth. At least they had been until they had talked to him in the forest and then walked from the trees. He looked into the cloudless sky and wondered if anyone would find them here.

He glanced around then, thinking of Ende and wondering just where he had gone. Did these people not like dragons, or could he not cope in the trees? He had lived on the mountain for so long; could he have flown home without anyone noticing?

How had such a man become friends with Mother? His thought was interrupted by Phillip barging from their hut beside his. His face dark, he glared at Ed, and then his expression became more worried.

"Where is Belle?" he demanded.

"I thought her still in bed," Ed said. "I haven't seen her."

"She wouldn't wander," Phillip murmured.

"Where is she?" Ed asked.

"That is my question," Phillip snapped, crossing his arms. "I thought she had snuck out to be with you."

"I…" Ed took a step back.

"She clings to you. She wants to be noticed by you," Phillip grumbled. "I don't know what her thoughts are, but there is something in you that she sees."

"That I am king," Ed said unkindly.

Phillip sighed. "She liked you well before then."

"Did she?" Ed asked, unsure if Phillip had read his daughter right.

"Where is my daughter, Your Majesty?" Phillip growled, and Dray appeared in the clearing from behind a hut.

"What has happened?" he asked.

"Belle has…" Ed started.

"Disappeared," Phillip finished for him. "I woke and she was gone. She wouldn't do anything silly."

Ed found his eyebrows rising in question.

"She is strong-willed, but not stupid."

"All right," Dray said, his hands raised to placate the old man. "I haven't seen her this morning, and she would have said something. Has anyone seen Ende?"

"Not since we entered the leader's house."

"I fear he has gone on without us. You didn't hear anything?" Dray asked Phillip.

"No. If someone took her, she would have screamed."

"If she could," Dray said, then turned an apologetic face towards Phillip.

"These people have taken her," Phillip said. "They offered help and now they are just taking what they want."

"We don't know that," Dray offered, but he looked around as though that was what he believed. "We should find someone."

Ed nodded and straightened his collar. He had thought these people wanted to help him, but maybe they wanted more than he realised. "Would they take her to give as tribute?"

"Do the Near Folk pay tribute?"

"The Near Forest is required to provide wives. I'm not sure my uncle would have stipulated who in the forest had to provide. The province, and that is all that matters."

Phillip closed his eyes and groaned.

"You should have headed home," Ed said. He didn't want to sound like he was apportioning blame. "Where did the others go?"

"You didn't help them?" Dray asked, and Ed cringed inwardly.

"They were determined to help themselves, or head home."

"How many women were there?" Dray asked.

Ed looked to Phillip. He had no recollection for the exact number; Belle had stolen his attention. He sighed as he ran a hand over his face. He was not a good leader. He had been selfishly searching for his own needs, his own assistance. For a man who had now left them.

"The trees were protecting them," he said weakly, knowing it was not enough to forgive what he had done.

"Let us find the Near Folk leader and see what can be done," Dray said, his hand on his sword. Ed wondered if the man ever took his armour off.

He allowed Dray to lead the way towards the leader's dwelling. And then as they drew closer, Ed had the same strange feeling he'd had outside the clearing that night, the women unheard beyond. His feet faltered and he stopped. Was the forest still playing with him? Was it protecting them from him?

The guide stood outside the house as they approached it and bowed his head in greeting.

"Where is my daughter?" Philip asked, rushing forward, his voice stern. The man simply indicated the building. Phillip pushed his way through the door. As it opened, Ed could hear the chatter, and he stepped forward to look.

The Near man turned his gaze on Ed, but said nothing. He wasn't sure if the man was trying to gauge his reaction, or if he blamed him in some way that all these women had been left in the forest. Ed turned his back and headed back to the hut. He couldn't face this, any of it, and he wondered what Ana was so sure she saw in him.

"You'll die," the Near man said.

Ed turned back to him. The chatter had ceased, and Dray had drawn his sword.

"That is what she knows."

"Ana?" Ed asked, stepping forward. Had the man read his thoughts?

He nodded once. Then closed his eyes and tilted his head to the side. "She thought you would die," he said, as though correcting himself. "She's scared."

"Now? For herself?" Dray asked, stepping between them.

"She fears she cannot help you."

"How do you know this?" Dray's voice was firm, and for the first time the guide looked at him rather than Ed.

"I sense her. I sensed her in you."

Ed glared at Dray as though his connection to Ana might be more, or stronger, than his own. Although those two had met and bonded first, Ed felt a jealousy he regretted.

"Both of you," the Near man said. "The forest is a part of us; she is a part of you. She came to you. She came to the forest and she didn't travel alone."

Ed stepped closer. "Salima?"

The man looked him up and down. "She saw it all."

"How?" Ed asked, the exasperation overwhelming.

The man looked back at the building behind him for a moment, then indicated that they follow him in another direction. Ed started without hesitation, but Dray grabbed at his arm. Ed glared at Dray's hand before looking up into the worried face of the soldier.

"How does he know this?" Dray mouthed silently.

"The fact that he does is all I need," Ed said, pulling from his hold.

"Or he is not being truthful with us."

Ed ignored the comment and followed the man along the dusty

street. The morning light grew brighter as more and more of the Near Folk started their daily chores. When he passed, they would pause in their activity and bow.

They ended up by a stream on the outskirts of the village, the trees looming nearby as though wanting to close the gap between them.

"Tell me of the hanging men," Dray demanded.

"They were not what we thought they were." The man sounded disappointed. "We thought it best to direct you."

"You could have tried another method. Asking works well," Ed suggested.

"Perhaps you should have gone around. It was only at your determination that I came for you."

"We were all quite determined to make it through the forest. To find Ana," Dray answered.

The man smiled. "You were all searching for something very different. Not all of you searched for the mage. Not all of you want her found."

"Ende?" Ed whispered.

"Belle," Dray said, and Ed looked at him.

"Really?"

They both turned back to the Near man.

He shook his head slowly. "I cannot say," he murmured. "But the mage has sacrificed herself for you."

Dray pulled his sword too quickly, and Ed threw an arm across his chest.

"Is that what she is?" Ed asked.

"She is called many things; the people call her witch, but it does not suit her. Magic lives in her."

"Lives in her?" Dray said. "She is gifted."

"She is more than gifted. She is…" He appeared to struggle for the right word.

"What are you called?" Ed asked.

The man blinked as though he didn't quite understand the

question. "We are all Near Folk."

"But what are *you* called, if someone needs you?"

"Eilke," he said

"I-el-ca," Ed sounded out. The wind moved through the trees, and the man smiled as he bowed his head.

"Not many need to call. I know when I am needed."

"The women in the forest?" Dray asked, glaring at Ed before turning back to the man.

"There is tribute owed," he said.

"You would send them to the capital?" Ed asked, confused for he had thought they would help them. "You would give them away?"

"It is for them to choose their path."

"But they were stolen," Ed stammered.

"Not all of them. And the king demands ten."

"I haven't demanded anything."

"The tribute is requested in your name; the people must show their allegiance. They must prove they are loyal to the kingdom and the king."

"You won't include any of your own women in that gift," Ed said.

Eilke smiled knowingly. "We are not wanted."

"Surely the Near Folk must be part of the kingdom, and so pay tribute."

"We are not like men," he said.

Ed ran a hand through his hair and blew out a breath. He had no idea of what he was doing, and he wasn't sure where to even start. "So, some of them are willing to go?"

The man nodded.

"We could travel with them," Dray said. "It could be a way into the capital."

"And then what do we do?" Ed asked. "I can hardly turn up at the castle gates and ask them to let me in."

"Do you need to ask when you are King?" Eilke asked.

Ed turned back to the man, taking in his height and build. "You offered assistance."

"And when you know what you want, we will provide." The man bowed and walked away. And although the soldier tried to hide it, Ed saw the disappointment in Dray's face.

7

The regent glared at the mage, only to get some sort of response. The man huffed and puffed as he moved around the dusty shelves of the cave he called a workshop. How he had managed to keep the witch here, Thom wasn't sure. How she had managed not to look as lost and dishevelled as the other creatures he had glimpsed also escaped him.

"Where are the girls?" he asked, sure that was what they had been at some time.

"What girls?" The mage looked up from the book he was scanning.

"The…" The regent waved his hand, unsure how to describe them. Hadn't the mage been searching for gifted ones throughout the kingdom? "Girls."

The mage looked confused for a moment and then nodded. "The girls," he said slowly. "I used them."

"Used them?"

"To bring the Merrin girl here. Although that was a waste of time."

"She may come around," Thom said, more hopeful than certain. He had the idea she would make a formidable queen, if he could keep her in check. She seemed so unsure of herself, so lost. And then she had scared him more than he would admit.

"She'll be dead by now, unless she could muster any magic in that cold."

"I wanted her," Thom said, allowing the anger and disappointment to be heard in his voice.

"As did some other young men, I should imagine," the mage said without looking up. "The soldier being one of them."

"The captain? He wasn't that young to be swayed by a girl. Maybe I could try again, now that her anger has had the chance to cool."

"Go if you must. I still think she will be dead."

"Why did you drag her here?" Thom asked, wondering if she might actually be gone.

"I thought she would be a help. With the boy she is too strong; without him she might be strong but not a threat, not like she was."

"I felt somewhat threatened," Thom murmured, touching his arm again. It hadn't felt right since the moment she had touched him. He would ensure that didn't happen again. Even if he had to hold her down. She certainly hadn't had any fight left in her the last time he had seen her.

"I'll send the maid," the mage said, his focus still on the book.

"I will go alone. If I need her out of the cell, I will send someone to you."

The mage looked up at him with hard eyes, a challenge he didn't usually offer. "Take the maid," he said.

Thom nodded begrudgingly and turned, finding the girl waiting when he exited the mage's room. How she did that, he wasn't sure. He had often wondered if the girl had some power of her own. She was loyal to the mage to a fault, he had discovered early on. He wouldn't risk the man finding out that he was trying to win her now.

They moved around the edge of the building and into another door that led to the cellar. Walking silently through the large dark space, they worked their way between bags and crates. Given the amount of supplies that were stored there, he wondered how many people moved through here every day without knowing what was beyond.

The maid reached for a hook on the wall and twisted it, opening the door. She stood back, her head bowed, and waited for him to head down the steps first. He wondered briefly if she might ever lock him down here, and if he would be discovered. He moved slowly down the slick steps into the increasing light. Another secret of the mage's, but it mattered not. Prisoners kept in the dark were just as damaged as those kept in eternal light. He held up his hand to shield his eyes as he reached the base of the stairs, thankful that he would never need to experience this himself.

He glanced around the cages and then took a step forward.

They were all empty, even the one he knew had held the girl only days before. He shivered from both the cold and the anger. He glanced back at the maid, but she was already racing up the stairs.

The regent stood in the middle of the large courtyard at the heart of the castle and glanced around the buildings that overlooked it. There was no sign of anyone at the windows, watching him or the world. The maid had disappeared, and yet he knew just where she had gone. Had the mage changed his mind? Had he missed the girl he had known long ago so much that he needed to keep her daughter for himself?

Closing his eyes, Thom allowed Mariela to form in his mind, her dark hair, brilliant eyes and captivating smile. Ana was an embodiment of her, and yet she was quite different. She lacked the same confidence, although Mariela had been distracted from what she could have been. Another soldier, one she had disappeared with. Again, the captain came to mind.

He wasn't the sort to do anything disloyal, no matter the enticement. And yet he had taken the girl and run. The mage had allowed it to happen. Could the captain have made it back to the capital and stolen her again?

How he might have made such a distance in so short a time was beyond Thom—unless the girl had found a way to bring him here. The regent shook his head slowly as he looked around the courtyard. The sword master caught his attention, stomping across the courtyard towards his practice halls as a young man joined him en route, although he didn't acknowledge the boy.

Master Forest always appeared angry to the regent. Was he disappointed that the king had disappeared, and that no one cared enough? He had been too close to Thom's brother, Barric. They had fought side by side and Barric had allowed Forest to retire to a wife Thom didn't know he had when Ter-essa had died.

When Barric had died, Forest had returned, wife gone, child in tow. Not that he paid much attention to the child. Girls were of little use, and although someone had suggested she could go into service, Forest's position as sword master allowed her to stay at home. Thom had worried for a time that the man might try to marry her off to raise his own status, but he didn't appear to want such a thing for her. She seemed a strange unruly girl when he had glimpsed her, and he doubted any man of standing would have her.

The sword master jumped as he reached the doors, as though he hadn't realised the boy stood beside him. And his glower grew more intense. He ushered the boy inside, muttering about swords and students. As he paused waiting for the student to enter the room, he glanced about and looked at Thom. He sucked in a deep breath, gave a half-hearted bow and followed the boy inside.

Thom wondered, not for the first time, if he would ever earn the respect of these men as Barric had. Not that he needed their respect, but he felt that loyalty to the crown should be a given. It was how these men had earned their status in the first place. And it appeared that the crown did have their loyalty, only it was to the boy.

Thom had managed to keep the boy locked away, out of everyone's thoughts, and then he had disappeared. It was just what Thom had needed him to do, and yet it had sparked far more trouble than he'd expected. He had managed to convince the people that Edwin was still a boy when he had long ago grown up. Thankfully, the boy hadn't tried to fight him on it.

Thom turned away from the practice hall and back for the mage's cave. He might have an idea now as to where the little witch had slipped off to. And perhaps how she had managed to escape a cell the mage had assured him no one could escape.

He paused mid-step, and a couple walking across the courtyard stopped to bow their heads. He nodded, focused more on his thoughts, but he noticed the glance that passed between them. Did they know the girl had escaped him as well?

He turned to watch them go, their heads together, but they paid him no further attention. The mage had said she was looking for the king, that she wanted to look for him, and that night she'd been certain the boy was the rightful heir and deserved the crown. Thom's hand moved to his still-tingling arm.

Did she know him? Had she somehow found a way to meet the boy?

He pushed into the mage's quarters, slamming the door closed behind him and searching for him through the dim light. The mage stood over a bowl, grey smoke rising from it, and pushed his hand through it, muttered something as Thom approached.

"Did she know the boy?"

"What boy?" the mage asked.

"Edwin."

The mage looked away from the smoke as a touch of red wove its way through the grey. As the regent stared at it, the mage returned his focus. "It isn't enough," he murmured. He moved his fingers through it again, then pushed the bowl to the floor. The clatter as it bounced across the stone floor echoed through the space, and as the cloak spilled onto the floor, the smoke dissipated.

"Why do you think she knows the boy?" the mage asked.

"She is sure he is a man, one who should be King."

"Perhaps she is better at determining his age than you give the kingdom credit."

The regent scowled at the man before him. "He will always be a boy."

"Where would she have met him? He cannot have reached Sheer Rock, nor even the mountains."

"How long was he gone? How long has he walked? Could he have found a horse, or ally to take him further beyond our reach?"

"No one knows the boy," the mage said, but the strength had gone from his voice. "There are no allies brave enough to go against you. Yet someone must have got him out of the castle. Out of the capital."

"I am still trying to determine how that happened."

"Then why are we surprised that he might make it so far? He is more resourceful than I imagined. There is more of his father in him than I thought."

The regent growled at the idea of his brother. "He wasn't as great as he thought he was. He was certainly easy enough to destroy."

"A friend of the king? Could that be the someone who would help the boy?"

Many of their friends had left, Thom thought. The Merrin soldier being one of them.

"The sword master?" the mage mused.

"He appears just as frustrated by the loss of the boy as I am. If he knew where he was, he would go after him, and he hasn't left the castle, let alone the capital."

"You could question him more closely."

"He came to me. Despite my reservations, I feel the man is genuine in his concern."

The mage looked back to the bowl for a moment and then closed his eyes.

The regent was tempted to ask him what his thoughts were, or he may have been searching for something.

The mage sighed. "I can't feel her," he murmured. "Maybe she was with the boy when we took her."

"The Lord of Edge Mountains would have sent word."

"Would he? If he was aligning with the king, he might not want to let us know his whereabouts."

The regent stomped from the room. One of his soldiers stood near the edge of the courtyard. Silent and foreboding. He waved the man to follow as he walked back to his rooms. His mind moved through various scenarios as he passed through silent passageways and up the stairs to what had once been his brother's home—his father's before that and the reason he was comfortable in them now. He had removed any sign of his brother and his family, as though they hadn't existed.

"I need you to take a small trusted group, Major Field," Thom said to the man once he was standing by the balcony, looking over what he was certain was his. He turned back to the tall soldier, who bowed his head.

"I understand," he said.

"Good. It appears my nephew might have travelled as far north as the mountains. Find the Lord's Seat, find the boy and…"

The soldier waited patiently, no indication as to what he thought. His face was hard but unreadable, even to the regent.

"Return him to the capital to stand trial for treason."

Major Field bowed his head again and left. The regent leaned onto the railing of the balcony, taking in the vast city beneath him. Beyond the houses and markets and smoke, he imagined the road that eventually led north. The distance was too great to see the mountains. "What was he thinking?" he murmured aloud. "What ally did he think he could find?"

# 8

Ana tried not to lean too heavily into the windowsill. She had found it difficult to look away, now that she had discovered her window overlooked the world. And yet she couldn't seem to muster enough energy to stand there. The cleric had been filling her with broth that helped somewhat. She wasn't shivering all the time, but she wasn't herself either.

There were times when she would shiver at the idea of the bright lights and ice-cold walls, so cold they burnt into her flesh. The sword master and the cleric had asked her many questions and she had done her best to answer them, although she wasn't sure they were satisfied with the responses. The child barely left her side, and the cleric visited often. The sword master's visits were now more to check on his daughter. Although Ana knew she wasn't his, as did the cleric.

The only one who didn't appear to know Salima's origins was the girl herself. But then, Ana thought, glancing at the cleric watching her from his chair by the fire, they didn't know her true origins.

"Tell me of the queen," she had asked. But there was little they were willing to tell. "You were her friend," she had prompted the sword master, but he either didn't know of her relationship with Ende or he wasn't sharing. The image Ed had drawn of his mother was beautiful, and yet Ende was an old man. How could such a friendship have produced the child it did?

Ana stretched out her fingers, trying to find the magic she had only recently discovered in her veins. Magic that had done her bidding so easily. Now she couldn't even raise a draft, let alone a breeze to move the thick curtains. She would be no use to anyone as she was. Not that she thought she was much use to Ed before. She still dreamt of him. She was unsure if it was just ideas or worry for him that drew him to her at night, or if she truly dreamt of him as she had before they met.

She closed her eyes, trying to refocus on the dream she'd had of him the night before. But it wasn't clear; trees and worry were all she could make out.

"Belle," she murmured. Belle should be helping him.

"What bell?" the child asked, coming to stand beside her. "There is said to be a bell in the old temple by the water," she said. "I've heard. I don't get out much into the city, let alone beyond."

"It is a warning," the cleric said, and Ana turned to take him in again. "In case invaders come across the sea."

She nodded and turned back to the city.

The child slipped her arms around Ana's waist, pulling in close. Ana wasn't sure which one of them she was trying to comfort. "What bell?"

"She is with Ed," Ana murmured. "At least she was."

"Is she a wit… like you?"

Ana looked down at the girl snuggled against her. She wasn't afraid of Ana anymore, or at least didn't appear to be.

"She is just a girl."

"And Ed likes her."

Ana nodded. Belle was difficult to read, but she would stand by Ed no matter what she had thought of him originally. Ana couldn't tell if she liked him or not; or was she not sure how to deal with him? Discovering he was the king would have made it even harder for Belle to voice her feelings. Ana remembered her clinging to his arm when they had arrived at the Seat of the Lord of Edge

Mountains. Did she cling to him still?

The door clicked open and the sword master slipped into the room. His daughter didn't move from her post, and Ana was thankful for the warmth.

"I think we might have a problem," he whispered, moving into the room. The girl released her hold. Ana felt the chilled air move around her where the warmth of the little dragon had been.

"They have discovered me gone," she said.

He nodded once.

"I'm surprised it has taken this long," the cleric offered.

"I don't think they were checking to ensure her health," Master Forest said.

Ana shook her head slowly, pulled the curtains closed and moved towards the fire and the cleric. "What would you like me to do?" she asked the sword master. She clasped her hands before her, unsure what else to do with them. They felt empty.

"I think it best to stay here for now. He sent men out."

Ana swayed a little before grabbing at the chair as Master Forest closed a tight hand around her arm. "Ed," she whispered.

"They don't know where he is," the master said.

"But they might have guessed. They might have realised we had found each other."

"Where did they find you?" the cleric asked.

"The Seat of the Lord of Edge Mountains."

"Lord Welcott. Would he hide the king?"

"He is gone," she said, nodding to the master. He released his hold on her, and she sat down slowly. "I don't think they would have stayed there. But if they know he was in the mountains…"

"If you were taken, would he not come for you?" Salima asked.

"It isn't safe," Ana murmured.

"But he might still come," the girl insisted.

"I don't know. I would hope that Dray and Ende would talk him around."

"Unless your soldier wanted to find you as badly."

She looked up at the sword master, unable to read his features. "What do you think I am to him?"

"More than a maid," he said. He sighed and squatted down beside her chair. "Either way, the regent has sent out men. I don't know if they will try to bring the king back or prevent his return."

"They may want to bring a body back to prove to the people that the regent is King." Ana hadn't meant to think it, let alone say it aloud, but if she were Regent and wanted to be King, it would make sense.

"They were trying to destroy you because of your strength," the cleric said, "and how you could help the king."

"Only I don't have any strength, and the gods only know where the king is."

"You say his name in your sleep," Salima offered. "Have you reached him again?"

Ana shook her head. "I can't make sense of the dreams," she admitted. "It may not be safe to reach him, even if I could."

"Try," Salima said, holding out her arm.

Ana shook her head and turned to the flames. She had used the girl enough, and she wasn't sure it would be enough to reach him. She turned slowly back and then rose unsteadily to her feet. As she took a step towards the girl, her father stood and blocked her path.

"What did you see?" Ana asked, although it was more to the sword master than the child behind him.

"What makes you think she saw anything?"

"You told me," she said. "You saw more than Ed."

Salima's face appeared around her father trying to shield her. She nodded once.

"What did you see?" Ana asked, too aware that the cleric was also standing.

"Trees," the girl murmured, suddenly unsure.

Ana waited, wondering if she feared what she might have seen.

"I saw them all," she said with a sigh. "As though you had dragged me through the campsite. I saw the old man, and the soldier." She glanced at her father. "He looked older than you," she said, turning back to Ana, her brow creased as though trying to determine as her father had what their relationship was. Although, Ana wasn't sure if she referred to Dray or Ende.

"Ed," Ana prompted.

She nodded. "Another girl, pretty and blonde, and her father?"

"Belle and Phillip Poales."

"She is pretty," Salima said, looking down. Then she chewed on her lip as she raised her eyes to Ana. "You are prettier," she said quickly.

Ana smiled despite herself. As her legs wobbled beneath her, she sat back in the chair. The girl was stronger than she realised. She wondered if Ende had seen her for what she was. He might have known; although he, like the rest of the kingdom, had possibly assumed she had died with her mother. If they knew she was with child… Ana had heard of the queen's death, but no one had mentioned another child. Was it because she had been conceived from an affair?

"Ed does not think of me like that. Nor I him," Ana said. "I am meant to keep him safe," she murmured.

"How?" the sword master's voice was sharp, and she was taken back to the first day she met him in Ed's room.

"I dreamt of his death." She wanted so much to lie down and close her eyes again. Would she ever be of use to him? So far, she had only made his journey more difficult. "I knew it was my task to prevent that."

"How?" the cleric asked.

She shook her head then. She had no idea what she could do. She didn't even understand what power she might have had. She was a useless maid who couldn't even carry tea, and there she was thinking she could save the king.

"Ana," the sword master said more gently, squatting down beside her again as she allowed the tears to run unchecked down her cheeks. "You knew this before you met him?"

"I thought so, but I don't know anymore. Ende thought I was powerful, dangerous even, but I don't have anything left. I don't know how to help him."

"It is the cold," the cleric said.

"I'm not cold anymore," Ana whispered.

"Then why do you continue to shiver?" the girl asked.

"It is better for him if I die," Ana said. "Dray should have let me go on the Walk. It was wrong to call to him, to drag him from his post."

"Did you call to him?"

"I didn't know I did. Ende said I called him too. This all started with Dray. If he hadn't looked so, with his face scarred as it was."

"Scarred?" the sword master asked.

Ana lifted her fingers to her wet cheek. They were cold to the touch. She felt along where the scar had marked Dray's face. "Here," she murmured, "and then it was gone."

"Had you seen something like that before?" the cleric asked.

She shook her head. "You knew my mother," she said, energy surging through her as she stood and moved towards him. "Did she see such things?"

He shook his head. "I don't know. I don't think so. She had feelings, and she may have seen things in her dreams, but she rarely saw what wasn't there."

"But it was there," Ana asserted. Even though she knew it wasn't, she knew it was. "It will be there." Her fingers moved back to her cheek, wondering if it would be her fault that he would be scarred in such a way.

"What else did you see?"

"Blood on his hands. Fighting in Ende's eyes. The crown in my hand."

The cleric leaned back.

"What is it?" she asked. "Do you see the danger that Ende did?"

"Your mother," he whispered. "She may not have seen much, but she saw herself at one point with the crown, a soldier and a king. Yet she knew it wasn't her."

9

Ed wondered where Ende might have disappeared to and what his disappearance meant. He had said he would help. At least that was the idea Ed had gotten from the man. But so far, he didn't feel like Ende had helped very much. And ever since Ana had appeared with Salima, he'd seemed somewhat distracted. Now they had no idea where he was at all.

He sat amongst a group of women he had thought he would never see again and waited. He expected frustration and hurt, even anger that he had left them. Although he wasn't sure now why he had been so sure they would be safe. They looked much better for their time with the Near Folk. They were clean, freshly clothed and fed. Many of them laughed amongst themselves; some even smiled at Ed.

He wasn't sure how to respond, and so he didn't. Dray stood in the doorway, his back to the group. He would know how to talk to women, Ed thought. Belle sat amongst her friends, talking, checking whether they were truly well, but she wouldn't raise her eyes to Ed.

"When?" he heard Belle ask, and he tried to focus more on the conversation around him.

"Soon. I'm not sure if we go on our own or if someone is coming. There was a man before who came to talk to the chief, but I think he was asked for something he didn't want to give."

"Like what?" Ed asked.

The girl—no, woman—turned a smiling face towards him, and he wondered if he deserved her attention.

"We aren't enough," she said, still smiling.

"Enough?" Belle asked.

"In number, for the tribute."

Belle met Ed's eyes then, and hers were wide. "Why would you agree to go as tribute?"

"We don't have much to return to. It may be a better life, even exciting with all the buildings and markets and people. We would be married off to the best of men. If I returned home, it would be some farmer's son I'd spend the rest of my days working for. In the capital I might have servants."

Belle looked at her with disbelief. "You are all willing to go?"

"Of course," she said. "We aren't being dragged by rope this time. The chief has shown us what we might encounter."

"It might be very different," Ed murmured.

"It would be better than what I had. My family already thinks me dead. Or worse, if I return to my father for him to…" She trailed off, and Ed wondered what life these girls had come from.

"We want to go," she said, turning to Belle and taking her hands. "You could join us. It will be exciting, and you might meet…" She turned back to take in Ed. They didn't know who he was, but they had an idea he was more important than he looked. "Or you might have met him already."

"You will not have a choice when you reach the capital. You will be selected by those the regent thinks deserve you, not the other way around."

"I understand that," she said. "They will all be men of power." She held her chin high as Belle clearly struggled for words she couldn't find. She stood quickly, stepped over the bench seat and pushed past Dray out into the sunshine.

The woman's attention turned to her friend. She whispered something, and they giggled as they glanced at Ed. He stood and followed Belle's path out of the building. She stood in the middle of the dusty path that led from the building. Her arms hung by her sides as she took a deep breath, her head tilted back looking up to the sky.

"Belle," he said quietly, coming up behind her. She jumped, wiped at her face and turned with a pained smile. "I don't think you can change their minds."

"It appears so," she said, bowing her head to him and then walking away. He grabbed her arm and halted her walk.

"I don't think it will be as they think, but it might not be so bad."

"You want to send them off," she snapped, but she didn't pull from his hold. "It isn't right," she added more quietly.

"I'm not in a position to change it."

"Will you ever be?"

He dropped her arm then. She was right; he didn't know what he was doing or how he was going to be King. Although Ana was so sure that he already was. He didn't feel like it. Although they had gotten closer to the capital and to Ana, Ed felt further away from being what she was so sure he was.

This woman didn't have any faith in him, not that he deserved it. He wondered, not for the first time, why she remained with him.

"Your Majesty," Dray asked behind him. Ed sighed before he turned.

"I don't know what I'm doing or where my focus should be. I don't even know how to get Ana back. I had…" He looked over the man before him, his façade calm. But there was something in the way he leaned forward that made Ed think he might listen to him. Might hope for something from him.

"When I was inside," he said, motioning back to the building he had just left, "I thought if they were so willing to go, we could go with them. But…" He turned to look after the path that Belle had taken. "I don't think we could risk taking Belle in amongst the tribute; they may want to keep her."

"You don't think she wants to be kept?"

There was a small smirk when he took in the soldier, but Ed shook his head. "Not like that," he said.

Dray nodded and stepped closer. "They will come for the tribute. The soldiers always collect."

"We could follow, but what good would it do us?" Ed tried not to whine. He had no idea what they would achieve if they made it to the capital. And they could find it easily enough without having to follow soldiers.

Dray waited beside him, trying to offer comfort perhaps, but so far he hadn't offered any options as to what they could do next. Ed had felt so sure in that moment when Ana had disappeared, dragged back to the capital by the mage and quite likely his uncle. He knew he had to reach her. And in the intervening days, she had reached him. But then there had been nothing, and he had no real idea if she had been turned to their cause or if she was lost.

"I trust that she is where she needs to be," Dray said softly.

"But what of Ende and us? We are no closer to the crown. I have no idea how to reach it and remain alive, and Ana is an unknown."

Dray shook his head. "She will never be an unknown."

"She called to you," Ed said.

"That does not mean I didn't want to save her, that I wouldn't follow her to the ends of the kingdom and beyond if that is what she needed from me."

"A maid," Ed said. It sounded as though she was not as important to him as she was to Dray, when he was sure she was more so. They were friends, and he needed her to regain the crown.

"Are you sure that is what you want?" a voice whispered from the trees.

"You have asked that before," Ed said, looking back to the chief's building. Dray looked confused.

"You are yet to answer."

"I thought I had," Ed murmured. But had he? Had he accepted

the Near Folk's help? And if he had, to do what?

"Bring her soldier with you."

Ed opened his mouth to protest, but instead motioned Dray back towards the building. The women were gone, and he wondered how they had left without his noticing.

"What do you know of Ana?" he asked as he stood at the end of the table. The room was empty but for them. Then a breeze blew through the door around them, and the chief appeared in the large chair at the end of the table.

Ed only just managed to keep his composure; the soldier beside him barely moved.

"Do you think I can be King?" he asked.

"It is not for me to say. Nor your reason for it."

"I was born heir of Ilia."

"There is more to being King than birth," Eilke said, appearing from the shadows beside the chair.

"I was not born to this," the chief said. "I strove for it. Only the strongest may be chief. When I am no longer strong enough, another will take my place."

"It doesn't work like that with the throne," Ed said, but he wondered how true his words were. His uncle had shown himself the stronger and thus ruled.

The chief looked at him as though he had read his mind.

"What do I need to do?" Ed asked.

"What do you want to do?" the chief asked in return. Ed tried not to let the frustration show on his face, although he was sure the chief knew just how he felt.

"I can't just walk into the capital."

"You walked out of it."

"I need allies. I need someone to stand with me, or my uncle will have me killed before the people can see me."

"How can he prevent the people from seeing you?"

Ed opened and closed his mouth. He wasn't quite sure what he had meant by the words, but he wondered if he wanted the people of the capital to see him as he was now. Would they consider him King? Would they if he made a stand against his uncle? The regent might use the mage against them.

He shook his head, unsure at the tumble of thoughts and bad ideas flooding through him.

"What if we raised the people against the regent?" Dray asked.

"Would that not put them in greater danger? We can't encourage the people to fight."

"If they will not, who will?"

Ed shook his head again and looked at the chief. "Why have you allowed us here?"

The chief looked him over, but said nothing. He couldn't very well march into the capital with the Near Folk behind him; he would put off more of the people than bring them on board.

"Why are you supporting the sending of tribute?" he asked.

The chief blinked for a moment, surprised by the question. "It is our duty as citizens of this kingdom to pay tribute that assures the crown we are loyal."

"Giving young women."

"There have been many different gifts provided to the crown over the history of this kingdom. Some are expected to ensure the kingdom remains strong; some are never asked for but gratefully accepted."

Ed looked at him carefully. "Every seven years, wives are sent."

The man nodded. "There are only six provinces."

"There is the capital as well," Dray answered, although he looked as though he was struggling to visualise something.

"They still take wives, only it is different when it is their turn. Lords and ladies and common folk will stand before the throne to offer their best. It is honour they seek as well as promising their loyalty."

Dray nodded once, and Ed wondered what he had seen.

"What else do you give?" Ed asked. "What else is demanded?"

"Will this help you decide who you are?" the chief asked.

"It may help me decide what kind of king I could be."

"You would not ask your kingdom to show its loyalty? You would not ask for proof that they will not remove you from the throne?"

"I'm not on the throne yet," Ed murmured.

10

"Has there been any word?" the regent asked, leaning over the balcony of his room and surveying the world beyond. When there was no answer, he turned back to the mage, who stood too close to the door.

The man shook his head and then closed his eyes. "They are not far enough from the castle yet," he murmured.

Thom wondered what the mage saw on the other side of his closed lids at times, but then he didn't want to know. Although he would have given anything for some knowledge as to where the boy was and with whom. Was he out there gathering troops? And if so, how had that happened?

The regent sighed and leaned into the railing, looking back at the view. This was his kingdom, and he wasn't going to let the boy take it. Although he couldn't for the life of him determine who might assist him. Sure, he was King, and he bore the title. But he didn't hold any of the power, and the soldiers all followed Thom— not that he would ask them to take the boy into one of those oddly lit cells.

"How did she get out?" he asked, distracted for a moment, wondering about the woman he had once wanted so desperately. For the idea of her being close again made him nervous.

"I cannot tell. There is no sign of her magic. The cold would have dragged her skill away, or at least made it hard for her to muster anything. She should have died in that cold." The mage screwed up his face. "She could not survive."

"She survived a fall from the Walk, and now the frozen cells. Perhaps she is as strong as you first feared and she…" Thom couldn't finish the words. He wasn't sure what he was about to say. That she would finish them all, destroy him as the mage had feared when he had first looked into her eyes. Help the boy regain his throne. The regent shuddered at the idea. Now they were both running free to do he didn't know what.

"Find them," he snapped. "I should have drowned the bastard at birth!"

"True heir, born in wedlock," the mage muttered.

The regent growled. Then he refocused on the mage. "Barric's friends weren't as loving of his wife."

The mage merely stared.

"When she died. So many of them left the capital, left his side, and in many ways it was how I managed to get close to him. The playful one, always causing trouble—Ende. He disappeared before she died. Maybe he didn't think she was as fun. And Forest was allowed to retire at the time of her death."

"I don't think your brother was thinking clearly when she fell ill."

The regent turned back to the view. Ter-essa had always been a fit woman, keeping pace with Barric easily enough, but her illness had surprised many, and her death from the unknown ailment even more. There had been something about it. Something unnatural.

"Your Highness?" the mage asked.

"When Barric needed his friends most, they left him. I doubt the boy could muster any further support." Thom turned and took the mage in. One of those friends had been Ana's mother, and still thoughts of her dark hair and green eyes made his heart skip.

He had been surprised when she had returned to her childhood home. He had doubted her sister would offer any safe place to hide. He had been further surprised when the same sister had contacted him in recent times to alert them to the child. Now a woman, he reminded himself, thinking of her in that dress. She might be half his age, but she was old enough. He cleared his throat and looked out over his view.

"I want this sorted. I want certainty that the king is dead and this girl stopped. Any means necessary."

"Any, Your Highness?"

He turned back to the man. The mage stood frozen by the door, his head cocked to the side, his finger extended. It was only as he blinked slowly that the regent realised he hadn't released some strange magic.

"What are you thinking?" Thom asked, taking a step closer.

"I may have a way."

The regent waited. Was the man unsure of his own skill, or was it something that may be worse than their current situation? Although he struggled to wonder what that could be. "He could die from an accident," he suggested. So far, the boy was proving far too elusive to allow them to get close enough to make it happen.

"We could seek assistance from the beyond."

The regent felt himself suspended in time. The magic was a link between the two, he knew—or had been told. He couldn't understand it himself, as he hadn't been gifted the ability to feel it out. Mariela had once told him about it, in a moment he had thought would lead to something else. He shook the idea away.

"How?" he asked.

"I will ask."

"You intend to bring something of magic here?" Thom didn't know how he felt about such an idea.

"It would not be connected to us. We give it the boy's scent, unleash it in the mountains and it does our job for us."

"That seems... too easy."

The mage shrugged. "I'll see what can be done." He moved through the door as though it had stood open for him.

Thom always got the feeling the man was somewhat nervous of

him, although he wasn't sure why. In many ways, the regent feared the mage. If the man had been loyal to his brother, there would have been no chance for Thom to get as close as he had, nor be the threat that he had been. But the mage had other interests his brother would not have approved of, and Thom didn't mind if the old man had to sacrifice a few girls to get him what he wanted.

He turned back to the view, wondering what kind of magic the old man could release and how tight a leash he should perhaps try to maintain over it. If Ana had survived, did she have any magic left? Could she drag something from beyond as well? He shook his head. She was too young. She didn't know what she had, if she had anything at all.

Ana could feel Ende calling to her, but although she stood in the forest, she couldn't see him. Nor could she see Ed or Dray. She flexed her fingers. Her bones ached, as though the cold had stiffened her joints and her body would never be her own again. Ende called again, and in some ways, she thought he was angry.

She had to be dreaming, like when she had seen Ende in her dreams of the Walk, because although he had heard her call that day, he wasn't there. He hadn't been there. The forest slipped away as she thought of the Walk, and the lord's office grew around her in its place.

The cold grey stone seemed to suck more of her warmth. She wondered if she was still trapped in the frozen cells of the mage, if this had all been a dream, including the warm bed, the little dragon and the cleric who had known her mother.

She took a deep breath and closed her eyes. She could smell the office, the sea breeze blowing through the window to the Walk, hot tea from a cup on her desk. But there had been no one in the room when it appeared around her, and she wasn't sure she wanted to look now.

Something rustled, paper or the like. She prised her eyes open to take in the room. The breeze blew at the papers on the desk, some of them weighted down, but a sheet had floated to the floor. She didn't want to be here. She didn't want to be reminded of what she had thought she had. She didn't have anything now. Not even Ende. She looked out towards the Walk, but he wasn't here, and she could no longer hear him calling.

She stepped forward, her hand braced on the curved stonework around the opening. Nothing but sea and sky before her. She released her hold and stepped out. The breeze tugged at her dress, pulled at her hair. She pushed against it to stand on the end of the stone platform. A mist closed in around her, the wind died and she took another step.

Ana didn't fall. The ground felt soft and muddy beneath her boot, and as the mist cleared, she found herself in the middle of a battlefield. The sounds of fighting closed in around her. Shouting, screaming, clashes of metal on metal, metal on wood. An arrow flew past her, the whistle of the wind indicating how close it came, and yet it thudded into something else. Something soft. She looked into the eyes of a man before her as he cried out and fell forward.

She looked around, trying to determine where she was and why this was important. A dark shadow flew above her, but when she looked up it was gone.

"Ende!" she cried out, but he no longer called to her.

Men in black armour fought around her. She couldn't see any colours, couldn't work out who was fighting whom. Then her desperate gaze found a man she recognised, a tall, broad soldier swinging a sword. She was taken aback by the power behind it, the determination or hatred that drove it. He turned dark eyes towards her, a bloody gash across his cheek.

"No!" she screamed and then a hand covered her mouth.

Ana blinked into the light, the sword master leaning over her, his hand across her face, his own features angry—or was it scared?

He glanced about, and as Ana blinked her way back to this world, she glanced at the girl standing on the other side of the bed. Salima looked weary, as though pulled from sleep.

Ana carefully put her hand over his and nodded. She gulped down the fear, her heart still beating too fast, as though she had stood in that battlefield. As she closed her eyes, she could see Dray again, his face bloody.

"Is it Ed?" Salima asked in a hoarse whisper.

Ana shook her head.

"We can't keep you hidden if you give us away." The sword master took a step back. His fear had been for their discovery, and it had now been replaced with open anger.

"I'm sorry," Ana murmured. "It was a dream."

"A bad dream?"

"I'm not sure what it was."

"You think the king in danger?" Master Forest asked.

She shook her head, tears welling before she could stop them.

"Ana?" Salima asked, uncertainty clear in her voice, but she didn't come closer or look as though she might return to the sheets. As much as the girl's father didn't want her here, Ana was thankful for the warmth. She couldn't feel the magic as she had before, or whatever it was that had woken in her body when she had first reached Ed, and she missed it more desperately than she thought she could. She had never wanted any gifts, and for the first time she wondered where it had come from.

"Dray," she murmured as the tears spilled over.

"Your soldier?" the child asked.

"He isn't mine," she said. Although she wasn't quite sure what he was. She wondered if she would have connected to another in the same way, or if they were already connected before she had seen him there that day. Had Ende mentioned something similar?

"What did you see?" the sword master asked.

"I'm not sure. It wasn't clear, and yet it was." Ana took a deep breath and closed her eyes again, but Dray's bloody face was burned into the world on the other side of her eyelids.

She sat up quickly. Although the man and the child looked at each other warily across her, they didn't move back.

"I think I should leave," she murmured.

"And go where?" Master Forest asked. "You are hardly well enough to stand."

She threw the blankets back as though to dispute his words. But the chill air seemed to hold her in place. Would she ever be warm again? Would she ever find what she had lost?

"If they find me here…"

"They won't," he said with a sigh. "I am sorry." He stepped forward. "You frightened me, calling out so."

"What do you think I can do?" she asked.

"In terms of what?" His tone was more friendly as he indicated that she nestle back into the bed.

"Why help me? How does that benefit you?"

He raised his eyebrows in surprise. "You are determined to save the king," he said, pulling the covers back up around her, although the child on the other side of the bed remained standing, her eyes wide. "That is all we hope for."

Ana looked from him to the girl. She longed for the girl's warmth, but Salima remained wide eyed. Ana sat up, allowing the covers to fall away again. "You saw it."

Salima shook her head, then nodded. "Some. The bridge to nowhere."

"The Walk," Ana said softly.

Salima nodded vigorously. "You fell from there."

"Yes," Ana whispered. "But Dray caught me. Did you see the trees?"

"It was like where we saw Ed," Salima whispered, closing her eyes. "But it wasn't him calling to us." She looked at Ana, her eyes flicking to her father. "You. He was calling you."

"He might have been calling you too," Ana said softly, reaching for her, but she stepped back.

"I don't want to see any more."

Ana looked down at her hands, and then to the man standing by the bed. Now it was his turn to look scared, and he staggered, falling to his knees. Salima raced around the bed and took him in her arms.

"Papa," she pleaded, desperation raising her voice. It was enough to draw him back from wherever his thoughts had taken him.

"Shh," he said, holding her close. He looked up at Ana, but she didn't know what she could tell him. He believed Salima to be the king's daughter. He held the girl too tightly for too long, and although she looked uncomfortable kneeling on the floor, she allowed it. Then he held her out, looking her over as though for the first time. "What can you do?" he asked, a slight wobble in his voice.

"I…" She looked up at Ana. Although Ana wanted to encourage the girl, it was for her alone to tell her father what she was. But it might be some time before she really understood it. "I freed Ana from the cell."

"Did you break the lock?"

"I bent the bars." She said it so softly, he leaned forward to hear her. "I have fire," she said, holding out her hands to him as though that might explain it. He surprised Ana by taking the outstretched hands in his own. "Ana knew it, but I melted them." She was somewhere between excited and scared as she relayed the story of the escape to her father.

"And the trees?"

She sighed and looked down. "When Ana dragged me across the kingdom to Ed, I saw it all as though I was there, like I said. But the old man looked like he saw what was inside me."

He looked up at Ana then, the question clearly written on his face. This was not her secret to tell.

"And now, when Ana dreamed of him calling her, of searching for Ed, and the…"

Ana leant forward. "What did you see?"

"You care for him." Salima's face flushed as though with Ana's emotions, or she had seen something Ana had not.

"I care for all of them," Ana said, wondering just whom Salima had thought of as she said it.

"I saw the soldier's face." She pulled her hand from her father's as her fingers flew to her cheek, marking the gash. Ana drew in a deep breath just to stop from crying out again. "What am I?" she asked Ana.

Ana shook her head.

"You have called me so many names. I thought they were in jest, but you know me, you know what I am. In the cell you said 'dragon.'"

"I might have said many things," Ana said hurriedly.

"But you knew I had fire. Do dragons have fire?" she asked her father, but his ability to speak had slipped away.

He stared at the girl as if truly understanding who and what she was.

"Papa?" she said, pulling at his hands to draw his attention.

"How could that have happened? She wouldn't have…"

"Tell me what I am," Salima pleaded.

"My perfect daughter," he said, pulling her into his arms. She gave up, allowing him to hold her again, and Ana wondered whom he shed the tears for.

11

Dray woke feeling unsettled. The cottage was dark, and the king lay sleeping in the small cot against the opposite wall. His even breaths were somewhat calming. As he stared into the darkness above him, the dream disappeared, although he was sure he'd heard Ana's desperate cry. Had she tried to reach them again?

He sighed and closed his eyes, but he couldn't find sleep. If she was trying to reach him, it was a sign that she was still alive. Or it was his desperate mind hoping she was, and his dreams were the only way to reach her. He threw back the blanket and swung his legs around. The king still slept.

Pulling his boots on, Dray crept from the hut to stand in the moonlight. Something moved in the shadows. He reached for his sword, only to curse himself for his distraction. He would do Ana no good if he was killed. He had removed his armour and sword to sleep, and he hadn't even thought to stop and collect them on his way out. He had become far too relaxed among the trees.

The shadows moved again, and he stepped back and pressed himself to the door. Then a man appeared before him. Near Folk, not man.

"Has he decided?" Eilke asked.

Dray looked over the man and then shook his head. The boy had no idea. He wanted to be King because that was what he thought he should want. But he didn't think he would make a good one, or at least that was how Dray interpreted his lack of confidence. He had no way to help the boy, and the decision could only be his. Even if he were clear on what he wanted, Dray would still be at a loss as to how they could return to the capital and reclaim the throne. And if these people were to help them, he wasn't sure what that help would entail. They were still keen to provide tribute in the form of young wives, but he doubted the Near Folk were prepared to leave the forest at all. And where was Ende?

"More men come this way."

Dray looked at the man in the dim light of the moon. The glow gave his skin an unnatural hue.

"Into the forest or towards this village?" Dray asked.

The man smiled. "You ask good questions."

Dray waited.

"They move through the forest, but they are as you are."

Dray looked down over his thick black shirt. He doubted anyone was as he was in that moment. "More King's Men."

The guide bowed his head in agreement. Dray thumped one hand in the palm of the other. What were they doing? "Have they determined where the king is?" he wondered aloud.

"I think they may consider where he was," the guide returned, and Dray looked at the man. "They pass through the forest."

"What will they do if they don't find him there?" Dray wondered aloud, hoping silently that Ana hadn't given anything away. "Your chief is sure she is alive."

The man looked at him confused for a moment. "You worry for the girl rather than your king."

"I know where my king is," Dray returned quickly. "Ana could be dead."

"The chief is sure she lives."

"How can he be sure?"

The man shook his head. It wasn't a skill he had, then. "Where is your dragon?"

"I don't know that either."

"Could he be on the outskirts of the forest?"

"Would you be willing to help me find him?" Dray asked, wondering where the questions were leading. Did the Near Folk want Ende gone, or did they want to ensure he wasn't going to cause them any problems? "You would know if he was in the forest."

The man bowed his head in agreement.

Ende hadn't been the same since they'd entered the forest, and Dray wasn't sure if it was the tight spaces beneath the trees or something else. He knew what lived beneath the branches. He headed back inside the hut to dress, trying to ensure he didn't wake the king as he strapped his armour on. It might be a bad idea to leave him here alone, but Dray was sure these people wouldn't hurt him. Although how he was so sure, he couldn't tell. He tied on his belt as he left the cottage, the thick cloak draped around his shoulders. Eilke still dressed only in leather trousers, his bare tanned chest exposed to the elements.

"Does your chief call you Eilke?" Dray asked.

"We have other ways of calling to each other. What does your king call you?"

"Captain, usually," Dray said.

"The girl you care for, she calls you something different."

"She calls me Dray. Yet she also calls the king by name."

The man looked him over as though trying to work out which name fitted him best. He nodded once and led the way past the cottage and towards the trees. Dray wondered what name he had decided on, but he would find out if the man needed to use it. He wondered how Eilke might get his attention otherwise, but he was sure the Near Folk were nothing like any other people he knew. He felt a strange sensation cross his skin, and then they were standing in the trees.

Dray followed Eilke through the trees. He didn't know if the man was leading him away from the village to find Ende as he'd suggested, or if this was to allow the Near Folk access to the king and Belle. He stopped and turned slowly, wondering if he could find his way back on his own and doubting it greatly. He had made a mistake.

He was distracted from the thought as the trees opened up before him, and he could see the meadows beyond. He leaned into a tree and took in the sight. Despite his concerns, he wasn't sure they should leave the safety of the forest.

"Do you see him?" Eilke asked.

Dray shook his head. "Do you sense him?"

"Not in the trees. I fear he has gone."

Did they need Ende in this? Did the Near Folk need him? He took in the man beside him. "Should we look for the soldiers?"

Eilke nodded, and they headed back into the dense forest, only to emerge near the edge again a short time later.

"They have moved beyond the trees," Eilke said.

Dray could see the dust in the dim light; the moonlight occasionally reflected from dark armour. The road from the forest led towards the mountains, which were darker shapes in the distance. The soldiers were moving fast.

"They look for the king," he said. "Not to help him."

"They are his men," Eilke said.

"His uncle's men, and I fear his uncle would rather the king dead."

"They will return," Eilke said, turning from the open world beyond. Then he stopped and turned back. "The dragon came from the mountains."

"I'm not sure he would return to them, but perhaps. He was willing to help us, although he wasn't sure it was a good idea. And yet he hasn't been the same since he entered the forest."

"The girl," Eilke said.

Dray nodded. It was when Ana had appeared to them that Ende had first seemed so unsettled. Maybe he had seen more in her than he wanted. Dray had as well. He shook the image away, fearing that the mage had won her over, although he was sure he couldn't have done so in this short amount of time. Unless he had something to offer, such as a way to learn, or information on her mother.

"What would she be willing to give for such information?" he murmured.

"Shall we try the southern border?" Eilke asked.

"It wouldn't hurt to try," Dray murmured, wondering if he was right. The world was starting to lighten around them. "Should we return?"

"He will be safe."

"Will we?"

Eilke looked him over seriously. "We are of the forest. There is nothing in the forest we do not know of."

What should have taken hours or days of walking took only minutes, and Dray wondered just what magic the Near Folk had that they could bend the forest to their will. Or did they manage to manipulate something else? The way Ed had talked of leaving the clearing and not hearing or seeing the girls within it… Maybe it was more of a gateway than he had understood. They appeared to simply walk between the trees, Eilke never overly hurried as he walked ahead of him. Now they looked out upon more fields, the mountain gone and therefore it could only be the southern border of the forest.

"He might not be a man," Dray said, looking beyond the fields and distant cottages. The road was far from here, but if Ende was determined to travel he wouldn't find his way slowly; he would disappear above them. He might already be in the capital. If that was his wish.

"He was never a man," Eilke said as though it had been a question. "Where do you think he has gone?"

Dray shook his head slowly and turned back into the trees. "He does as he does."

Eilke looked at him.

"Would it matter?" Dray asked him, trying to read his steady features. "Why do you need to know where he has gone?"

"He has purpose. The chief worries that it may conflict with our purpose."

"And what is your purpose?" Dray asked.

"To survive," Eilke said, turning and walking into the trees. Within minutes, Dray felt the strange tingle across his skin, and he was standing beside the small hut again. Ed stood in the doorway, looking warily over the world before him.

"Did you find him?" he asked.

Dray shook his head.

"Do you think he is more worried for Ana? That he fears she has become the danger he sensed?"

"I don't know," Dray said. "We may not know, for he wasn't willing to share."

The king ran his fingers through his hair. "What do we do now?"

"That is up to you."

"Have you made your decision?" Eilke asked, his tone neutral.

Ed glanced towards the neighbouring building.

"You wait for the decision of others to influence you?" Eilke asked.

When the king opened his mouth, Eilke held up a hand to silence him. "We can wait," he said. "Others may not." He stalked away.

Dray watched him go, wondering what they would get from this, why they were concerned for Ende. Or was it that they worried where he might be and whom he might be talking with?

Dray could only hope that he returned.

12

The mage looked over the shelves and regretted, again, bringing the girl from the mountains. The effort had used the last of his options, and with the girl herself now gone, he would have to find more. The maid slipped a cup of tea silently onto his desk, and he turned towards her as she walked towards the door. There was something to her. It may be enough, although he doubted it. She had longed to be more—he had sensed it in her—and she was loyal.

"Child," he called, and she stopped.

She turned slowly and bowed her head. "How can I be of assistance?" she asked.

"Will you review the cell for me?"

"Review it?" she asked, with a slight wobble of uncertainty.

"Look over where the girl was held. See what might be different in that cell that would have allowed her to escape. Then tell me what you find."

She bowed her head again and disappeared between the shelves. He squatted before a stack of books, which rose from the floor to create part of a makeshift wall. He ran a finger down the spines and wondered when he had aged as he had. A quiet groan paused his movement before he tugged at the book, which slid easily from the pile. Once he held the book in his hand, those above it dropped down with a thud.

He closed his eyes and pulled the book to his chest before returning to his desk. He pushed everything else to the floor, including the fresh cup, and with his eyes still closed he dropped the book. When he opened his eyes, the book had opened to a page with strange markings. Not letters or even the script he used. They were more like what an animal might make scratching across a surface. He laid his fingers over several marks and then pulled his hand back at the sharp pain that raced up his arm.

He leaned over the page and whispered, "I would only offer you one who was worthy." Although he regretted the loss, the marks glowed a little darker, more a deep red than the brown black they had been before. They had been written in blood, whose he didn't know. It didn't matter.

It was some time before the girl reappeared, and he wasn't sure if she had been avoiding returning or if she had found something. There was a nervousness to her that he hadn't seen since she was a small girl standing before his desk.

"What is it?" he asked, wondering if there had been a mistake and Ana was in fact inside the cell trying to talk her way out.

The girl chewed on her lower lip. "There is no sign of a door," she said quickly.

"There never is," he answered.

"Sometimes I can sense where you have opened the cell."

He stared at her, wondering why he had not fully appreciated her before.

She swallowed loudly and cleared her throat. "Something has moved the bars."

"Something?"

She shook her head. "I tried, but I can't tell what it is or was. But it was hot. The ice has melted and then refrozen. It looks different. It feels different."

He squinted at her then. He should have gone himself. But he needed to know just what this girl was, although he was already wondering if this was the best use of her. He wouldn't be able to replace her so easily.

"What do you see here?" he asked, pointing at the page.

She leaned forward and then sucked in a frightened breath, but as she stepped back, he caught her hand and pushed it down onto the page. She screamed out.

"You wanted power," he murmured. "Now you have it."

Something growled within her, something that was not the child he knew, and he released his hold as she smacked the other hand down onto the page. She closed her eyes and drew in a deep breath. And then she smiled.

"What would you have me do?" she asked as she slowly lifted her hands from the page. The markings were gone.

He held out the image of the queen that the boy had sketched, one Ana had used to try and reach him. The maid leaned forward and licked the image, then closed her eyes. She rolled her shoulders, and her body shifted. She, whatever she had become, was no longer the child he knew. She licked her dark lips with a tongue now as black as the ink the image had been created with. She slowly blinked large ink-black eyes, which shimmered red around their edges.

"Kill him and anyone who stands in the way."

The strange girl bowed, reminding him of the maid he had lost, and then winked out of existence. He placed the picture into the now-blank pages and closed the book. Then he rested his hand on the worn leather cover and patted it gently. It was a small price he had paid, he thought, rubbing at his still-sore fingers that had brushed over the page. Now he needed to see the cell for himself and discover how she had managed to free herself.

She had heard him talking to the regent of the mountains, but she stood in the shadows behind the stables, and she wasn't alone. Nor was she what she had been. She closed her eyes, remembering the mage's grey eyes. Sorrow filled his face as he gave her what she had always wanted. And yet he didn't. She pulled back further into the shadows as a stable boy walked past in the early morning light.

The mage had given her something of power. Her body was no longer her own. She looked down over long dark fingers, thick claws extending them further. They were the hands of the creature that had created the marks on the page. She wondered if she would give that power back to the mage at some future point. She clenched the hand. For now. she was free.

She wanted to return to the cells, taste the scent of the girl and find her out. She knew the ice would have dulled any senses and skills she might have had. But the taste of the king pushed her, and whatever she had become, forward. She closed her eyes and breathed in the world around her.

The boy had been here, standing in the shadows, his heart pounding too fast. She wondered if he was scared of what he might find, or of leaving. She could taste the answer on the air. The fear of staying drove him forward.

She would do as they were bid and find the king. Kill the king. And then they could find the girl. They wanted the girl more.

13

Ana felt an uneasiness she couldn't explain cross her skin. It was different from the shivering she continued to have, and it was not reassuring.

"Ana?" the cleric asked, as though he'd noticed the movement. She turned from the window to take in his concern. "What is it?"

She shook her head.

"It was as though you called out, but didn't," he said slowly, his brow creasing as he tried to determine what he had heard.

"I felt something, but I couldn't tell you what. Just a feeling."

"Your mother had feelings."

Ana smiled, missing the woman she hadn't known all the more. "You said she had visions."

"Not often, more that her dreams were clear. I understand you have clear dreams too."

"And ones I am no better at understanding. What are we to do?" she asked, still looking out over the dark world beyond the cold glass. The sun had started to rise, but the sky was deep blue and there was no warmth in the golden glow that tinted the horizon.

"What do you ask?"

She allowed the heavy curtain to slip from her fingers and turned her full attention to the cleric. "I can't stay in this room forever."

"No," he agreed, leaning forward and patting the other seat by the fire. "But until you are what you were, I think we should cosset you away for a time."

"And if I am never as I was?"

"Your dreams are getting stronger."

"Did I call out again?"

"Yes, although it is almost as though you know you must hide yourself. I can see the stress on your face, the fear, the worry and sometimes wonder, but your lips move without sound."

Ana sat back in the chair, clasped her hands in her lap and closed her eyes. She felt as though she had screamed all night, although she couldn't clearly remember what she had dreamt of. It wasn't as clear as it had been when she'd seen Dray on the battlefield. At the thought of him, she saw him again, standing amongst the mud, splattered with blood, his face sliced and bleeding. He looked towards her, but she had no idea if he saw her. If he knew she was there.

"What if I'm not able to get to him?"

"There is much to happen in the world before you should fear for your soldier on the battlefield," the cleric said as though they'd had the conversation before. He had described him as her soldier. Although she knew the words to be true, Ana couldn't accept that he put himself in danger solely for her. Whether to save her or to fight on her behalf.

She sighed and looked towards the door. Master Forest had taken his daughter and disappeared. Whether it was because of what he had discovered or because he feared what else the child might learn from her, she couldn't tell. But she missed the girl's warmth. She could feel something, she realised, her focus still on the door. But she wasn't sure it was close.

"You have made that noise again," the cleric said, and she looked to him with confusion.

"I didn't say anything."

"No, and yet it was as though you spoke." He looked more confused by his words than she was.

"I am not what I was, not that I was anything for very long. But

I felt something else, something like the certainty I felt within my heart when I unlocked the power within me. Although it is frozen solid now, or gone. Could it have escaped and is wandering on its own?"

"You think your gift an entity?"

"It was as though I had to find a way to unlock the barrier between us. It had always been there. Could there be another like me?"

"I don't know," he said slowly, inching forward on his seat and leaning towards her to study her face. "Was this what your mother had?"

"You knew her, not me," she said quickly. Although she didn't want to sound as though she were accusing him of anything, it certainly sounded to her own ears that this was what she meant.

"She never told me," he said. "I wonder if she told your father."

"That too is a mystery. He didn't even tell me what I was, let alone what she was. I only learnt of her when I was in the mountains. In a castle magicked—it showed me things."

"What did it show you?" he asked kindly, leaning back again.

"My parents, her fear for me, his sadness at her leaving." Ana sucked in a breath. She hadn't known how true what she had seen was until she had arrived at the mage's workshop. The cleric watched her expectantly. "I also saw the mage's rooms," she said. "The magic he used to bring me here."

"Why?" he asked.

She looked at him. That was a question that opened up so many more questions; why had he brought her here? Why had she seen what she had? Why did he want her dead, again? Why had he helped her find what she was?

"We may never know," she murmured, standing again and looking at the bed. She should be doing more, being more help than sleeping and shivering and hiding.

"You must get better before you can find what you are," the cleric said.

The orange glow of the sunrise rimmed the curtains in the dimly lit room. She rubbed a hand over her forehead to find it still sticky with sweat. She climbed back into the bed, slipping into the cool space between the sheets, and pulled the covers up. The cleric surprised her by appearing at her shoulder and pulling the heavy blankets up higher.

"Sleep, child."

She closed her eyes as he bid, although she didn't think she wanted to sleep again. For she would dream, and the dreams only scared her more.

Ana stood amidst the fighting again, her heart pounding the same panic she had felt before. It pushed at her chest, the hard lump in her throat making it hard to breathe and swallow. Then a strong hand closed around her shoulder, and calm washed over her as she turned. She was standing in a dark forest with Dray.

He grinned at her and pulled her tight into his arms, her face against his chest. She wondered at the sensation, for he lived in his armour. The strangeness of it returned the panic. She pushed out of his arms and stood back, looking him over. His face was as perfect as it had been when she had last seen him in the flesh, and her fingers brushed across his warm cheek.

The smile he wore turned to worry, and he pressed her hand to his skin. "You are so cold," he murmured, wrapping the other arm around her.

"Where are you?" she asked.

"I'm coming."

The same fear filled her again. She wanted him near, needed him near, and yet she feared what she might do to him or bring upon him.

"Stay away," she whispered. "Stay with the king."

He sighed, his strong hold loosening, and she missed his embrace. "He does not know what he wants without you."

She looked up into his dark eyes, the stars twinkling strangely above him. "He knows what he is," she said. "I'm not sure I have the strength to help him. He must help himself. Be the man I know he is."

Dray pulled her close again, wrapping both arms around her. She did the same, surprised that she could reach so much further around him with the armour gone. He felt less intimidating, and yet more so in that moment. As she pulled herself into his chest, taking in the scent of him, his warm lips pressed into her hair.

Ana blinked into the light and sat up with a sigh.

"Another dream?" the cleric asked.

"Different," she murmured. "My mind playing some strange trick. It is daytime, I can't have…" She looked towards the window, the glow around the curtains gone. She looked back at the cleric, who stood and lifted a bowl from the table by his chair. "It is night again. Your body clearly needs the rest."

Ana sighed again, took the bowl he held out to her and wondered if she would ever reach them again.

Dray sat slowly and threw his legs over the side of the narrow bed. He ran his fingers through his hair and blew out a soft breath.

"I thought you slept with it on." The sound of the king's voice made him look up.

He looked from the king to the armour at the end of the bed. "Usually," he muttered.

"You look more like a man without it," the king said.

Dray raised his eyebrows. "What do I look like with it?"

"It is hard to say."

"Try," Dray suggested, attempting to keep his voice level. He wasn't sure why the words offended him, but he was still staggering from the strange dream. He could still feel the pressure against his skin where Ana had been pressed against his body, her arms wrapped tight and clinging to him as though she would never get the chance to see him again.

"What happened?" the king asked instead.

Dray refocused on the worried face of the king. And without thought, he rubbed his hand over his cheek where she so often indicated the scar had been, and where it might be again. He could still feel her icy fingers against his face, and as his fingers worked over it now, he was somehow disappointed that he could feel the stubbly growth of their travels.

"Are you worried about Ana?" the king asked.

"She was so cold," Dray murmured, then leant back as the king sprang to his feet.

"Did she come to you?" he asked, leaning over Dray.

Dray shook his head, but he wasn't sure. He wished he had his armour on. There was something he couldn't read in the king's face. Was it jealousy that she would come to him rather than the king? Or worry? He pushed out another slow breath. He couldn't explain what it was, and it may have simply been a dream. One where he had wanted to hold on to her forever.

"It wasn't her," he stammered, thinking of the feel of her in his arms. She had always been slender, but the smooth, tight-fitting dress was different, and he could feel heat pushing up his neck at the thought of her. What was Ana to him?

"Who was it?" the king demanded.

Dray shook his head and pushed him out of the way as he stood and collected his armour. "I don't know what it was. I thought it was Ana, but it wasn't. I don't know if she was calling to me or if it was a trick—or simply a dream because we want to find her so desperately."

The king was staring at him when he turned back, his armour over his head, pulling the tie tight.

"We do want to find her," Dray prompted.

The king nodded.

"And yet we remain here."

"I…"

Dray sighed. He didn't mean to push the king. He had decisions of his own to make. Support to find. They couldn't barrel into the capital and demand the return of a girl the mage had taken.

14

The inn smelt musty, as though the walls were damp, and although the maid screwed up her nose, the darkness wrapped around her felt at home. The scent of animals hung thick in the air, almost hiding the smell of the people it clung to. She hungered for it.

Closing her eyes, she allowed the dark to take control. She was the passenger now, and although she felt the pull of her task, they were now one. The room was loud with conversation, but none of it was important. The scent of the boy only travelled through the space. She looked up at the ceiling and then blinked, reappearing in a small room with a narrow bed and a small round table.

He had lingered here. A dark, clawed hand rested on the back of the chair. They could feel his wet cloak as though it lay there still. But it was long ago. Weeks ago. They looked out of the window, the mountains visible in the distance. Could he be there still?

The door squeaked open, but they maintained the place by the window. The long dark cloak would hide them until they were ready to be found. They were taller than she had been, broader than she had been. A lock clicked into place, and then there was the sharp intake of breath as the person realised they were not alone.

In a blink, they appeared between the short, round woman and the door, preventing an escape. She glared at them with angry eyes. As they tasted the air with a long black tongue, the glare turned to fear. They drank it in, and the maid's heartbeat quickened with excitement. Before the scream formed on the woman's lips, dark claws dragged across her throat, silencing the scream and pulling her closer.

Lost in his own thoughts, the regent only just registered the noise around him. But it was a general murmur; he couldn't focus on or hear any one voice above another. He glanced across the room, his gaze resting on the sword master, who was focused on his food and barely appeared to be listening to the man beside him. He seemed eager for some news or other, and in the end the regent stood and moved towards the table. He noticed the drop in voices as he passed.

He stopped by the sword master's table and stood beside him. The man continued to shovel meat into his mouth, his eyes unfocused.

"Is everything well?" Thom asked the sword master, who jumped, dropped his knife and looked up at him as though he had just appeared from nowhere.

"Your Highness," he said hastily, pushing his chair back and leaping to his feet.

"There is no need for such…" The regent waved his hand, unsure what he could call the movement, and indicated the man sit back down as Thom sat opposite him in a newly vacated space, an abandoned meal before him.

The man who had been eagerly talking before now sat back, an uncertain look on his face.

"Are you worried for the king?" the regent asked.

"Aren't we all?" Master Forest said, sitting slowly. "My daughter has been unwell," he murmured. "I'm afraid it has distracted me somewhat."

"Girls need a mother," the regent said.

The man nodded, the vacant look appearing again as he gazed at his plate.

"I am surprised you have not remarried."

The man looked clearly confused for a moment, then nodded. "I am too busy with my students to find a wife."

"The tribute will arrive soon enough. Perhaps you will not need to trouble yourself."

The sword master opened his mouth and then closed it.

"You do not long for a woman?"

"Too busy," he murmured. "The tributes are young girls. Close to my daughter in age. If I were to take the time to marry again, I would want a woman closer to my years."

"I see," the regent said slowly.

"Has there been any news on the king?" the man beside the sword master asked.

"News?"

The man opened and closed his mouth before getting brave. "The witch said he had run because you would not let him be King."

"You would believe a witch over the King's Regent?"

"She seemed to know."

"She did appear determined," Thom admitted. "But what did the witch want from such a show?"

"We could ask her?" the sword master suggested.

"Ask her?" Now he was confused.

"You had her arrested and locked away?" the sword master said. "Surely you would interrogate such a woman. She might have been behind the king's disappearance all along and was trying to divert attention."

"Perhaps," the regent said, wondering just what the man opposite him was thinking.

"I could assist," he offered.

"I'm sure I have the right men on the task."

"Is she talking?"

"I'm afraid not," the regent said carefully. The girl had been seen talking with him. The mage had suggested he might be involved in her escape, although he doubted the man capable of such a thing.

"If you need my service, I am at your disposal." The sword master bowed his head.

"And your daughter?"

He shook his head. "I do worry, but the cleric is keeping a close eye on her."

"I'm glad to hear it," the regent murmured, pushing the chair back. Without a glance at either man, he headed back to his own table.

The sound of the room remained hushed, and he wondered if others feared or expected a visit from him. Perhaps he should make the effort to talk to more men of the kingdom, find out what they thought. Although he wasn't really interested, unless they were hiding the girl from him. If he should find her before the tributes arrived, he might be able to slip her amongst their number and claim her where she had no choice.

He absently rubbed at his arm. She might make it clear what her choices were. He would have to find another way to break her. Once he found her.

The mage wasn't in his rooms when Thom searched him out later in the evening. The room was dark; only one candle burned, and he couldn't tell where it was placed. There was no sign of the maid either. He swung around and headed back out into the courtyard. The torches had been lit, and there were few walking the grounds.

He glanced towards the cellar. When he was sure no one was looking, he headed that way, moving easily through the main store. He released the door and descended into the too-bright light of the cells.

The mage stood before a cage and ran his hands over the bars.

"How did she escape?" the regent asked. The mage barely

flinched at his voice, his focus still on the bars. "Was she as strong as you feared?"

The mage continued his assessment, then rubbed his hands together and tucked them into his tunic. "She is not as strong as she thinks she is."

"Then how?"

"Someone helped her."

"Someone in the castle?"

The old man scowled at him and then, as though remembering himself, rearranged his face and sighed. "Someone came into the cells and released her."

"How did they know she was here?"

"That I don't know, but it was someone very strong."

"More magic," the regent whispered, "and not on our side."

"It appears not. But I do have some I can use to benefit us."

"The soldiers, have they reported in?"

"They continue to search."

"Then they should—"

The mage held up a hand and Thom bit his tongue, wondering if this was the place he should risk angering the man. He shivered and pulled his cloak tighter around him. Perhaps they would be better discussing this elsewhere.

"I have sent someone I trust to complete the task required."

"I trust the soldiers I sent."

"There is no other I would trust more," the mage said, looking again at the bars.

"Except your little maid, perhaps," the regent quipped, and the mage turned an angry glare his way. He thought something flashed within the man's grey eyes, but it might have been the light. "It is cold," Thom murmured, heading for the stairs. "I trust the one you sent will report."

"You will know when the task is complete."

The regent nodded and moved quickly up the steps. In his haste, he slipped a little and nearly tumbled forward.

"Be careful," the mage whispered too close behind him. "If you die there will be no question as to who should wear the crown."

When Thom swung around, the man was gone. He sucked in a deep breath and looked up into the darkness above him. He had always managed to make his way into the cells when he wished, but there was always the small niggling fear at the back of his mind that one day he would find himself trapped down here. He glanced around once more, then moved as quickly as he could up the slick steps and out into the cellar. The door clicked shut behind him, and then he heard something else. But as he strained in the darkness to determine if anyone else was there, he heard nothing further. He headed back to his tower and the safety of his balcony.

15

Ana sighed against the glass. Her breath fogged the small pane and obscured her view of the lights below. "I need to get out," she murmured.

"You are not yet well enough," the cleric said from his usual chair by the fire.

"Surely you have other things to be doing," she said, not turning from the window despite losing her view.

"Nothing as important as this."

"I feel much better," she said, finally turning and trying to smile for him.

"Your long hours of restless sleep tell a different story."

"The fever is gone."

"But you aren't yourself," he said, looking at her through squinty eyes.

She sighed and sat in the chair. "I have always had strange dreams."

"But they have become more so."

"How do you know that?" she asked too loudly. "I don't tell you everything," she added more quietly, glancing at the door.

"I see enough that they concern you, confuse you even, as though you don't expect to see or experience what you do. Salima saw much of that battle and the Walk, and it scared her."

"She is a girl," Ana said gently. A girl who hadn't returned to her since. "Is she sick?" she asked, worried that she may have taken too much from the little dragon.

"Her father is worried."

Ana nodded and looked down at her hands. She had dreamt of Dray again, as though she had found him, but it wasn't as it should have been. And yet, she felt more at peace.

"Do you want to talk about what you saw?"

She flushed at the idea. He had been without his armour again. She had felt the man he was through his shirt, the strength of his muscles, and her fingers had moved beneath the soft material to brush across his warm skin. She was still so cold, yet he hadn't flinched away from the touch as she had feared he might. Instead he held her closer, tighter, as though he didn't want her to leave him again.

"Are you confused by what you saw?" the cleric asked.

Ana nodded, but talking about it would not help. "I need to get out of this room," she tried again.

"Not until I know you have regained yourself."

"That is an odd thing to say," she said.

He looked to the flames. "You said that you felt the magic wake inside you. I think the cold has kept it from awakening again. Until we know that you can be what you were, I think we should wait."

"And if I am never again what I was? What if I was never meant to be? I only truly felt that power once I reached out to Ed, and I only had it a short time. Days. Maybe it wasn't mine at all."

"Do you truly believe that?" he asked.

"I don't know. I don't know what I am." Ana put a hand to her chest as she felt a strange stirring sensation. The cleric sat forward and looked at her closely. She shook her head, then looked up as the door opened and Master Forest slipped quickly into the room. He took a moment to close the door and then turned to take them in.

"The regent has suggested I marry one of the tributes."

The cleric sat back, a smile splitting his face. "Is he trying to win your favour?"

The man shook his head.

"Did you accept his offer?"

"I told him that if I had the time or inclination to marry again, it would be to a woman of my own age and choosing."

The cleric nodded his approval.

"What happened to your wife?" Ana asked, then chewed on her lip as he turned a hard glare her way. "I'm sorry," she said quickly.

"I was not married," he said with a sigh. "It was a story the king and I concocted to allow me to escape with the child."

"Salima," Ana said, thankful she wasn't present; although it was the first time, for she missed the heat. "I understand you want to protect her."

"You are to stay away from her."

"And will you keep her from me?"

"I just said…" He turned as she indicated behind him with a tip of her head. Salima crept silently into the room and closed the door without a sound. She turned to find the three of them looking at her, then straightened and smiled.

Ana settled back into bed reluctantly, with the three of them watching over her. She was still cold. She longed for the girl to warm her, but her father was having none of it. He guided Salima from the room as the old cleric ran his hand across her forehead and ensured she was tucked in.

It was a surprise then when she woke, unsure what had woken her, to find herself alone in the room. The fire crackled in the hearth, a single candle burning beside the bed. Two empty chairs and no one snuggled in beside her. Did they trust her more, or was there more pressing business for them to attend? Perhaps the regent had become suspicious, if he was suggesting wives or the like for Master Forest.

Ana put her hand to her chest. She wasn't sure what it was that she had felt before, but it wasn't there anymore. The emptiness that had replaced whatever had been inside her appeared to remain in strength.

Why had they thought she had some gift? What had the mage done to bring the idea of it to the surface, only to take it away? She lay back, pulled the covers up around her neck and closed her eyes.

Her mother came to mind, sitting at the table with the baby in her arms. Her father determined that she shouldn't go.

"What did she think I was?" Ana wondered aloud as her mother's fears replayed for her, as they had that day in the castle on the mountain. "Don't let them discover what she is?" Was that what she had said? *What am I?*

What do you want to be? a voice asked inside her head. Not quite her own, and yet it was hers.

Ana squeezed her eyes closed tighter, trying hard to picture the question.

A set of shining eyes looked back at her. Bright-green, round eyes that blinked slowly. *Well?* the voice asked impatiently. *What do you want to be?*

"I don't know," Ana whispered.

I can help you. Do you want to be the strongest mage in the land? Do you want to be Queen?

Ana saw herself as Ende had so long ago, standing before a throne, a crown in her hand. And then she was in the smoke in the mage's rooms, as a woman she didn't quite recognise, with the crown on her head.

"How did you find me?" she asked, her voice a hushed whisper in fear someone would return.

I never lost you. I have been with you always. We are linked across the veil.

"The veil?"

Do you not sense the world beyond? You are one of the few who can feel it, sense it and connect to it. You only had to call me forth. The ice tried to separate us, but we are together now. I am you and you are me. Together we can be anything.

"I'm not sure I want to be anything in particular. I just want to protect my friends, help Ed be King."

You will be his queen.

Ana shook her head. "That is not what I want. I don't want the crown. I want to help him be what he already is."

A strange cackle filled her senses, making her shiver. *If he is already King, he does not need your help.*

If only it were that easy, Ana thought. What did she want for herself? Dray flashed into her mind again, dressed as he had been without his armour the last few times she had seen him. The voice inside her didn't speak, and she wondered what it could see of her thoughts.

Everything.

Ana sighed and looked up at the ceiling, too scared to close her eyes again.

We worked together before, with the little maid, the regent.

"I didn't know you were there."

Child, the voice chided, *you knew something was there inside you, giving you the power.*

"So, it is your power, not mine."

It is ours. You may use it how you wish.

Ana had no idea how she wanted to use it, other than to help Ed. She was more confused than she had been before, and as she closed her eyes, the large green eyes stared back at her again. She didn't feel afraid, though, and she thought that was something she should feel.

The darkness had been comfortable, and despite the strange smell, she was no longer repulsed by it. And although there were moments of clarity, as though she were lost in the hold of something greater than herself, she knew she was part of that new being. That they were one.

They blinked as one now into the light in the cold empty castle. If it could be called such, for it was small in comparison to what either of them had known in a previous life. The scent of the world was similar to what it had been in the dark. Empty.

A long black tongue licked over their lips, tasting the air. Sensing the boy.

They turned from the castle towards the view from the mountain across the kingdom. The green world beyond was so unlike the worlds that surrounded the castles of their past.

The green trees of the forest appeared more unnatural than the creature looking towards them. And they took a step forward. The tongue flicked again. She had been here, the witch who wasn't.

They dragged their interest away from the trees and back to the castle, pushing through the weathered door. The scrape of claws on flagstones echoed through the hallways. Inside a larger room, the scent of the girl stopped. As though it had been dragged with her from this very spot. A growl of frustration filled the space.

She had been pulled from here. The boy had been here as well, and something else. Something unexpected, something hot.

Who did the boy travel with?

The forest would know. The trees would know. But would they share such secrets? Would they keep him for themselves or give him up?

They would find a way. The growl of frustration echoed through the room long after the creature had winked back to the darkness.

Salima tried not to grumble as she headed for the practice hall. A couple of young men were already headed that way, and she knew her father would be busy. But he had asked for her to attend. Not because he thought the young men would need her assistance in any way, but because he didn't want her anywhere near Ana.

He had been saying that for days, but the night before he had been very clear. She'd almost had the feeling that she had walked in on something, a discussion he did not want her to be a part of, because he had looked even angrier than she'd expected when she'd entered the room.

She had been careful. Between the three of them, they had been coming and going, and they needed to ensure no one saw them. Very few used the hallway outside the room, but being so close to the royal suite did mean more soldiers and risk.

Salima stopped as a tall, handsome man appeared at the edge of the courtyard. He appeared to be looking for something or someone. When his searching gaze fell on her, her heart beat so fast she was sure it would leap from her chest.

It was as though she knew him. Something on his face changed, softened, and he walked quickly towards her. Salima was frozen to the spot. Something about him scared her, and yet she had to talk to him, had to be near him. As she took a step forward, a hand closed around her arm.

She looked up at her father, his face unreadable. When she looked back at the man walking towards her, he was moving faster—very fast. She sucked in a breath as he stepped in close.

He bowed his head, his feet together. And when he looked up, he had the blackest eyes Salima had seen. In fact, they were solid black. She stepped forward again, pulling from Papa's grip and towards the man.

He smiled at her, his perfect straight white teeth catching the light. He was handsome, with a strong square jaw and dark ruffled hair. It was short but wayward, as though the wind had blown through it. His clothes were dated but bright. She looked back to her father, who appeared unsure of what to do. He looked more afraid than Salima had ever seen him.

"Do you know me, child?" the tall, handsome man asked, his voice much deeper than she expected. It vibrated through her.

She nodded, although she wasn't sure why. She didn't know

this man. Did she?

"Papa?" she asked, turning back to her father. "What is it?"

He sucked in a deep breath and took a step forward to stand beside her again, his hand finding hers. "Ende," he said politely, bowing his head. "Why are you here?"

"Ende?" Salima asked. "But he is an old man."

"I am what I need to be," Ende said, his deep voice rumbling through her. She felt comforted by it, despite not knowing him. She wanted to put her arms around him and see how warm he was.

"You know Ana," she said instead. "Have you come to find her?"

"She found you," he said, his voice soft and gentle. Salima felt he appreciated what Ana had done, although she wasn't sure why.

"I don't think we should do anything right now," Papa murmured.

"You have students," she said, and he flinched. "And I am to help you," she added quickly, fearing he thought she was trying to get rid of him and spend time with this man, although she wasn't sure why that would matter.

"I can find Ana," Ende said.

She shook her head and stepped closer to him. "It is not safe," she whispered. "The mage is trying to kill her, and we have hidden her away."

Ende looked at her seriously, and then at her father, who nodded once. "You have not hidden her very well," he said, looking towards the tower.

"How?" she asked.

"She called to me once, and I can find her again."

"Did you bring Ed with you?" she asked hurriedly, looking around to ensure they weren't being overheard as Ende shook his head.

"Is he safe?" Papa asked.

"Do you think I would harm the boy, given who he is?"

Her father remained steadfast, and she nudged him. "Papa?"

"We have class," he said, taking her hand and pulling her away from the strange tall man. Ende watched them go, his dark eyes shining in the light.

Once they were inside the room, she pulled from his hold. "He was old," she said.

Her father glared at her as several students looked their way.

"What is he?" she asked.

"I don't know," he murmured.

16

Ed felt completely at a loss. They had spent too long in the forest, and he didn't feel they had achieved anything. He knew what he should be doing, but he didn't think he had the strength, nor the understanding as to how these people might help him find it. Belle looked just as lost as he watched her standing by the hut, staring into the trees. Did she want to go with her friends, or did she want him to stop them? He wasn't sure how to do that, or whether he should. The tribute was set, and they were willing to go.

He didn't want that life for Belle, despite how she frustrated him at times. But he had nothing he could offer her instead. With her they would have the ten needed, and he wasn't sure when the soldiers were coming. Although he was sure the exchange would not occur around the Near Folk.

Dray emerged from the hut. He looked as he always did, armour polished, although how he managed that in these conditions Ed didn't know. His cloak about his shoulders, his hand on his sword, he looked the part of a man ready to face whatever might threaten his king.

Ed was also sure the man could last for days without sleep, and yet he had appeared more tired over the last few days. When he did sleep, it was fitful. Ed had heard him calling out in the night, and he appeared somewhat spooked when he woke, as though having seen something that worried him.

"Where is Ende, do you think?" Ed asked the soldier, startling the man who appeared ready for anything.

Dray shook his head. "Where he thinks he needs to be," he said, rubbing at his face.

Ed had noticed that his hand moved to his cheek too often, where Ana had been so sure she had seen the scar. Did he feel something? Had he seen something in those dreams?

"What if I did go?" Belle asked, still looking at the trees. Her father murmured something Ed couldn't hear.

"I can't even keep a small group together," Ed lamented. "How could I keep a kingdom together?" He sighed and looked at Dray, hoping for some words of support.

"Is that a decision?" the soldier asked instead.

"I need Ana," Ed said. She was the only one who had been sure of what he was. And without her, he couldn't see that himself.

"Of course you do," Belle groaned. "Come with me, Pa," she said, taking her father's hand. "Come to the capital. I will find a good husband who will provide, and you will be cared for. You will never have to work another day."

The older man's jaw dropped open.

"It is the only way I can help you."

Ed looked from them to Dray and gulped down his regret. He didn't want her married to some strange man in the capital. Some man selected by his uncle to win his favour. But what could he offer? Did he even want to make her an offer? She was right; it might be the best chance she had.

"Your decision is to give up," the chief said, appearing beside him. It wasn't even framed as a question.

He knew Ed's heart and mind. And although Ed wanted to be something more, he was just the insignificant boy his uncle had always known him to be. He wiped quickly at the tear that surprised him. He had made the decision, and it hurt to do so. It was what was best for the kingdom.

"Truly?" the chief asked. This time it was a question, and Ed slowly nodded his head. He looked at the faces around him. Phillip looked at the ground. Belle looked beyond him, tears clearly shining in her eyes, even across the gap between them. Dray dragged a hand across his jaw and sighed.

"None of us are what we should be," Ed murmured. "They should have a chance. It would only bring them harm to follow me anywhere."

"Where would we go but with you?" It was Dray who asked the question, but Ed's gaze rested on Belle.

She shook her head once. "You don't care what happens to us," she said.

"I do. I want you to have a life you deserve. Not trapped here, waiting on me to come to a decision I never will. You want the chance at a family, and to help your father."

"I had thought the king might help him, given his service."

Ed ran a hand through his hair. "I can't even get back to the capital, let alone a throne. What use am I?"

She huffed, her back straightening as though she was going to say something, like she would have when they'd first met. Like the time she'd slapped his arm when Ana had told them they were to help the king. He blinked back the tears, showing he was a boy, just what they all thought he was.

"What do you want to be?" the chief asked, his voice like a whisper of wind in Ed's ear.

"I want to be of use," he admitted, "but I'm not." He turned from the group and headed towards the trees.

Something dark flashed in the corner of his eye. He searched the trees trying to find it and found Dray standing beside him, his sword drawn.

"Did you see that?" Ed asked.

Dray didn't move, his eyes trained on the trees. His arm stretched out across Ed's chest as though he might push Ed behind if something threatened. Ed glanced around to find Belle and her father had moved back towards the hut. The chief closed his eyes and tilted his head to the side.

"Is it Ende?"

"I don't think it can reach us."

"You don't think?" Belle asked, her voice high and scratchy, making Ed smile. She still had some fight, it seemed. "What is it?"

The chief shook his head. "I don't think it is only one."

Ed drew his own sword then, and Dray gave him a sideways glance.

"You might be good," Ed murmured. "But can you take on two?"

"We are surrounded by Near Folk," Phillip said.

"They don't want us," the chief said, staring into the dark.

Ed's heart beat loud in his ears as he pushed Dray's arm down. He closed both hands around the sword and nodded to the man beside him.

The longer Ana spent in the room, the more desperate she was to get out. The magic that filled her—however it had come to be, or from where—pushed at her extremities. It wanted to be far from this room as well.

"Where would you go?" the sword master asked, staring into the flames. He had been distracted since he had arrived in the late morning. The girl was not with him, and for the first time Ana missed the child rather than the heat of her. She had finally warmed enough to allow the magic to awaken, not that she had shared that yet. And it had stopped the ache in her bones.

She had found herself again, just as the cleric had suggested she needed to do. He hadn't been near since he had tucked her in the night before, and she wondered what he knew of her that she didn't know herself.

"Maybe I could find Ed," she said.

"And what would you do with him? Bring him back? Send him

away?"

"Master Forest," she said, remaining where she was standing in the middle of the room, "what do you think should be done for the king?"

He looked up at her then, as though not quite listening to what she was saying. "Have you had a visitor?" he asked instead.

She was honestly confused by the question. "Outside of yourself and the cleric, who I have not seen today? No." She took a small step forward. "Do they know where I am?"

Despite the concern, calm filled her. She knew she could escape the mage. He would not get the same chance again, and she might also ensure that the regent kept his distance.

At the idea that someone might have found them, the door quietly swung open. Ana turned to find a grinning Salima slipping into the room, a tall man following her in. As she closed the door and ushered him forward, she said, "I have brought you a visitor."

Ana looked from the grinning girl and the tall man to the sword master, who had pushed out of the chair and now stood before the fire. He shook his head.

"He would have found her anyway, and this way I could be sure that no one noticed him."

"I think there may be more than one who has noticed he is back in the castle."

"Ende?" Ana breathed, stepping forward. His dark eyes flashed, but he remained still and unmoving. It all made sense, the man the queen had fallen for, loved, and what she would risk for him. Which had ended up being her life.

"Say something," Salima said, giving the tall man a nudge. Her father stepped forward again.

"I can see it," he said, his voice deep, his face unreadable.

Ana nodded once. What else could she do? Was this what he had feared for her? Of what she would become? An image of the crown appeared in her mind, her standing before the throne, and Ende growled. The noise filled the room, rattled the windows and pushed out the fire. Salima rushed across the room to Ana, throwing her arms around her and burying her head in her shoulder.

"I'm sorry," she murmured. "I thought he was your friend."

"He is," Ana soothed, patting her back. "He, like all good friends, wishes the best for me."

Ende grumbled something else, which similarly came out as a growl, but not to the same extent. If not for his angry heat, the temperature in the room would have dropped, and the girl in Ana's arms turned to him as though she could feel it.

But Ana pulled her closer as something dark swam in her vision. A strange creature, and yet she knew it. The magic surged angrily inside her. She clutched at her chest, pushing Salima out of reach in the same movement. Ende's hand wrapped around her arm and pulled her clear.

"No!" she yelled as the room around her vanished.

She was in a forest amidst thick dark trees, and yet she stood in a clearing. The darkness drew closer. She could feel it in the trees, and yet she couldn't see it. How close was it?

"Ana?" Ed's voice broke through her searching concentration, and she turned to take in the group staring at her. Ed, Belle, Phillip, a strange man she did not know and Dray, standing close to his king and yet unable to look at her. Had they been more than dreams?

Ed rushed forward and threw his arms around her. She held him tight, looking over his shoulder at the man who would have been the first to find her as he studied the ground.

"Come and meet the chief," he said, pulling her towards the other man.

"I'm not here to visit," she said quickly.

"You know what it is," Belle said, looking towards the trees.

Ana stepped forward and touched her arm, and then Phillip's, reassuring herself that they were real. "I am glad you are safe."

"We've lost Ende," Dray said, maintaining his distance. Ed

looked at him strangely.

"I think I know where he is. And why," she said, looking back at Ed.

She turned to the chief and bowed her head.

"They want you too," he said, and she turned back to the darkness she could feel in the trees.

She stepped forward and closed her eyes, reaching out between the trees. She glanced back at the chief. The trees were infused with their magic, or their magic came from the trees, a very different place than her own. It confused her for a moment.

"You may use it," the chief said, bowing his head. "They will do more harm if they reach us."

She sucked in a deep breath and turned back. She could feel the trees, and she stretched her senses along them. The darkness drew closer. Two and yet one.

Large green eyes blinked behind her lids, and she could see the shadows like she had seen the magic within her. It came from beyond the veil, from the other realm, as her magic had. Was her magic this dark?

Focus, or it will kill us all.

"How can I stop them?"

A hand rested on her shoulder, and she sucked in a shuddering breath. Ed. They had always been something together. Were they the force she saw coming? Although the creature was coming for the king first, and she couldn't save Ed by putting him forward.

Before she could determine how to save any of them, the shadows moved from the trees and a large black creature stood before them. Ana could feel the trees holding it back, but she didn't know how she might use that. A wide grin split its face in half, and a dark tongue licked over it. Red-rimmed eyes stared at her as the hunched figure took a step forward. It was at least seven feet tall, slender, and as the cloak fell from its shoulders—no, their shoulders—the creature stood taller and almost feminine in shape.

She closed her eyes as Belle started to whimper behind her.

Reaching out, she could feel the two souls intertwined, becoming one within the creature. One she knew; the other knew her.

She pushed Ed around behind her, or at least tried as he was determined to stand beside her. "She is after you," Ana hissed. "Allow me to protect you."

"She?" he asked.

"They. There are two within."

"How do you know?" he asked as the creature remained focused on Ed, staring and flicking the long tongue.

"She is the same," the chief whispered behind her. Then the creature pounced, moving forward incredibly quickly, sharp claws outstretched.

Ana closed her eyes again, stretched out her hand and hoped she had something of the magic within her to stop it. As another hand rested on her shoulder, an ear-splitting scream filled their world. And the hold squeezed tighter.

The creature was on its knees. Long fingers covered its face; the claws scratched at its eyes.

"Stop," Ana said. And it did, dropping its hands to the ground and bowing its head.

"Forgive us," it hissed.

"Who sent you?" she asked, although she knew the answer.

It looked up, an unnatural grin spreading across its face. But when Ana scowled, it looked down again. "We did not know you were here, Majesty."

"But I thought…" Belle said behind her.

"I only want the boy," it hissed.

"He is mine," Ana said. She felt Dray's hand lighten its hold, and the creature flicked its dark eyes to him. "They are both mine," she added.

"The child wants your blood," the creature said, twitching and crying out again, as though in a battle with itself.

"She is yours," Ana continued. "Do not make me take her."

The creature pulled back, hissing again, and then it was gone.

Ana sighed, putting her hands to her face. "What are you?" she asked.

I am you.

"Ana?" Ed asked, pulling her towards him, and Dray's hand slipped away.

"Where did you come from?" Belle asked, and turning to Ana. "Where did that come from?" She held out her arm towards the trees.

Ana shook her head. "I don't think it will return, not yet. The trees help keep you safe." She glanced at the chief then, his face unreadable. He nodded once. "I can't stay," she said to him.

"The trees struggle with your kind."

"I understand," she said as Ed gripped her tighter, pulling her back into his arms.

"You can't leave us."

"I must. I can't keep you safe in the trees. They have a magic of their own."

"Do you want to be Queen?" Ed asked, his low voice whispered in her ear.

She pulled out of his arms, confused by the question. Then she glanced at Belle, standing back. "No," she said too quickly.

"She already is," the chief said, bowing his head once more.

"That is not what I want," she said. "That is not who I am."

"You are as you are. She and you are one."

She spun on Dray, still at her back, still silent. She looked at him, willing him to say something that would help, but he only shook his head.

"What is she?" Belle asked.

Ana closed her eyes. "It no longer matters," she whispered. And when she opened her eyes, she was too close to the mage and too far from those she only wanted to help.

17

"What is she?" the king asked the chief as Dray stared at the space Ana had filled not so long before.

He had known something was coming, something dark. Then she had appeared and his first thought, other than to throw his arms around her and drag her to his chest, was that she was the darkness.

Then the king had done just that, holding her tight, and although she had returned the hold, she'd looked at Dray. Willing him to do the same, and yet he couldn't.

"What is wrong with you?" Belle asked, tapping his arm.

"What?" He shook Ana from his mind and stared down at the blonde girl.

She stared up at him, her hands finding her hips. "What is wrong with you?"

"Nothing," he said quickly. But Ana hadn't looked like the girl he remembered, and she felt different beneath his hold. As she did in his dreams. Although he couldn't understand such dreams, he wondered if she had shared them.

"You hesitated. You never hesitate when it comes to Ana," Belle said, her voice accusing him, of what he wasn't sure.

"Belle?" the king asked. "He stepped up when he needed to, as he does. Did he hesitate?" Now he was watching Dray closely as well.

"I was surprised," Dray said. The girl nodded as though

agreeing with him. He had hesitated. He had not wanted them to know what he felt. He didn't want her to be confused. He was confused.

"She is like that creature," he said, making eye contact with the chief of the Near Folk. "Yet you allowed her access to the trees."

"She is alike and yet very different."

"She is two souls, joined as one."

The chief sighed. "It is not something I can explain. I know of it, but not what it is. Her magic has come from… beyond," he added as though searching for a word. "They work together, for a common goal."

"The crown," Dray said. "That creature called her Majesty."

"It may be that the other is just that, but whether that is what your Ana wants is unknown."

He wanted to say that she wasn't his, that he claimed no ownership, and yet they were connected. He looked back at the man and then his hand.

"You are connected, and she draws from you. Although, which one draws that power we may never know."

"Until the king is handing him her crown and we are all lost."

Dray glanced at Belle. Did she really think that Ana would betray them in such a way?

"I don't…" the king started, but Belle turned an angry glare on him, and he stopped.

"You don't know her. She suddenly appeared in our midst when we thought she couldn't return to us, and then she was gone again. She could have taken you with her. She could have taken you to the capital and magicked you onto the throne."

"She may think us safer away from the capital," Dray offered. Ana would have had a reason. She had come to save them, after all, sensing the creature. But he had hardly understood what she had said to it, other than that he was hers as well. He pushed out a breath. He would be sleeping in his armour tonight. If she did visit him in his dreams, rather than an idea of her, that might slow things down enough for them to talk.

"What do we do now then?" Belle asked with a strength he hadn't seen in her since they had entered the forest. "Do we wait for that creature to return? Do we try for the capital?"

Dray sighed. He had no idea what to do. He looked to the king, who was studying her.

"What will you do?" the king asked.

"I don't know," she snapped, and he grinned at her. She wasn't quite sure how to respond and looked down. "I'm sorry," she murmured.

"Don't be," the king said quickly, stepping forward. "It is nice to see some spirit. I wish I had the same passion."

"Do you think Ende has gone to the capital? Did Ana know where he was?"

Dray nodded. "She knows, although she didn't say where or why." Dray turned back to the chief. "What do you say?"

"You are to follow your king, not I."

"I know what is to be done," the king said, his voice calm. Dray wondered when he had finally determined what he was to do, or if it had only happened when Ana had appeared before them. "I am unsure how to achieve it. And I don't want to bring death to the kingdom in my attempt to retake it."

"It may not be avoidable," Dray said.

"We can't hide here forever," the king said. "Can you help me?" he asked the chief.

"We can guide you, help in some ways, but it is you who must find a way to defeat your uncle and reclaim your throne."

"I have some allies within the capital."

"Enough?" the chief asked.

"I hope so," the king said, turning to Dray, who hoped the look he was trying to give was confidence.

Ende watched the girl by the window, her hands fidgeting, and he wondered how safe they really were in this room. He glanced around. It had a familiar feel to it, and he wondered if it was just the castle. Being back stirred more in him than he'd expected.

She glanced at him and then back to the view beyond. She looked so like her mother, and yet there was something very different. Her hair was more red than blonde, but its wayward nature caused his breath to catch. He looked over at the sword master watching him closely. He knew the truth, it seemed by the way he watched Ende, as though he might take the child and run.

Ende had no idea why he needed to be here, why he had to come and see the child for himself. But that was the reason—not Ana, not a need to help the king, but to see that the child he was so sure had killed Essa had lived.

"When will she return?" she asked, a longing in her voice he did not expect. Too much was not as he had thought.

"It is hard to know how far she has gone," Ende said, trying to keep his voice soft. Forest feared they would be discovered. Even with Ana gone, the regent would make them pay for taking residence in his tower.

"She went for Ed," the child said, as though it were obvious to all. "Will she bring him back?"

"Is it safe to return him?"

"That is what Ana says."

"What is she to you?" Ende asked.

She shrugged then, one shoulder lifting higher than the other, and he wondered at the wings hidden within her. Would he need to help her find them, or did she already know they were there?

"She is trouble," Forest murmured.

"Really Papa," the girl said, turning a smile on him that lit up the room. "She needed us, and she will help Ed."

"That is why you help her," Ende said aloud, "because she is the way to help the king."

"That is not the only reason," she said quickly, a flush rising to her cheeks.

"Then explain it."

"I can't…" she stammered. "I need her."

The sword master sighed. "Whatever she is, she feared something."

"We are hiding."

"The threat is not what it was, at least for now," Ana said calmly, appearing in the middle of the room. Ende flinched despite himself. She locked her gaze on him. "I still scare you, at least," she said, then slumped to the floor.

"Where is Ed?" Salima asked, rushing forward and throwing her arms around the woman.

She sighed and leaned into the girl. "Safe," she murmured.

"What did you do?" Ende asked, squatting before her.

"Not as much as I could have. The mage has sent something after Ed; I think they mean to kill him."

"Why did you scream?" Forest asked, standing back from the group.

"I wasn't sure what it was. Dark, hateful. There is a lust for power hidden within the compliant servant."

The man looked at the girl, who was too busy holding on to Ana to fully understand what was being said.

"I don't have anything they would want," she said, and Ende realised she was listening very closely.

Ana ran a hand over her hair. "You have a fire that could destroy them all."

Salima sat back, looking at the sword master nervously. Then she looked over her own hands.

"Have you seen it?" Ende asked.

She nodded, her gaze still down.

"Can you direct it?"

"Not always. I haven't really tried." She looked back to the man she saw as her father, and something sharp pierced Ende's heart. Would he have had any more time with this child if he had remained in the capital, if his queen had not died? He should have taken them both away, far away, and yet he would have lost her still.

"I could teach you," he said softly, holding his breath in fear of her response.

But instead of looking up at him, she looked to Ana, who nodded once. Then she closed her eyes and sighed.

"Did you find the Near Folk with them?" Ende asked.

Ana nodded again. Whatever she had done had taken more from her than she'd been prepared for. When she had first disappeared, Forest had claimed that her magic hadn't returned, that she had been too damaged by her time with the mage in his cells. She must have kept it hidden from them, but was that because she didn't trust them or because she worried they wouldn't trust her?

"Who else knows you are here?" Ende asked, focused on Ana.

"A cleric," she murmured. "The Near Folk?"

"The trees," he answered.

"They shared the magic."

"They wish to protect the king as well."

"Do you think he should come?" she asked.

"He needs to make a stand of some kind if he wishes to be seen as the true king, if for no other reason but to be seen. Does she want you to help the boy?" he asked, reaching out a hand and placing it on Ana's knee.

She nodded again, leaning more on the child than the child was on her. He left his hand where it was, closed his eyes and blew out a soft breath. Large green eyes stared back at him from the darkness. Strange images flashed through his mind, but he couldn't grasp on to any of them.

He removed his hand, opened his eyes and found Ana and the child both staring at him. "I needed to be sure of what you are," he said, trying to smile.

"And?"

He shook his head. "I think you should rest. Whatever you have done has drained more than your energy. I have some old friends to reacquaint myself with."

"I can show you the way," the girl said, jumping to her feet. The man behind her took a step forward.

Ende smiled, wanting desperately to run his hand through her hair. "I thank you for your kindness," he said. "I know my way around the castle, and I'll be sure to only let those I want to know that I am here see me."

Ende didn't know who he wanted to see. It had been so long since he had been in the capital, he didn't even know if those he'd known then were still around. Forest had been Barric's closest friend, more dear to the king than his own brother. Ende stopped in the middle of the courtyard and looked up.

Thom had been a boy himself when they were all together, when Barric had become king. And there'd been no real friendship there. Was that why he'd stolen the crown and locked the boy away?

He wasn't a man on the inner circle, and he barely knew what was going on in the kingdom, let alone amongst the friends. So much had happened in that time. Long before he and Essa...

But that was a whole lifetime ago, and much more had changed in that time. If it had been any other king asking for his help, Ende would have turned them away. And despite the boy's uncertainty, he was the king. Ana was certain he was to be on the throne, wearing the crown his father had worn before him.

Ende headed towards the main rooms, hoping he could find the throne room as easily as he used to. As he stood in the doorway, taking in the people, bowing and talking with the man who sat solidly within the wooden frame, Ende knew it would not be as easy as Ana had first thought. Ed could not simply stand before the people, thank his uncle for his help and have him step aside.

The King's Regent was very comfortable and didn't appear to consider the boy a threat at all, although Ende was sure the man had asked for the mage's help and wouldn't shy away from some beast being sent to kill him. The regent locked eyes with him across the room, and a confused look crossed his face.

Thom had been interested in Mariela, Ende remembered. But she only ever had eyes for her soldier.

"Endeavour," the man said loudly, pushing up from the throne. The people around him stepped back. "It has been an age."

Ende bowed his head in the respect the man expected and smiled. "That it has."

"You don't appear to have suffered from the time as I have," Thom said, looking Ende up and down.

"I am surprised to see you here," Ende said.

"You have been gone so long." The man stepped forward and reached out a hand to him as though they were long-lost friends. "You left before our dear Ter-essa's illness, and I'm afraid Barric died a few short years later."

Ende nodded slowly, wondering what excuse this man would give for their deaths, particularly that of his brother. The friendly approach stopped, and although he held his hands out, he didn't try to touch Ende. An idea flashed through Ende's mind, that he could burn the man where he stood and fix all their problems.

"I had travelled far," Ende said, "but news still travels."

Thom nodded slowly, as though understanding his grief.

"Edwin?" Ende asked, and there was the smallest flinch from the man.

"Missing." He waved his hand. "It has all been too much for the boy; it appears he has run away from his responsibilities."

"Truly? I would have thought you would have guided him in his understanding of what was required of him, and that he would already sit upon the throne."

Thom cleared his throat. "I tried very hard," he said. "The boy is not what his father would have hoped," he added in a loud whisper.

"Trying to discredit him?" Ende asked softly, leaning forward.

Thom scowled, straightened and turned back for the throne. "How long will you stay, old friend?"

"I'm not sure. But I see I am needed more than I realised when I set out for the capital."

"Where have you been?" Thom asked, sitting down and wrapping a hand around the armrest as though taking ownership of the chair. For that was all it was, unless someone else sat upon it. In Ende's visions of Ana and the crown, she didn't sit down. She stood before it. He would need to take another look.

18

Dray stood outside the chief's dwelling and watched the dark forest around him. The king had called him in, but he couldn't face further discussion of the day—of what had happened to Ana, where she had come from, and where she might have returned to. Belle kept looking at him as though he was as different as Ana appeared to be.

"Do we know who we can trust?" Belle asked in a loud whisper, and he was tempted to turn and let her know just what he could hear.

"He saved her," Ed returned in the same hoarse voice. "She trusts him."

"Does she?" the girl continued. "She didn't try to step up to him."

"She was facing a monster," Ed said more clearly.

Dray grimaced. She would have found a way to greet him, no matter what they were facing, he thought. She had hung back in the same way he had. Did she avoid him for a reason? Was she guilty of something, or had she been so connected to him that she could read his dreams?

He blew out a long breath. She was a girl, one he had been called to protect. And he would protect her no matter what. The idea that he wanted anything more from her was uncomfortable. He was sure it stemmed from a need to be near her. That was all it was. For in the dreams, she held him tight. They stood together. That was all they needed. But the feel of her body against his and his hands over the silky material caused his face to flush again. She had run her fingers over his skin, her hand too confident beneath his shirt.

He blew out another frustrated breath.

"Dray?"

He turned then as the king appeared in the doorway.

"Do you see something?"

"No," Dray murmured, turning back to look over the world around them. Had he missed something? He was far more distracted than he should be. He had managed to look after her and stay alert previously. Now he couldn't even stay alert.

"I thought you called out."

He grumbled something under his breath, and the king watched him for a moment longer before turning back to the room. Then he surprised Dray by stepping out and into the night with him.

"Are you worried?"

"About the beast?"

"About Ana," the king said, his eyes focused on the night beyond the light of the doorway. Their shadows stretched away until they disappeared into the night.

"There aren't any lights," Dray said, looking around the village.

"They don't feel the need. They can feel the forest and what is around them."

Dray nodded.

"Ana," the king prompted.

"She is not what she was."

"No, she's not. But we always knew she wasn't a maid."

"I wonder if she sees herself differently," Dray mused.

"She certainly spoke differently. I couldn't understand half of what she said."

"What do you want to do?" Dray asked seriously, turning to the king. He certainly seemed to hold himself as one now, although

Dray could still see the scared and grubby boy who had stood in the cottage in the mountains.

"I think I have to return. But how and with whom, I don't know."

"You want an army."

"I want to keep the peace if I can."

Dray shook his head. "I doubt you will take the crown back without bloodshed."

Now it was the boy's turn to sigh. "I don't know what I'm doing."

"None of us do," Dray admitted. "We started this by following a maid certain you should be King, with a dragon who feared her and has since disappeared. You have one old soldier, one old man and a girl probably brighter than the rest of us put together."

"Thank you," Belle said, "but I don't think you are as old as you pretend."

"I am not pretending. I have seen far more years than you."

"Why didn't you talk to Ana?" she pressed again.

He shook his head, walking away from the door and into the dark, glancing over his shoulder. The girl stood in the light; the boy stood down a step and watched him walk away. Although Dray was sure he could stop and they wouldn't even know he was there.

He didn't want to explain himself to the girl, because he couldn't. The woman who had appeared before them, calm and confident and powerful, was not the Ana he had lost in the mountains. And he didn't know how to get her back.

Standing in the doorway to the hut, Dray did not want to go in, nor did he want to sleep. He didn't know what he might dream of, and he didn't want to face her again. Not after he had struggled today. Although, he had stepped up when he'd needed to.

Something shimmered in the moonlight. He thought it part of the magic that protected them, but the world beyond was dark. He didn't know if that creature was still out there, nor if her words were enough to keep it from consuming him. Yet he was tempted to push his way through the barrier and explore the world beyond.

What else might the mage and the regent send after them? He took a step and placed his hand out towards the shimmering barrier. They had to see the boy as a threat. They must have thought the only way to stop him was to destroy him. Had they attempted to discredit him within the capital? Were the people worried, or had they come to accept that he was gone?

Dray looked back towards the building he had left the king in. Could they just walk back into the capital? That was where they had been headed when they were waylaid by the forest. Was the forest trying to protect him now, or did it have an agenda of its own? He needed someone to advise him. Someone he could talk to about what was happening, for he had no idea at all. He ran a hand over his face, the fingers finding the scar that wasn't there, and he turned in frustration to find himself lost in the dark.

The night sky had disappeared. The forest he was sure pressed on the edges of the village was gone. Large green eyes blinked at him from the darkness, and his hand rested on his sword.

"What is your plan, little soldier?" a voice asked. It vibrated through him, as though it spoke inside him rather than to him.

Was this something else the mage had sent?

It laughed, and he gulped down the rising fear, drawing his sword. Although he doubted it would have much impact on whatever this was before him.

"I could use you," the voice whispered, and he shivered.

"Enough," Ana's voice snapped through the fog. The world cleared a little, but the lights were not the same. It was as though he stood somewhere else, somewhere outside the forest.

The silhouette of a woman moved from the darkness, but she stopped as he maintained his hold on the sword. "I'm sorry," she murmured.

"Are you really here?" he asked, lowering the sword.

"In some sense, but no."

He waited, but she didn't come any closer. "What happened today?" he eventually asked. "What have you become?"

"I don't know," she said, her soft voice sad. He was reminded of her following him through the brush on the mountains and scratching her arms to pieces.

"Does Ed know?"

"What I am?" she asked, something catching in her throat. "He struggles with what he is."

"I meant that you are here."

"I am sorry," she whispered, and he could hear the tears in her voice. He stepped forward, unsure whether she was herself, what danger she posed now and whom she worked for. As he watched her unmoving silhouette, it suddenly seemed too easy for her to have scared away such a beast.

"Ana," he said, sliding the sword back into place. But it felt as though she moved further away from him rather than towards him. "Ana?"

"I know I cannot expect you to trust me. But you will watch over him, won't you?"

He nodded, disappointment flowing through him. Had she come all this way to ensure he was doing as he was designed to do? "I am the king's man."

The moon moved from behind a cloud, shining brightly and illuminating her too-slim frame and the tears on her cheeks. He closed the gap between them before he realised what he was doing and wrapped his arms around her. For the first time, he wished he wasn't wearing the armour, which would be cold on her skin.

"I won't let her hurt you," she whispered.

"Who is she?" he asked.

"Me." She pushed against him and wiped a hand across her cheek. "She is me and I am her."

He tried to smile, to reassure her in some way that he trusted her above all others. "Will you talk with me? I miss you."

Something shuddered in her chest, as though she was trying to hold in a sob, but as he reached for her again, she was gone.

19

The mage leaned over his notes, trying to determine what he might be able to do from his workshop to assist the maid in her task, when she appeared before him. He sat back from the book and looked at her, back to the book and then back again.

"Have you done what you were sent to do?"

"No. It is not possible." Her voice was not her own, and yet she looked just as she had any other day standing before him, waiting for instructions.

"Why is it not possible? Did I not give you the means?"

"He is protected."

"By whom?" the mage asked too loudly.

"Many," she said, her features giving nothing away.

He sucked in an angry breath and stood to look down on her, but she changed before his eyes. Growing taller and darker, the creature before him was one he had not seen for a very long time.

"The forest keeps him safe."

"He is in the Near Forest?"

The creature bowed its head.

"Do *they* help keep him safe?"

"I do not know. There is another involved."

He waited.

"You created her and sent her to stop me."

"Ana?" he asked, stepping back.

The creature licked its lips in response. The forked tongue was unsettling.

"She is dead," the mage insisted, but he already knew that she wasn't. She had escaped from the cells. He stared at the creature before him. Had he given Ana the skills to allow her to escape?

"She is royalty," the creature hissed.

The mage refocused on the creature before him. What had she managed to do? "She has not…"

"She is who she is. I must obey her. Yet the child wants her dead even more than you do."

"Really?" he asked. "Can she come forward and speak?"

"We do not wish to."

The mage looked over the creature before him, then glanced at the book to the side of the desk.

"If we return that way, she will be lost."

"It is a risk I am willing to take," the mage said, resting his hand on the worn leather cover.

"It is not one *we* are willing to take," the creature hissed.

"You must kill the boy."

"I have promised my queen." The creature remained unmoving before him.

"What of your promise to me? I gave you the child to bring you to our world."

"We thank you," it hissed, then disappeared.

The mage thumped the desk. There must be a way around this impediment; he just had to find it. The creature's words confirmed that Ana had survived, and he assumed she must be in the forest with the king. That was disappointing, if they had been reunited, although it would surprise him if she had made it that far. He sat slowly at the desk, his hands resting on the book he had been reading. If Ana's magic had awoken, she might be far more powerful than he had anticipated. His first images of her when he had met her at the Seat of Sheer Rock returned. Darkness and blood surrounded him. And the boy ripping the crown from his uncle's dying hand. She would be the cause of such action; he had seen her as the darkness that closed in around them. He should have watched over her more closely to ensure she died. He wouldn't make the same mistake again.

That might be why the cloak and magic he had kept had not been able to find her—not that it was not strong enough or he had used it up, but because he had been searching for the wrong magic.

He shook his head. That didn't make sense. He'd known what she was the moment he saw her. A vessel as her mother had been, one with a connection that needed only for the magic to find her. And it had. He didn't know what had woken it, for she didn't know herself. Or did she?

He made his way through the piles of books and shelves that formed pathways through the workroom until he came to the dish upturned on the floor. The green cloak, faded from his use of it, spilled across the floor. It had remained just where it had landed when he'd upended the bowl in his frustration.

He squatted down over the cloak, lifted it to his nose and closed his eyes. He had a similar sense, although his magic would never be as strong as Ana's, nor as her mother's. He could call upon the world beyond the veil, but he would never be able to work with it as closely as the women could. The little girls he had found almost had a similar ability, yet they weren't able to clearly sense the magic or use it. For these women, it possessed them.

He breathed in again. Magic filled his senses, but where it came from or from whom he could no longer detect. He had initially felt her in the power that surrounded the cloth, but it was long gone. He dropped it and kicked the upturned bowl across the space. It bounced loudly from a bookshelf, causing it to wobble and several bottles to fall and smash. Their voices called in pain before they disappeared.

Ana had heard them, the voices of the other. Those children had no such skill, and yet he had been able to use them. Perhaps he could find another child with which to find her. If the creature he had released from beyond would not deal with her, he would find a way to destroy Ana. His little maid had wished her dead, and the idea caused a small smirk to lift one corner of his mouth upward. She was worthy of the gift he had given her.

He had threatened to separate the creature from his little one. Perhaps he could do the same for Ana. It would not matter if one of them survived the separation or not, for it would be enough to solve the problem.

Whatever magic lived in her had not come from a book but been gifted at birth. He would need to find another way to cleave them, he thought as he allowed the cloak to fall back to the floor.

"What is the plan?" Forest asked, finding Ende in the courtyard. Some people moved around them, but not many, and no one paid them any attention. Or at least he hoped that was the case, and not that he was being watched. Could someone have worked out that he had helped the girl? The idea that she was a witch returned, that she was something darker than a mage. She had kept the return of her magic hidden from him, from all of them, and the idea made him nervous. His daughter continually sought her out, despite his warnings, and he was scared of what the woman might do to her.

The man before him stared but said nothing, a single eyebrow raised to the sky.

"Do you have a plan?" Forest asked again.

"Do I need one?"

"Ende!" he cried, allowing the frustration to boil over.

Ende held up his hands in defence and smiled, his perfect teeth distracting the sword master for a moment. "You are so easy to tease."

"Is that why you are here? To cause more havoc and run?" Forest barely regretted the words, for he knew they needed to work together, but the hurt that flashed across Ende's face was a surprise. "The king," he prompted to divert attention from his own words.

"I don't know," Ende admitted with a shrug, looking around the courtyard. "I wasn't really thinking when I returned. I didn't know…"

The sword master found himself looking around then, worried that his daughter might be nearby. He knew why the man had returned. He had discovered that the child had survived. Although he hadn't known she wasn't Barric's daughter until Salima had spoken of how she had found a fire within and used it to help Ana escape.

He only hoped no one else within the castle had Ana's skills and could determine the truth as well. "Where is Ana?" he wondered aloud, then glanced around again to be sure no one was near.

"Resting," Ende said softly, looking back towards the tower. "It took far more from her than she would admit."

"I saw her for myself," Forest growled. He didn't need Ende to tell him anything about the woman. He had no idea what had occurred, but it was enough that if she had not returned amongst friends it might have been the end of her. If a friend was what he was to her.

"Emotionally as well as physically, it seems. She continues to murmur in her sleep."

Forest looked seriously at the tall man before him, wondering what he might be keeping from him.

"I can't see. Whatever it was that has woken her magic will not let me."

"You think she is dangerous."

"One of them is." Ende looked back again to the tower.

"Is Salima with her?"

Ende nodded. "But she will not harm her."

Forest wasn't sure if he should believe this man or determine it for himself. As invested as Ende was, Salima was still his daughter. "The king," the sword master prompted again.

"I don't know what the boy should do, or what we can do for him."

"We could help him," Forest implored.

"How? Kill the uncle, help raise an army against his own family and people?"

"He is the king. That man will have him killed if we can't find a way to get him here."

"And then what?"

"The people want their rightful king."

"Do they? Once the important men of the land are supplied with new wives, the best the kingdom has to offer, they will remain loyal to the man who provides."

"It is the crown that provides."

Ende laughed, a booming sound that ricocheted off the buildings.

The sword master shook his head and walked away. He was almost back at the practice halls when he stopped, sure that something lurked in the shadows. Yet when he looked closer, there was nothing there. What had been sent after the king? And if it refrained from taking him, what might it take instead? Forest shivered again at the thought of Salima. She was much stronger than he had ever imagined. She might be just what some strange creature searching for power would want. And it had been sent after the king. She shared his blood, and that might be enough.

He was about to turn on his heel and return to the room, and to the woman who might have a way to protect her, when there was a scream from inside the practice halls. He raced forward and pulled the door, only vaguely aware of someone running with him as he searched the dimly lit space. The tall windows usually allowed daylight to light the space and avoid the need for torches during the day, but despite the hour, the room was dark and the air unnaturally hot.

"Hello!" he called out.

Someone had been inside, for the scream had reached across the courtyard, high and desperate.

"Sir," a shaky voice whispered, and a hand rested on his shoulder. He glanced around at the soldier, wondering if this was the man who had followed him in or a man who had been inside the room all along.

He pointed to the room before them, and Forest stopped. Something dark marked the floor. The usually pale grass-woven mats looked as though something had been spilled across them. Perhaps a sack of something, for there was a larger lump in the middle of the space.

"Why can't I see anything?" he murmured.

A torch flared to life behind him, and he wished it were dark again. Someone, and he couldn't even guess at whom, had been pulled apart. The remains of a torso lay in the middle of the floor, blood both pooled around the pieces and spattered across the mats and walls.

The soldier beside him made a noise of trying to stop his lunch returning. They had all seen war in some form. But Forest had never seen this. He looked down to notice part of a limb at his feet. He couldn't tell if it was arm or leg, but he squatted and put his hand to it. Still very warm. This had just happened. They had heard the scream. Long deep cuts covered what might have been the torso. The head was crushed.

He looked up at Ende, who stood behind him with the torch.

"Do you think this is the darkness she sensed?" Ende asked.

Forest shook his head. He had no idea what might have caused this. He had once seen the mark on another, but it was too long ago. And it had been three scratches across an arm. Not *this*.

He looked up then to the strangely shrouded windows. He looked at Ende, then back to them as he stood. Did whatever had done this need the shadows? Was this a message? And if so, for whom?

"Papa?" Salima's voice called from the doorway, but before he could find a way to stop her coming, the torch was thrust into his hand with such force it nearly knocked him over. And then Ende's voice carried from the doorway as he pushed her outside.

Forest handed the torch to the soldier and followed Ende out. The man stood in the courtyard, his arm around Salima's shoulders, and Forest wanted to squeeze between them. She would have to know at some point who and what she was. He wasn't ready for that to be anytime soon, despite what might be lurking in the shadows.

The soldier appeared not long after. "I'm not waiting in there alone," he said.

"Then go for more help," Forest directed.

He bowed his head and disappeared at a run towards the barracks. What help anyone could be, the sword master couldn't guess.

20

The noise of the room was overwhelming, and no matter what he did, the regent couldn't get the attention of the people. Despite his cries for silence and their want for his attention.

He glanced around, wishing the mage would appear from the shadows, but he was nowhere to be found. This might very well be his own fault, but he wouldn't be admitting that to anyone.

Thom tried to focus on a single person, to get their attention and so hopefully bring the focus back to where it should be. Him. Not that he knew where to begin to explain what had occurred or how they could stop it. He locked eyes with Ende, staring at him over the head of the child, and found himself taking a second look. The sword master's daughter was pressed against Ende's side, his hand firmly on her shoulder. The sword master stood beside Ende, the child's hand in his. Were they friends?

He didn't think Ende had made too many true friends during his time in the capital all those years ago, and no one had seen him since before Ter-essa's death.

Thom studied the child then, as though seeing her for the first time. There was something familiar in her, and yet he couldn't place her. Then his view was obscured as the sword master moved and Ende put his fingers to his lips.

A sharp whistle cut through the air, and the room dropped into silence.

"Thank you," the regent said, stepping forward to the edge of the platform. "I understand that you are all…" He stopped as the people in the room focused on the tall slender man. Ende. He scowled. "Are you responsible for this?" he asked, allowing the hatred to show in his voice.

"The visitor," a soldier said clearly, indicating Ende, "and Sword Master Forest were talking in the courtyard when the victim screamed."

"Have we determined who he was?" the regent asked, ignoring the grin across the room that showed too many perfect teeth.

The soldier shook his head.

Another man made his way through the crowd. "My son is missing," he cried, looking through the crowd around him. "I have searched, but…"

The sword master paled. Did he know, or was he guessing? "He wasn't due for a lesson for two days," he stammered.

"He wanted the extra practice; he wanted to make you proud," the older man said, his voice cracking.

The sword master closed his eyes and nodded once. The man who believed his son the victim teetered back and forth, and another man stepped in to support him. Thom was sure Ende was strong enough that he could have held the man up with one hand on his own. But he didn't move from the child.

All Thom needed now was for the witch to reappear. Not that he thought she would, but the idea of her made him rub at his arm. There was something far more unnatural about her than he had considered when he had pictured her as his wife. He might have to select someone from the coming group for himself. A young bride might be just what he needed to help cement himself as the rightful ruler of this world.

Murmurs moved through the crowd, but most eyes were on him. He cleared his throat. "We have some understanding of the events," he said softly, although he had no idea at all as to what was going on. "I think I should see the place for myself."

The murmuring increased.

"Do you think that necessary?" someone asked.

"Your mage might have more idea." Ende spoke softly, and yet his voice filled the room.

"Where is the mage?" someone else asked.

"Is there magic involved?"

"Something unnatural," the sword master said before looking around and swallowing down his regret.

The regent wasn't sure that he really wanted to see what was out there in the practice halls. If only it had been the boy he so desperately needed gone.

"I have seen something similar before," the sword master said, his stare vacant.

"Truly?" the regent asked, stepping down to stand before him while trying to ignore Ende moving between him and the girl. It was a subtle movement, but one all the same. Again, he found himself looking at the girl.

"On an arm," the sword master murmured, moving three fingers across the skin.

The regent studied the man's arm. "It is not possible," he whispered.

"What is it?" someone asked.

He shook his head. He had no idea what had been present when he had last seen Mariela, but the idea of the described marks reminded him of her. It was after she had left the capital, and it was as though she shouldn't have been there. He had walked into the mage's workshop and been caught by surprise. Three deep scratches sliced into her arm. And he hadn't seen her again.

He looked up at the sword master. "You saw her," he said, feeling like a lost boy himself.

The sword master looked somewhat confused for a moment, as though they were talking of someone else, and he glanced at Ende without answering the question. Thom was starting to wonder if he really had seen Mariela that day.

"A child," the sword master said, and Ende nodded. "A small boy who had roamed out by the river."

Murmuring moved through the crowd again.

"Just the one mark?" the regent asked.

The man nodded again, but his attention was on Ende. Thom wanted to take him by the shoulders and shake him, but he was too aware of the room full of people wanting answers. "Was the man in the practice hall similarly marked?"

"It was hard to say," Forest said.

"I need to see," the regent said, waving people from the room, although they didn't move. He made his way out of the throne room and towards the courtyard. The soldier who had found the body followed him, and he wondered if this man could be trusted. He wasn't one Thom would have sent out with the major to find the boy. And they were yet to return.

The sword master pushed ahead of him and pulled out a large brass key. He inserted it into the door. The regent wondered if the room was locked at other times, or if it was left open for the young men of the capital to practice whenever they wanted. Perhaps if the young man inside had thought to ask his friends to join him, he would not have found himself alone with a killer.

The stench of blood and death reached the regent as the door swung open, and he tried not to gag. He might not have seen the battlefield like these other men, but he was a man—a royal one, at that—and he needed to at least look like he could hold himself.

No matter what he thought lay in the dark room ahead of him, he wasn't ready for it.

"Surely whoever did this would be covered in blood," he murmured once he was standing inside the room. Several soldiers stood around him with torches. He looked up. "Why is it dark?"

"Someone has covered the windows." The soldier beside him held the torch higher, although it did little to tell him what covered them. He nodded to show understanding, tried not to look at the remains of the body before him and headed back out into the air.

He found the sword master and Ende standing together looking out across the courtyard. The child was no longer with them.

"You didn't want to see?" Thom asked.

"We've seen it," Forest said. "It stays with you."

The regent nodded despite himself. He feared the sword master might be right. Even with the poor lighting, it was too clear just what had happened. "It was fast?"

"The boy screamed; we entered and found…" The sword master held his hand out towards the door.

The regent nodded. He could still smell the blood, and he wanted to be further away. Could something do this to the king? He hadn't heard back from the mage on that front yet. Maybe whatever he had sent after the boy had developed a taste.

"Did that answer your questions?" the sword master asked.

The regent shook his head. "Could it be that the young man upset someone, was in debt…" He stopped at the incredulous look on the sword master's face. "You have seen this before. Tell me the details."

Forest looked at Ende first. Thom wondered why, after all these years, the man had decided to return now. And he had barely changed in the sixteen or seventeen years since he had seen him. He was unsure if it had been that long. Maybe there was something a little unnatural about him. But his own men had seen him when the killing had occurred. He tried not to sigh.

"It wasn't much, although the boy's death couldn't be explained. He was found by the river, but did not drown. The only marks on his body were three deep cuts across his arm. It was thought to be an animal attack; there was nothing else, and we couldn't identify the animal that might have created such a mark."

"You have seen this yourself," Ende said, and the regent looked up at the intense gaze, eyes much darker than he had thought they were. Maybe the man could be in two places at once.

"Have you?" the sword master asked.

"Once, but the person lived. Or so I thought."

"Who was it and where?"

"That I can't remember." Ende narrowed his eyes, and the regent knew he didn't believe him. "I only remember the marks were on a forearm. And when I noticed them, thinking how deep and painful they appeared, the person covered them with the other hand."

"Did you see them again?"

He shook his head.

"Where?" Ende asked, his deep voice commanding.

"Somewhere in the castle."

"When?"

"Long ago. Fifteen years." The regent looked them over for a moment and then turned back to the room he didn't want to re-enter. He sucked in a deep breath, took the torch from the soldier beside him and headed back into the room. He wasn't sure it was a good idea to head in alone. But if it was the creature the mage had sent, he hoped it was on his side. Although if the mage was behind this, did that mean he was responsible for Mariela's disappearance?

Thom stopped by the body, trying not to breathe as the bitter coppery scent overwhelmed him. He held the torch out. There was little left of the boy, but some scratches sliced through the clothing across his torso. They were similar to what he was sure he had seen on Mariela's arm that day. Across one leg, torn free of the pants that had covered it, there was another. Was this frustration—a beast unable to take what it had been created to take?

He shivered and looked around the room. The strange light filtering through the covered windows drew his eye upwards. Something was smeared across the windows, all of them, something dark that didn't stop the sunlight, but made a dark halo of light. He wondered if the boy had entered the space to find it like that, or if it had been done after. He shook his head. There hadn't been the time. It had all been very fast. It was waiting, whatever it was, in the hall. Who was it waiting for?

21

"The soldiers come," Eilke said.

Ed turned to Dray, but he was looking at Belle. She was staring down at the table. The room looked as it always did, although the stars above had changed to sunlight pushing through the leaves of tall trees. Belle took her father's hands and nodded once.

"You need to say goodbye to your friends," Ed said, trying to draw her attention. He wasn't sure why, but he felt very uncertain. She pushed up from the table, her father following.

"I am to go with them," she said.

"No," Ed stammered, looking to the soldier again for some confirmation that this was not her decision. But Dray only watched her.

"Why not?" she asked, glaring at him, the fire back in her eyes. He had longed for that look, and yet he wasn't sure what to do with it now. "It might be my only chance at a life," she said, her focus still on him and him alone. "We have nothing to return to in the Grassland. Your focus is Ana."

"I want to find her," Ed said quickly, "but not at the risk of losing you along the way."

She smiled then, but it was sad. No matter what he said now, she was going.

"What if you end up marrying some old man?" he asked. "Or if he is cruel?"

"What if he is young and handsome?" she returned, and Ed felt his face burn. She was right. What was he making her stay for? He had nothing to offer her.

He bowed his head and ran a hand around a knot in the surface of the table.

"You are the king," the wind whispered in his ear. He looked up again to see she had already left, and he pushed at Dray to move so that he could follow her.

"Maybe we should come too," Ed called after her as she met with her friends. Some of the girls whispered amongst themselves.

"Is it safe?" Dray asked.

"For them or me?" Ed returned.

"Something is trying to kill you."

"And it hasn't yet. I need to…"

Dray looked at him with almost the same intensity as Belle had.

"What do you need?" she asked then, stepping away from the group of girls. "To be king? To save Ana?"

"I…" he started, but the words wouldn't form. He still had no idea of what he should do. No, he told himself, that was a lie. He knew what he should do; he just didn't know if that was what he wanted or how he would achieve it. Although, he'd had the discussion with the chief after the creature had disappeared. He was the king, and it was time he started to act like it.

He wouldn't have the same options as Belle, living a normal life, his choice in a family. And he wasn't sure if that was what he wanted or not. He did understand that he was to be King, and he would have to find a way to the throne. He glanced back at Eilke standing by the building.

"You will come too?" he asked.

"I shall lead the tribute to the Seat."

Ed nodded slowly. They still had time; he just had to work out what to do with it. The Near Folk had asked him what he wanted. They had offered him help. And yet he didn't know what that would be. "You won't leave the forest," he said.

Eilke smiled, but made no other movement.

"We will travel with them," Ed said to Dray.

"To what end?" Belle asked, clearly exasperated with him.

"I don't know," he admitted, "but it is what I need to do."

She studied him for too long, trying to understand him, which he doubted she could do, for he didn't understand himself. Then she turned and, taking her father by the hand, joined the other girls. They had very little with them. Some carried a piece of cloth tied around a bulge, maybe clothing, with the four corners knotted together to act as a handle.

"I'll need my cloak," Ed said, striding back towards the huts. He wasn't sure what else he could take, and his father's sword stared up at him from its place on the cot. He had become complacent, he realised as he strapped it on. They all had, to some degree. Dray had been seen without his armour. Although it had only been a couple of nights before he had gone back to the sturdy, unshakable man.

Ed glanced at the other man's side of the room, and there was nothing there. He truly carried everything with him. Knives, swords, armour. He must have been wearing his cloak already, for it wasn't there. As Ed approached the group, he noticed that the soldier was staring out into the trees around the village. Did he worry for what might be there? Or was he looking for Ana?

Belle was right; he was distracted and not himself. He would have been the first to greet Ana, no matter the circumstances, embracing her and claiming her for himself. Yet he stood back, as though he was wary of her and what she might do, when she had appeared in the forest. There was one night when Ed had thought she had appeared, as Dray had called out to her, but when he rose from his own cot, the large soldier was still sleeping. Maybe he was worried.

"Do we worry about Ende?" Ed asked as he rejoined the group. The girls, women, were talking amongst themselves, and Eilke was moving along the road. The group had started to form a line as it followed him.

"Ana knew where he was," Dray said without looking around.

Ed nodded. Ende could look after himself. Although Ed had hoped he would help look after him. He was his mother's friend, after all. It might have been the forest, for he hadn't been the same since they had entered it. Or it might be Salima. Ende really hadn't known of his sister. Perhaps he didn't understand what had happened to Mother, or he blamed her for her death. Ed shivered at the idea. But she had died to protect her, or so Ed had thought at one point. If his mother had wanted Salima to survive, Ende would want that too.

Ed looked through the slowly moving group for Belle, but she was closer to the front. "Is it safe to have only one of the Near with us?" he asked, then wondered if he should have taken the time to say his goodbyes to the chief.

Something whispered against his skin. The chief might know far more than Ed could ever explain.

"You and I both have a sword," Dray said, looking Ed over, his brow creased. "Do you know what you do?"

"Would you rather stay?"

"I will do as you do."

"Because Ana asked?"

The man stared ahead at the women and then turned back to Ed, far more serious than he remembered the soldier being. "Because you are my king."

Ed nodded once, and they followed the women through the shimmering edge of the village into the forest. None of it looked familiar. He wondered how close they were to the Seat of the Forest and what the lord might think when he arrived.

Despite strange dreams of a world she didn't know, Ana felt quite refreshed when she woke. The room was as she had imagined it, only there was no one present, and she was surprised that they would trust her alone again. She should have told them about the magic, she thought as she climbed from the bed and looked down at the unfamiliar nightshirt. Was that to slow her down? She had been wearing the same silky dress since she had attacked the regent and been locked in the ice cells.

She had no idea how long ago that was, and she had no idea how long she had slept. She had returned from the forest drained, as though someone or something had dragged all the energy from her.

The darkness had called her. It wasn't just that she knew it was out there—something that scared her beyond words, something that was a danger to Ed and those with him—but that it had called to her. As it did now.

She stepped forward, closed her eyes and dragged in a deep breath. It was here in the castle, and it wanted her to see what it had become.

The little maid came to mind, the one with the strange link to the mage and the understanding of what he wanted. As did Ana's mistrust and dislike of her, even though the girl had dressed her and bathed her as instructed. Despite the darkness wanting to impress her, part of it still wanted to use its power to destroy her.

She smiled at the idea. She had wanted to slap the girl before; she certainly could now. The remains of the dress hung over the back of a chair by the fire. She ran a hand over it, feeling the fine material, but it was torn and worn. She wondered if the wardrobe remained in her room by the mage's workshop, and she shook her head at the silliness of it as she pushed herself there.

She pulled open the wardrobe door and stood back to look over its contents. The room was just as it had been left, except the image Ana had taken of the queen from Ed's room was no longer there. Had she put that somewhere, or had the mage used it to find Ed? Or to send the creature after him?

The fine dresses were there as she remembered, and she moved through them searching for something a little thicker than the fine one she had been wearing for so long. She realised then that it was still in her hand, and she put it down on the bed to reach for another.

They were all the same, or at least very similar. She removed the nightshirt and pulled on a fresh dress. She looked herself over in the mirror on the inside of the door. It certainly made a difference. No one would mistake her for a maid now. She wondered if her own aunt would even recognise her. Her new look had certainly unsettled Dray.

He had looked so unsure the last time she had seen him. But she hadn't returned to him in her dreams, not since the beast. She had longed for him, but she couldn't remember seeing him.

She saw the hairbrush on the mantle and picked it up, turning it over slowly, then returned to the mirror to drag it through her hair. The other women of the court had worn their hair up in a similar fashion to Belle when they were at the Seat of the Lord in the mountains. Ana could do something similar, but then who would see her? And if anyone did see her, after what had happened last time she was in the castle, it wouldn't matter what she wore or how she looked. She appeared too pale, she thought, leaning forward to study herself in the glass. Her dark hair made her look even paler. She tucked it behind her ears, straightened up and smoothed over the dress.

She moved to the door that led to the rest of the castle and wondered if it was open. She leaned against it, but no one stood on the other side. She sighed as the darkness called again. She turned back to the other door and knew that the other side would be covered, although if she wished it, she could open the door and appear in the mage's workshop as she had done so many times before.

Instead, she answered the call that continued at the back of her mind.

As the cool wind whipped around her hair and shoulders, Ana

regretted the dress. Surely there was something that would keep her warm. She missed Ende's cloak, and her own green cloak to keep the chill at bay. The cold wall of the castle stood at her back and the river flowed before her, barely a walkway between the two. Someone else was here, not the darkness that called but another.

She suddenly wanted Dray and his warmth. Not like the little dragon's heat, she wanted his arms around her. And then a cloak, very much like his, black and thick and a little prickly, rested on her shoulders. She pulled it tight. She put her nose to her shoulder and breathed in the scent of the wool. No hint of Dray. At least she hadn't stolen his cloak.

Ana moved carefully along the path, too aware of the fast-flowing river beside the narrow bank. A little further along the path, she noticed a man standing on the opposite bank. Fishing, she assumed, a rod held over the water and a basket by his feet. He didn't seem to notice her. She closed her eyes and breathed in the smell of muddy water. There was something else. As she looked up, the man sighed and started to pack away his rod. Then he looked up as though just noticing her. He lifted a hand in greeting and then turned away.

Blood. She could smell blood. It was oddly calming, and the idea made her nervous.

She followed the path, knowing that the darkness had been there before her and that it was gone. The small body by the water was not as damaged as she expected when she drew closer, and yet she knew it had gone. The soul, that was. Not just that the child was dead, but that his very essence had been pulled from his body.

She knelt over him and pulled him over, worried that he would come out near such a fast-flowing river alone and dressed in so little. His bare feet appeared blue from the cold; or was that because he was already dead? His stomach had been sliced open, the cause of the blood.

She glanced behind her at a sense of the darkness, but it wasn't the same as she had felt before. She wasn't sure exactly what that meant. Were there more of these creatures, and could she direct them in the same way? Not that she was sure she had directed the other, but she appeared to have stopped it taking Ed.

She looked back over the child. Would the creature have taken Ed, or would it have killed him? She tried to understand what it had been; it was two in one. The maid and something else had become something new, something darker than either of them had been alone. Had something similar tried to claim the child? Was that a way for it to come to this side of the world? *The veil*, an idea breathed in her mind. She had heard that before.

"Is this your doing?" she asked herself.

Others wish to come.

"If the child is not like me, then is that possible?"

The maid.

"Mmm," Ana said, looking at the body before her. But someone had fed that child to the darkness, and she had taken it in. Had someone tried to feed this child to the darkness before it killed him? Was the mage experimenting with the kingdom's children? She should have stayed and sought him out.

Would you have won?

"I don't know," Ana admitted.

A cry from the wall above her made Ana pull back against the wall. "Are there more?" she whispered.

A whole army.

Ana shivered despite herself. Pulling the cloak around her tighter, she disappeared to the mage's workshop before she was seen near the child. Was it truly a gift as the feeling had suggested? Or was it a threat?

We work together. What do you seek here?

Answers, she thought, although she didn't know where to start. The room was strangely quiet. Despite her magic being stronger than it had ever been, she couldn't hear the world that lived in here, somewhere on the border between worlds.

She had barely taken a step when the door banged open.

"You better explain this," the regent shouted.

She cursed the interruption and went back in the room Salima and her father had found for her before the regent saw her. She still didn't know if the mage was there, or if he was responsible for any of what she had seen in the last few days. She moved towards the fire, but as she heard the approach of Ende, Master Forest and the little dragon working their way up the stairs towards her, she felt something else. Not the darkness that had called to her, but something very similar.

The room she found herself in was strangely dark, as though someone had painted over the windows. She looked up, seeing the light pushing through the darkness, or at least trying. She raised her hand and then stopped.

Another body torn open by the shadows was present, and judging by the stench there was a lot more blood. Despite the queasy feeling, Ana stepped forward as the body spread out before her started to twitch.

Someone made a strange sound in the darkness. A torch flared to life, the soldier catching her unawares, appearing too much like Dray in his shiny armour before she waved her hand towards him and the torch died.

"Is someone there?" he asked, sounding nothing like Dray.

She sighed and turned back to the body as it pulled together. Not in a form anyone would recognise. The blood was the only thing not moving. The shadows closed in around her, yet she could see very clearly.

"Hello? Miss?"

"Shh," she hissed.

He took a step closer, his armour squeaking, and she wondered why they had left such a man to watch over the body. He was not the soldier Dray was. If only they were all Dray, she found herself thinking. She shook her head as the shadows disappeared.

"Where did it go?" he asked. And then the shadows formed into something far more solid. The creature, very similar to the one she had seen in the forest. But this had not been accepted by a cruel girl. This had been accepted later. She could feel them both, the confused boy and the darkness surrounding him.

"How did you capture his soul?" she asked.

A strange hiss-like laughter filled the space, and the soldier dropped the dead torch. She could hear him clanking towards the door. As the light spilled into the room, the creature before her leant forward. "Why would my queen ask what she already knows?" it hissed. They hissed.

"What do you want?" she asked, trying to sound confident when she was sure her legs would buckle. The amount of blood splashed around the room made her wonder just what these creatures were capable of.

"What you want," they said, a forked tongue flicking over reptilian lips. The large dark eyes blinked in the dim light, and then it was gone.

She turned back to the door. The soldier stood in the doorway, and although she couldn't make out his face with the light behind him, she knew that he watched her. Behind him, she felt Ende approach across the courtyard. She wondered if he had sensed her here, or if he'd guessed when he hadn't found her in the room. She needed them, and yet she couldn't face him and his questions.

As he stepped up to the soldier in the doorway, she disappeared, hoping to be gone before his eyes could adjust to the dark room.

22

Dray walked along behind the girls, trying to pay attention to the trees around them and what might be lurking behind them. They had camped for the night amongst the trees, and he got the feeling they were further from the Near Folk village than the amount of travel would have taken them. He wondered then if the Near Folk had not only directed their travel through the trees but moved them, as he had moved with Eilke when they had searched for Ende.

The trees didn't appear too different to him. And just as before, he couldn't tell where they were. There was no real path, yet he trusted the man to lead them where they were meant to go.

The king didn't appear quite as certain. But Dray guessed it was more about what lay ahead than how they passed through the forest. Belle, on the other hand, looked more confident than he had seen her for some time. The self-assured young woman who had punched the young man in the arm before she knew just who he was appeared to have returned. She hadn't been the same since she had learnt of the king's true identity. He doubted the other women knew just who they were travelling with.

Within only an hour of waking, they moved onto a clearer track, and then he could hear more people within the trees. Dray looked up into the canopy at walkways and huts built around the trunks, between the branches and leaves. If it hadn't been for the noise of the people moving around, he might not have realised they were there.

Eilke appeared to sigh as he rested his hand on a broad tree in which a large door had been carved. Dray wondered if these people had worked with the Near Folk, or if they could have helped each other to manipulate the forest. Eilke glanced back at Dray and then turned to the women at the front of the line.

"Please wait," he said, then disappeared through the doorway. Dray was curious as to where it led, but rather than follow he stepped forward, nudging the king to move with him as a quiet filled the world around them.

He glanced up at men lining the walkways, men that could have come from anywhere in the kingdom. They didn't appear to share any similarities with the Near Folk. Women stood in doorways, with small children at their legs or with babies in their arms, peering down at the women below. Older children leaned over the ropes of the walkways, openly staring at the group in the small space between the trees.

Eilke appeared on one of the walkways and bowed to a tall, dark-haired man. He appeared younger than Dray would have expected for a lord, but he might be someone else. Yet there was something about him that gave Dray the understanding that he was more important than the other men lining the walkways. He nodded slowly, looking over the group of women as Eilke continued to talk quietly to the man, who then turned a hard jaw towards the Near man.

"Something he doesn't like," Dray muttered.

"Probably a king sneaking into the ranks," the king returned.

"At least the people appear to be real," Dray added as the man waved them forward and Dray prodded the king towards the door.

It swung open before they reached it. They looked at each other, Dray unsure if he should go first or follow. The king made up his mind for them and pushed ahead. Dray shouldn't be struggling this much, but he still felt as though he was distracted, not quite paying the attention he should. Ana hadn't visited him in his sleep the night before, and he was both relieved and disappointed. She had not been herself the last time.

He shook his head and refocused in the dimly lit stairwell. The king pushed open a door and emerged into the green light of the walkway to face the young lord and Eilke.

"You are no boy," the lord said simply.

The king snorted with laughter. "Not many people seem to think so."

The man looked him over and then held out a hand. As the king reached for it, the lord reached beyond his hand and took the king by the forearm. The king hesitated only a moment before clasping the man's arm in return. Then the lord bowed his head, still holding on to the king. "Your Majesty," he said.

"My lord," he returned.

Several of the women below murmured something, and Dray glanced down at the group as a couple of glares turned towards Belle. Her face burned red. She hadn't shared the information then.

"Shall I give you the tribute now?" the lord asked with a smirk. "Or are you simply here to tell me it is already accepted?"

"Neither," the king said. "My uncle expects it, and the tribute is willing, although I don't like how it was done."

"There are nine; the crown demands ten. One of our own will go."

The king looked down at the group. Now that Belle had joined them, Dray thought the ten were present.

"Do you steal all your tribute?" the king asked. Dray wondered if he had considered the numbers himself.

"The soldiers come tomorrow to collect."

The king actually sighed, and Dray wondered just what these men might be able to negotiate.

"Dahli," the lord called. A beautiful young woman appeared in the doorway behind them. "Show the king to our best room, and then the tribute to the waiting house."

She bowed her head. "Your Majesty," she said softly, indicating back the way they had come.

The king stared for a moment and then followed, Dray a step behind. They moved back through the doorway to appear on another walkway. The men who had lined them appeared to have moved on, and they followed the young woman from tree to tree before a hut appeared at the end of a walkway. She stood to the side of the doorway, almost lost in the leaves of the tree it appeared to be built around, and held out a hand. The king moved past her and pulled open the door. A room that might have been in any castle opened up before them, and Dray was tempted to push past the king. Which, after too long standing in the doorway, he did.

Windows looked out over the green world around them. Several had been set into the ceiling above them and looked up into the trees. The effect was to give the room a green glow. It was a large, comfortable space. A long table with two bench seats running either side could easily have seated ten. Then he noticed that the tree he'd thought would be growing through the middle of the room wasn't there.

He walked over to where it should have been and reached out a hand. A huge square bed stood against one wall. Soft, deep chairs were pulled together in another part of the room, and several cupboards lined the walls. There was no fire, but the space was comfortably warm.

"How?" he asked.

"It just is," she said.

The king stood inside the door staring, but Dray wasn't sure if it was at the strange space or the girl. She smiled and bowed her head before turning back to the door.

"Who is the other tribute?" the king asked as she moved through the door.

"Your Majesty," she said with a bow of her head.

"Why?" he asked.

She blinked at him for a moment, and Dray wondered if she was offended by the questions. Or was she trying to find a way to explain it?

"I am the lord's sister," she said.

"Duty?" the king asked.

"It may be my only chance for a life of my own," she answered, standing tall. Dray was reminded of Belle. "No one would risk my brother's ire by courting me or asking for my hand. If I stay, I will live my life alone in servitude to the lord, or to the man of his choosing."

"You may find your life similar in the capital. You may not get the choices you expect."

"No, but it would be for me alone that they would choose, and not for my brother's favour."

The king bowed his head.

"I understand it will not be ideal," she went on. "Women have so few options."

"So I am learning," the king admitted. "I wish you well."

She bowed her head and left, pulling the door closed behind her.

"I think they are trying to win your favour," Dray said.

"Were there not ten girls?" the king asked. He stepped carefully into the room, as though the tree that should have grown through the floor would suddenly appear.

Dray nodded and wondered if the lord intended to keep one of the intended tribute for himself. Sending his sister seemed a strange choice. Although it appeared that the women of the kingdom were stronger than he had anticipated. They were being sold on like bags of wheat, and yet they had turned such a thing into an option, as though they would be better for it. He was beginning to believe that they might. Many of them were poor and, like Belle, didn't have much of a life to return to. Marrying well in the capital could change their lives, and those of their future children.

Dray would like a chance to talk to the lord himself. But that wasn't what soldiers did. If Ana had been there, she would have included Dray in any discussions, but he wondered if this young lord did things differently, and if he might have seen the benefit of keeping Ana for himself. She certainly wasn't a maid any longer.

"Dray?" the king asked. Dray wondered if he had been trying to get his attention for a time.

"Ten," he said.

"Which one does the sister replace?" the king asked more urgently.

"I don't know," Dray said honestly, and far too loudly, as there was a knock at the door.

Eilke stood on the other side when Dray stepped forward and opened it. He entered the space without acknowledgement and turned serious eyes to the king.

"What is it?" Dray asked, not sure he wanted to know.

"They wish to keep the farmer in payment for the lost men."

"Ahh," the king said, his shoulders slumping. "The fight and deaths are on my hands as well."

"You are the king; they will not ask of you. They are willing to continue with the tribute, but families have requested retribution."

"How many did you kill?" Dray asked.

"Three or four," the king murmured. "What has Belle said?"

"She does not know. For the moment, they have her separated from the others."

The king sighed again. "Why?"

"It appears that the tribute offered by the Forest Lord will include his sister. He said that Belle is the least beautiful and at risk of offending the crown."

"What will he do?" the king asked, desperation clear in his voice.

Eilke shook his head.

"I could talk with him."

"Not until he is ready to see you."

"But he would want an answer to the farmer, if we are willing to give him up. I was to blame for as much as he was. They stole the girls."

"As girls have been stolen before. Such things occur each time a province is to give this tribute."

"I understood them willing," the king snapped.

"They may be when the time comes, but this is the way of it."

"You or your chief talked those girls into wanting to come."

"We gave them the options."

"Has he seen anything in the forest?" the king asked, and Dray wondered for a moment what he was asking.

"The creature of shadows has not returned."

"You are sure?"

"The trees cry out here," Eilke said, a pained expression on his face, "but they would still tell of such an intruder."

Dray nodded once, looking back to the middle of the room.

"This was created long ago, by a magic that no one understands within the lord's seat. Yet it continues, and the trees grow up around the space. They cry, but they have always cried."

The king nodded, although he looked around the room as though trying to determine how it might occur.

"There is magic in the trees," Dray said, remembering something Ana had asked.

"This is different."

Dray bowed his head to the man. He wondered who could have harnessed it, but he might never know. "Let us see the lord," the king said.

"I cannot help you," Eilke said, bowing his head. "I must return."

Ed bowed his head to the lord, who sat at the head of a long table. His sister, Dahli, sat to one side and Belle the other, but he did not look happy that Ed would come to him before being sent for. He was the king, after all; perhaps it was time he started acting like it.

"What is it you want from us?" Ed asked before the man could say anything.

He raised his eyebrows a little, clearly surprised that the boy king would speak out. But he said nothing, only glancing at the woman to his right. Belle. Ed tried not to show the anger that was building in his chest. She had chosen to join the others and go to the capital. The lord was choosing a different path for her.

"I was involved in the death of those men."

"I understand," the lord said, indicating the bench beside his sister. But Ed shook his head, only to have the other man's face darken.

"What do you want of Phillip?"

"Payment," the man said simply.

"He has nothing he could pay you with," Ed said. "He is a poor farmer."

"He has much he could pay for those men's lives with." The lord rested his hand on Belle's, and she looked down at the table. Dray came up to stand beside him, but he couldn't take his eyes from Belle. She would sacrifice herself for her father, but he couldn't let it happen.

"Your men had taken her in the first place."

"You would want her for yourself."

"She is tribute for my uncle," Ed said quickly. He didn't want his words to endanger her further, but he had no understanding of how such negotiations occurred. He might very well be putting her in more danger. He half expected her accusing eyes to glare at him, but she hadn't raised them from the table.

"Then you will leave me the father," the lord said.

As Ed shook his head, she raised sad eyes and gave the smallest nod. She would sacrifice herself for him when he had gone through so much, and travelled so far to save her. Although Ed would have done the same for Salima, he knew Master Forest would keep her safe.

"What will you take in exchange?"

"There is no exchange," the lord said, standing. He released his hold, and Belle quickly pulled her hands from the table into her lap. "Although…" He said it as though just finding an idea, but Ed was sure the man had it already planned. He looked to the sister on the other side of the table. A beautiful woman, olive skin, her dark eyes on her brother. A flush filled her cheeks. Ed wasn't sure if that was because she realised what he was suggesting and was shy or angry.

"I am tribute," she said, her voice strong and determined.

"To the crown," the lord said, grinning.

"You would use me, still."

He scowled at her.

"I suppose if your sister sat on the throne beside me," Ed said, "you would think that an advantage. But it would elevate her above your station, and I would heed her word above yours."

"She is a woman," the lord snapped.

"No, you propose she would be Queen. I can't even reach my own throne, so I fail to see how you would see that an advantage."

Dray growled something under his breath. Ed was sure it was a warning, but he was flying by the seat of his pants here.

"Dahli," Ed said carefully, taking a step forward and holding out his hand to her.

She took it and stood from the table.

"If you were to be Queen, what would you do for your brother?"

She turned a dark look back his way. "Nothing. It is the lord's place to show fealty. It would not be for you or I to bow down to his whims."

"Whims?" The lord scowled, raising a hand quickly towards the woman, and Ed pulled her behind him. Belle leaned back from the table.

"I may have to talk to my uncle about how willing your tribute is," Ed mused.

"Then I keep the farmer and his daughter."

"And if I have your sister, you are short on what you owe the kingdom."

The man growled, and Dray stood before him, his sword drawn. "You might reconsider how you address your king."

"There must be ten. If you keep my sister for yourself, I will claim you stole the best of the tribute for yourself."

"You offered your sister. If I leave her, and I meet her in the capital, it would be nothing."

"You would take from the tribute?" the man sneered. "Can you not find better?"

"Are the tribute not the best you have to offer? And who better than the sister of a province lord?"

The man growled and the woman flinched, still pressed into his side with her hand tight in his.

"I will stay," Belle said, bowing her head.

Ed took in her sad face. "I will not accept that either."

"You are hard to please," she murmured, a small smile lighting her face as she lifted her eyes.

"I am King. Aren't kings fickle?"

Her smile broadened.

"We will discuss it with the soldiers tomorrow," Ed said. "In the meantime, the women are to stay with the tribute."

The lord scowled, but he bowed his head.

Ed nodded to the girl and released her hand. Without looking at her brother, she took Belle's arm and pulled her from the room.

"We shall discuss payment for your men later. I would talk to the farmer."

"You have no rights here. No one knows you are here."

"Someone knows I'm in the forest, someone you don't want searching your trees for me."

The lord's look changed, and although Ed couldn't quite read it, the man nodded.

"I will eat in my rooms. Send the farmer directly."

He turned and walked out, Dray following close behind. Once he was back in the privacy of his own room, he leaned heavily against the table, his legs threatening to give way.

"Well, you certainly sounded like a king," Dray said, and Ed looked up at the grinning man.

"Do you think it will work?"

"Hard to tell. Are you sure you don't want the sister for a queen? She is very beautiful."

Ed smiled and shook his head. No matter how he had treated Belle, he feared she would not approve. But he had to find a way to take one of them out of the tribute and save Phillip. There was a knock at the door, and it swung open before Dray could reach it. Ed stood straight up from the table and saw Belle in the doorway, tears streaking down her cheeks.

"He's gone," she blurted.

Disbelief washed over Ed as he crossed the room and took her in his arms. She clung to him while sobs wracked her body.

"He's gone," she murmured into his chest.

23

Salima watched Papa pace before the fire. He would stop occasionally and look towards the door, but Salima doubted Ana would use the door if she returned. Still, she turned towards it expectantly when it clicked.

The tall man, Ende, was almost a disappointment. Salima sighed and turned back to her father, who had started to pace again. Sitting cross-legged in the middle of the bed, Salima was itching to get out and see what she could find for herself. But she didn't want to risk running across whatever it was that had caused the death in the practice halls.

She hadn't seen much, but she had smelt the blood—a lot of blood. And the look on her father's face, and the soldier's, was enough to tell her she didn't want to see anything.

"You don't think Ana did this?" she asked.

"The body has gone." Ende's voice was low to prevent their being discovered, and yet it vibrated through her. She longed to know more about him. She sensed a heat from him that both drew her forward and pushed her away. It was an odd sensation.

"Gone where?" Papa asked, stopping mid-step.

The tall man shook his head. Salima could feel something from him, ebbing like his heat. Concern? Uncertainty? Fear.

"You think Ana did this," she said.

"She may have been there, but I think this is something very different."

The door swung open, and the cleric stood in the doorway, motioning them forward. "There has been another," the old man wheezed, as though he had run all the way to the room. "By the river."

"A child," Ende said, not a question.

The cleric nodded. "As before."

Papa growled something as they all raced from the room. Salima took a moment to lock the door behind them before she followed along the hallway. Papa suddenly stopped and looked back.

"I am not staying on my own," Salima said before he could order her back. He glanced at the tall man before he nodded.

They followed the cleric through the castle and into the courtyard, where too many people were gathered. Her father pushed his way forward, Ende behind him, and Salima followed in their wake.

Lying face down amidst the silent crowd was a small boy. He looked as though he had been pulled from the river, although he wasn't wet. His skin was pale, blue from the cold—or perhaps because he was dead. His face looked as though he rested, his eyes closed, his lips pressed together. A scratch crossed his arm, three scratches, as though some animal had clawed at him. But they were broad, indicating a large animal. This was just as her father had described to the regent.

The cleric rolled the child over, and Salima pushed a hand to her face. His stomach was torn open. The beast had fought back, or devoured him. She could feel the hot tears running over her cheeks and fingers as she pressed her hand tighter over her mouth, fearing she would cry out in the odd silence.

Where was his mother? Where had this boy come from? Was this the same creature that had torn the man to pieces in the practice halls?

A hand rested on her shoulder, and she looked up into the

worried eyes of the tall man. He nodded once, and she threw her arms around him. As she buried her face in his side, somehow the heat of him distorted the smell of blood.

"Take her back," Papa was saying.

"She is safer amongst the crowd," Ende said, his arm pulling her closer.

She couldn't be anywhere on her own right now, and she really wanted Ana. What if something had happened to her? What if this beast was a danger to her? No matter what magic she had, Salima didn't think the woman could defeat such a beast.

She took a steadying breath and looked back towards the body. A soldier stood nearby, shaking his head.

"There is another," he said, his eyes wide as he focused on her father. A murmur started through the crowd as she was guided away from the people.

"Is this wise?" she asked Ende. He kept her close at his side, as though he might keep her safe, and she knew he would.

"Another?" Papa asked.

The soldier nodded. Salima pulled back from the warmth of the tall man. "He…" The soldier gestured back across the courtyard to the practice rooms, but he couldn't seem to come up with any other words.

"Another what?" Salima prompted.

"The body," the man went on, as though he didn't realise it was her who had asked the question. "The boy." He gulped down his fears. "He disappeared into the shadows, and then the shadow moved."

"I thought I saw something," Ende said. "You didn't say anything," he continued, his voice accusing.

"She was there, and then she wasn't. And when you arrived, I was called away." He gestured back to the group surrounding the little boy.

"Who?" Salima asked.

"The witch," he whispered, glancing around as though she

might appear at the mention of her. "It was like she knew it was there, the shadow. She asked why it was here."

"Did it answer her?" Ende asked. Something dark in his voice made Salima shiver, and he glanced at her as though he had forgotten she was there.

The soldier nodded.

The tall man sighed, and Salima felt the warm air wrap around her. It felt angry, hot and yet comforting. "What did it say?" he prompted.

"That it wanted what she wanted. It was there but not there. Dark. And by the time you arrived at the door, the witch was gone, and so was the shadow."

"Who else have you told about the witch?" Salima asked, worried for her.

He shook his head. "Who would believe me? She appeared from nowhere and then went away again. It might have been my imagination."

"Someone may say that she took the body," Salima whispered.

"Not unless she made the shadow."

"Someone killed the boy for a reason, and then something else used it. Or was it the same beast?" Papa asked.

"The same darkness that she felt," Salima said. When the soldier turned his attention to her, she chewed her lip.

"Have you seen the witch?" he asked, his voice accusing.

She shook her head. What was Ana? Someone thought her a mage, someone who had magic but wasn't ruled by it. Wasn't that a witch? She looked up at the tall man beside her, wanting to step into his warmth again. He could explain to her what Ana was. He seemed to know her best. Her father moved between her and the soldier.

"We haven't seen her," he said. "How do we know that you didn't do something to the body? You were on watch. How could it simply disappear?"

"It didn't disappear," the man said, desperation clear in his voice. "It moved into the shadows and then became the shadows."

"You have seen this before," Salima said slowly, looking between her father and Ende.

Papa sighed but nodded. "Many years ago," he whispered. "Long before you were born."

"What happened?"

"It disappeared."

"To where?"

"Does it matter?" he asked, turning on her.

She shook her head. "Unless that is part of the reason it has returned."

"There is much in the world we don't understand. Has the regent been made aware of the boy?" Papa asked the soldier.

The man shrugged and looked back to the crowd. It appeared no one was brave enough to lift the child from the ground, yet someone had carried him here from the river. "Who found him?" Salima asked.

"The watch on the wall," the soldier answered. "There was a cloaked figure, maybe."

"Maybe?" Salima asked.

"The soldier wasn't sure, and when he got down to the child, he wasn't very sure of anything."

"Cloaked?" she asked.

"He thought it another soldier. But maybe they couldn't bring themselves to bring the child into the castle, for fear they would bring the evil with them."

"We are a far more superstitious people than I expected," Salima said softly. It can't have been Ana with the boy, for she didn't have a cloak. Did she? She had worn that same dress for so long. If she'd had a cloak, she might not have frozen so quickly in the cells. Salima was tempted to sigh now. For all the work they had done, it seemed people knew Ana had survived and was free somewhere in the capital.

"Can we go home now?" she asked her father.

He nodded and held out a hand. Salima was reluctant to leave the tall man's side, but she stepped forward and put her arm through her father's, allowing him to lead her away. When she looked back at the group, the cleric had the child in his arms and was carrying him towards the library. She had a sudden image of him lying amongst the books on the tables where the cleric read of an evening, but she was aware that the cleric's workrooms were near the library, and he was most likely taking him there. She wondered if they would be able to determine just what they were facing. Or if it was similar to what they had seen before. They might be superstitious people, but how short were their memories?

It was nice to enter their own small rooms rather than the other room they had hidden in for so long. She was surprised that it was as warm and cosy as it had always been, rather than the cool she feared would have filled the space in their absence. The curtains were pulled closed, and her father lit a candle as she stepped forward to pull them open. She stopped, the hairs rising on her skin as something moved in the shadows. She swallowed down her fear and dragged the curtain back to allow the afternoon sun to fill the room.

A cloaked figure stood against the wall, slender yet hidden in the depths of the thick black wool. Salima could understand why the watch had thought it a soldier, for it wore a soldier's cloak.

Her father frightened her, taking her hand. He had inched around as she stared at the figure. The door banged open, and Ende stood in the doorway, seeming even bigger than he usually did. The figure moved, raising a head, and the greenest eyes shone from within the darkness.

There was too much happening inside Ana's head for her to keep up. She had thought the space the only quiet and safe place she could find. Everyone else was busy looking for her or the creatures that appeared to have followed her here. Or followed something else of her here. She still didn't quite understand the beyond, and yet she knew it more clearly than much of her own history.

Had they abandoned hope of her return in coming back to their little space? The neat, open living room had only two small bedrooms leading off it. Although small, it was comfortable for the sword master and his daughter. There was a warmth to it that drew her, like that of the little dragon. But it had still been a surprise to hear them return, and Ende had felt the little one's fear. Ana had felt it herself. Perhaps she was on edge due to the events of the day.

Ana didn't have any understanding of it. And yet she understood it all. The maid had been given and went willingly. The boy, though, was another matter. He was already gone—or had some deal been made in his final moments and the sudden appearance of the sword master had delayed what was wanted, needed, for the joining to occur?

Ana shook her head. She pulled the cloak tighter around her. She looked between the faces, the uncertainty of the sword master, the relief of his daughter and the anger—Or was it fear?—on Ende's face. Again, she thought of him as someone different, not the dragon she had met on the mountain, not the old man who had seen her dreams.

"I didn't call you," she murmured.

"Not this time," he said, his anger rolling out. Ana wondered if he could bring the castle down around them if necessary.

"But you knew," she said.

He looked at the child. Strange that he hadn't sensed her before now. Or he hadn't tried because she'd been thought lost with her mother.

"You are taller than I remember," she said.

He turned his glare on her and, reluctantly, she stepped away from the wall.

"I'm so glad you are safe," the child said, throwing herself at Ana, who gripped her tightly in return. "Could you bring Ed back?" she asked. Ana released her hold. Everyone wanted something, she thought. It must have shown on her face, for the dragon was there between them, pulling the child to safety.

Ana sighed. "He will do what he must. And he needs to find his own way." She sounded harsher than she had intended. Dray might have cautioned her. Might have. She doubted he would take the time. It was only at the open mouth of the sword master that she wiped at the tear. Dray was still pulling her, and she wasn't sure why.

"You found the child," she said.

Ende nodded once as the sword master stepped forward, almost between her and the girl again. They did think her a threat. "The watch brought him in. The other body has disappeared."

"Not exactly, just moved."

"How?" he asked.

"They are two shadows from the beyond that have become solid because someone on this side is willing to help them."

"That body was willing?" the sword master asked, shuddering.

"It may have offered a deal, before the death. I don't know how it works."

"You have an idea."

"I could sense the girl in the one I met in the forest."

"The girl?"

"The maid," Ana said with a sigh. Had he given her up or offered her something more? She doubted he would give himself up in such a way, but there must be a way to undo it.

"There are two," the sword master said slowly, as though trying to process the information.

"There may be more. The shadow can only become solid once it has something to cling to. One must have killed the boy to bring another forth."

"And the little boy?"

"He might not have been willing, or his soul was used to strengthen another."

"They can take souls?" Salima asked, her voice too high and squeaky. Ende pulled her closer.

"I don't understand what they can do, but the child's soul was… removed."

The sword master sat heavily in a chair. "We don't want the king in the middle of this."

"The regent may be responsible in some way," Ende said. "Do we want him remaining in a position of power?"

"Putting Ed on the throne may not stop it."

They all looked up at her. "I thought you wanted that. I thought you saw him as King," Ende said, his voice accusing.

"He is the king," Ana said, "and I think he will find his way to us whether it is safe or not."

"Can you stop them?" Salima asked. "Can you defeat these shadows?"

Ana shook her head. She had no idea. They wanted what she wanted. Was that to put Ed on the throne? Were they removing his enemies? Although it appeared that the mage and regent had sent them. "I can slow them down."

"How?"

Ana put her hand to her chest. She wasn't sure what lived inside her, and she could only hope it wasn't the dark shadows. But they had listened because of her magic, because of the strength inside her. The queen inside her. "They listened when I said not to harm them."

"But can you do that for everyone?" Salima asked.

"I don't know," she said too loudly, exasperated.

The sword master surprised her by stepping forward and resting his hands on her shoulders, then pulled her hood back. "Have you slept?" he asked. "Eaten?"

She shook her head. She didn't have time for such things; she had been busy trying to find her way to… where? What?

Understanding?

"Go to the kitchens," he said to Salima, and she was on her feet and gone.

"You can't send her out into that?" Ende said sharply, making to follow her.

"She knows the way, and I think she can protect herself better than you imagine."

"It might want her," Ende said, a dangerous rumble behind his words.

"I know that. But I have kept her safe this long. And Ana wouldn't let that happen."

"I don't know that I can stop it," Ana admitted as the sword master directed her across the room and into a chair. As she sat, her cloak moved, and he studied her leg for a moment. She pulled at the cloak, but he put his hand on hers to stop the movement.

"Where did you get that?" he asked.

She looked down at the mud on her skirts. When she made to brush it off, she noticed the blood on her hands. Had she touched the child? Had she touched Salima with that hand?

"The river," she murmured.

He turned to the fire and then looked at Ende, who stepped forward with a huff and started it quickly. And as the sword master watched him, it blazed to life, warming the little room further along with the kettle that hung over the flame.

"I meant the new clothes," he said, walking to the stand by the wall with the basin, which he carried to the small table before her. He looked again at Ende, then lifted the kettle and poured the steaming water into the basin.

"The regent had sent dresses when I stayed with the mage."

"You went to the mage?" Ende asked.

She shook her head and then nodded. "He didn't know I was there. I can put myself wherever I like," she said. "I don't quite understand it."

She leaned forward and submerged her hands in the water,

rubbing at the blood as though it stained her skin. The sword master submerged a small cloth and then rubbed at her knee where the mud marked her dress.

"It doesn't matter," she said.

"Let's make you appear somewhat respectable."

She wanted to laugh. She was anything but. He couldn't make her into a lady of the court. She would never be that. "They will always see me as a witch," she whispered.

"What is the difference?" Salima asked, rushing through the door, a large bowl in her hands and a loaf under her arm. "I kept it hot," she said, grinning as she sat the bowl down beside the basin.

"Serve it out," her father said, and she lifted it back to the side board. Then she opened it to retrieve a small stack of bowls.

"Some call you a witch," she said. "Some a mage."

"A mage is someone with magic; a witch is something else," the sword master said.

"What sort of something?" Ana asked before the child could.

"Something dark."

She looked up at Ende then, who was looking down at her over the sword master as though he was still trying to read her. "You think I'm a witch."

"I always thought you a mage," he said, "but I don't know what your magic is."

"Like my mother's." Ana took the towel the sword master offered to dry her hands, leaving streaks across it. What if she was a vessel for something darker, something like the shadows that consumed all around them? Yet it chose not to change her, to use her to hide in. "What happened to her?" she asked as the girl handed her a small bowl. The smell of stew filled her senses, and she realised just how hungry she was.

"She ran away with your father," Ende said.

"After that?" Ana asked, looking up.

He shook his head. "She had you."

"She left us," Ana said, looking back to the bowl. "I saw it, her leaving to keep us safe."

Ende studied her but said nothing else. The girl sat at her feet with a bowl of her own, and the sword master rubbed the towel over her knee, drying the material he had cleaned. "I could get another," Salima said.

He shook his head, and she nodded once.

Ana woke, still in the chair. Someone had draped a blanket over her, and the bowls and basin had been removed from the table in front of her. Someone had even taken her boots off. The memory of the sword master's gentle hand on her knee made her wonder if there was something else. Or was he hoping his kindness would be returned and she wouldn't kill the child? She wouldn't. Ana knew what Salima was, and she would keep the secret. She wondered if Ende would be able to. She stood slowly and stretched, the blanket falling around her feet, and found her cloak over the back of the chair. She turned, wanting the rough wool against her face, and Dray's face appeared in the darkness.

He sat at a window—not one looking over the capital, as was the one in the room she was in, but one that overlooked a forest through dense leaves, the moonlight barely lighting his features. He continued to stare as she stepped closer. Did he know she was there? Was she, or was it an idea of being there, of being with him? Everything seemed to make her think of him.

She turned and took in the room. Ed slept on a large bed. The room felt familiar and yet was unknown. But they were the only two in it. She took another step towards Dray and rested her hand on his shoulder. He felt so real, and she sighed. He rested his hand on hers, and she looked from it to his dark eyes. She wanted desperately to reach for his face, but she kept her other hand at her side.

"Where are the others?" she whispered.

"They want payment."

"For the forest?"

He nodded, turning back to the window, his hand still on hers. She could feel the warm, calloused skin. "I wish you were here," he whispered.

"Ed will find a way," she said.

"We are coming to you." He startled her by standing quickly, her hand still in his. "We will find you."

She shook her head. "I'm not safe."

He smiled then, and her fears subsided a little. "You wouldn't harm Ed."

She glanced back to the sleeping king. She hoped Dray was right. "I'm scared," she admitted, knowing he was the only one she could truly be honest with.

"You control them," he said, his voice a little hard.

"No."

He let her hand go then, and she was looking out the window of the master's rooms over the city surrounding the castle. A different view from her last room, and yet it all felt like a prison. Would they truly work together? Could she save them from whatever the mage had called forward? Would Dray ever forgive her if she failed?

24

Dray was roused from sleep by the sound of horses and armour. He looked out the edge of the window at the group below, unsure if he wanted to be seen or not. There was no sign of the forest men, but it appeared that the soldiers knew to wait. He rolled his shoulders, stiff from his night sleeping against the window. It wasn't that he had intended to keep watch; it was more that he couldn't face sleep. And Ana had found him anyway.

"It is time," the king said behind him. He nodded before he turned. Belle had returned to the tribute, and there had been no explanation given as to why Phillip hadn't been presented to the king as requested. Nor was it clear where he had gone.

Belle was sure he had been taken and murdered in retaliation for freeing the girls and killing some of those men who had taken them. But he may have escaped another way. It was only as Dray looked at the king straightening his jerkin that he hoped Eilke had managed to take him back to the Near Folk, despite his parting words.

"This might not be a good idea," the king said.

"Only one way to find out," Dray admitted, opening the door for him.

"Bring out the tribute," a soldier called, and Dray paused in the doorway.

"Is that usual?"

"I don't know," the king said.

A line of women moved below them across the forest floor towards the soldiers. Dray looked down on the heads that passed beneath them, nine in total, and wondered what the lord was playing at.

"Are you trying to cheat the kingdom?" the same soldier asked. His voice was stern, but there was something a little rehearsed in his words, and for a moment Dray wondered if there was a play that went along with such a tribute. He had been to collect enough of it himself over the years, yet he had never been selected to collect this tribute. He also wished he could see the man through the leaves to see who he might be.

"There is a question as to the tenth. For I have two beauties good enough for a king."

"Bring them forward," the soldier called.

The king made to step forward, but Dray caught him by the arm. "Wait," he whispered.

"Why not offer both?" the soldier said as the two heads moved out, walking closely together, one dark and one light. An uneasy feeling filled Dray's chest.

"This isn't going to end well," he murmured.

"The greater the tribute, the greater your loyalty to the crown," the soldier said.

Dray tried to place the voice. He was sure he would know the man, but he wasn't sure he was ready to stand before the group and find out.

"Why not ask the king yourself what he thinks?" the lord said.

They wouldn't get the chance to meet the group on their own terms.

"Your Majesty?" the lord called. "Care to make the decision now?"

The king growled. Dray pushed ahead of him along the narrow walkways and down through the tree. He pushed the door open carefully, taking in the two women, who were surprisingly calm.

Although he knew that Belle had been crying most of the night in fear of what had happened to her father, she looked refreshed. The lord's sister stared ahead. The group of soldiers before Dray was made up of twelve men. Fitting, he thought, although he wondered if they thought there was a chance they would need to convince the tribute to travel with them. There were two carriages, which he should have expected, and Dray wondered if he had been too long out of the capital.

"Captain Sterling?" A soldier Dray knew well stepped forward, then saluted with a fist across his chest and a controlled bow.

"Captain Barlow," he returned.

"Why are you…" the soldier started, then saw the man behind him step out from the tree. He stared for a moment before looking to Dray. Dray nodded once, and the man dropped to his knee, the men behind him following. "Your Majesty," he stammered. "We did not expect to find you here."

"I was taking some time to visit the provinces," Ed said, as though it were perfectly normal. "You may rise."

"We had heard…" the man continued to stammer.

"What did you hear?" the king asked, sounding far more like the king he was meant to be than Dray had ever heard him.

"That you had run away," Barlow said matter-of-factly as he climbed to his feet.

"As though I were a child?" the king asked.

The man looked him over, and a murmuring started amongst the men behind him. They might have seen him for more than what he was before. But Dray still wondered if they were more the regent's men than the king's men. He cleared his throat.

"The tribute, Your Majesty."

The king turned and looked over the group. "You may guide them to the carriages, Captain. Is that not what you are here for?"

"There need only be ten."

The king nodded.

"There are eleven," the soldier said slowly, as though

explaining it to a child. The king sighed, and the man snapped to attention.

"There are ten," the king said calmly, "and a companion of mine. I would appreciate it if you would allow her ride with the others. We lost our horses. I would not wish to make the lady walk any further."

Well done, Dray thought. He had saved them both without naming which he was to take. Although after the hours Ed had held the crying woman last night, Dray imagined it was Belle he would not let give herself away. He wondered how long it would take for her to become what she had been in the forest. Annoying. Dray leaned forward and indicated the carriages to the two women with an outstretched hand.

"You would steal my sister?" the lord demanded.

"Is she not tribute?" the king asked. Dray wondered at the calm façade and how much longer he would be able to maintain it. The captain had his hand on his sword, Dray noticed. Did they expect a fight for these women?

"My lord," Captain Barlow said, stepping forward as he gestured to his men with a short wave. "You were to provide tribute and have done so. Are you no longer willing to give to the kingdom?"

"Of course not," the lord said through clenched teeth.

"My father is safe?" Belle asked as she was ushered into a carriage with the other women. It appeared the soldiers were ready to take the tribute whether it was being given willingly or not.

Dray nodded and could only hope he was right. She looked at him with such hope he wondered if it had been a mistake. Eilke may have returned to his people alone. He didn't owe them anything.

"You cannot take them all," the lord called.

"Your Majesty," Captain Barlow said, indicating one of the carriages. "There is room for you to ride inside. I think it best at this stage."

The king looked to Dray, who gave him a small nod. This was going better than he had expected, but it could be a very different matter once they were on the road. These men might have other ideas.

"You cannot take them," the lord roared. Men appeared from the trees, swords and arrows trained on the soldiers.

Captain Barlow looked at Dray and then sighed. "There is always a drama with this tribute. Their fathers don't want to give them up, their mothers try to give away girls not worthy of the tribute, or lords don't want to show their loyalty to the crown."

"I am loyal," the man spat. "I give willingly to be part of this kingdom. But you have a selfish boy of a king who would steal my sister."

"She is tribute," the soldier said simply.

"And the other?" the lord sneered.

"His friend. Forgive me, my lord. I am but a captain in the King's Men. I am his to do as he directs. It is not for me to question his choice of friends." He bowed again.

The lord scowled down at them but did not call off his men. Dray had developed a new respect for Barlow. At the smell of smoke, he turned and noticed two soldiers towards the back of the group armed with bows; each had a flaming arrow nocked. Definitely a man brighter than Dray had previously given him credit for.

"Would you like a horse, Sterling, or will you ride above?"

"I'll ride above for now."

Barlow nodded and, as Dray climbed up onto the front of the carriage the king had climbed into, he looked back to the paling face of the lord.

"I ask again, my lord: do you offer this tribute willingly?"

"Yes," he growled.

"Excellent," Barlow said with a clap of his hands. The soldiers moved to the carriages and their mounts, and the convoy started to move out. Dray could still smell the smoke of the flaming arrows, and he wondered if they were still trained on the men of the forest.

They travelled in silence for a time, and then Dray climbed down along the edge of the carriage as they made their way through the trees towards the main road that cut through the kingdom towards the capital. He opened the door and edged inside.

All ten girls could have easily fit into the one carriage, but they had spaced them out. It might take a day or two, and Dray imagined they could rest. Or if they played difficult, the soldiers would fit as well. Every face turned to him, and a girl stood and offered her seat, as it was close to the king. Dray held out a hand to allow her to hold on as she made her way down the carriage to another seat. When a wheel hit something, the whole carriage swayed and someone gasped. Dray searched the ceiling for a hand hold.

"Sit down before you squash someone," the king said. Dray nodded and sat heavily into the vacated seat.

"So," he said, unsure where to start. "This is a nice way to travel."

Belle started to laugh and then rubbed her hand across her eyes. He wasn't sure if she had any tears left. "It is better than walking, perhaps."

"It isn't as smooth a journey as it appears," one of the girls said. Dray looked up as they were all jostled about. It might have been better if they were squashed in together to prevent such movement. The seats were unpadded wooden benches.

"We could ask for a horse," he said to the king, who smiled.

"And miss this adventure? We will be fine."

"I am sorry, Your Majesty."

"We seem to have found a group of soldiers not trying to kill me, yet. And we managed to save both Dahli and Belle from the lord. Things are looking up."

They went over another bump, and Belle was almost bounced off the seat. The king reached out and pulled her close. "You can hang on," he said, pulling her arm through his.

"What shall we do when we reach the capital?" Dray asked, trying to ignore the rising heat in the young woman's face as she smiled at the king.

"Find Ana first," he said, and Belle's smile slipped.

"We may not get that chance. I think your uncle will have other ideas."

"Well, I doubt he can lock me in my room," the king said, sounding like a child.

"Where do you think Ende is?" Belle asked.

"He might very well be there waiting for us," Dray said. "He seems to know where he is needed."

"He's not good in castles."

"He might not be that willing to help," the king said softly. Dray looked around at the women, wondering what they thought of the conversation. "He hasn't been himself since we entered the forest."

"Let's just wait until we are out of the forest before we breathe too easily," Dray said softly. "The lord is not so happy about his sister joining us, and that he could not keep Belle for himself."

"The king said she was to come," one of the women offered. "He can't go against the king."

"I haven't been heard too much so far."

"We know you," the woman said, smiling shyly.

"More and more know who you are," Dray said. "That may work in our favour."

The king sighed and nodded once.

"I think I'll stay close for now," Dray continued. "I'll talk to Barlow when we stop."

"When will that be?" one of the other young women asked.

"Once we are out of the forest," he said, looking at the faces focused on him. The lord's sister must have been in the other carriage. He would need to check that for sure and ensure she hadn't been left behind. He looked at Belle, her arm through the king's and her head resting on his shoulder as they silently bumped their way out of the forest. He wasn't sure that the young man would give her up now, whether she was willing tribute or not.

25

Ed tried to look like the king he hoped they thought he was as he sat amongst the women in the carriage. He was starting to feel quite claustrophobic. The dim lighting through the narrow windows, the heat of the bodies, Dray watching him too closely…

He glanced at the man from time to time and tried to determine what he was thinking. Dray might have been doing just what he was designed for, watching over Ed. But the number of soldiers around them made him far more nervous than he anticipated, and if they turned on him, he wasn't sure what he could do. Or what danger that might put the women in.

The captain had seemed very sure of himself when he'd collected the tribute. It might be that he would claim the lord refused to hand them over. But would the women be heard if they spoke against them? If there was a chance the men could turn on him, Ed doubted the women would survive.

He glanced down at Belle on his shoulder. She sighed softly in her sleep, her body relaxed against his. Her hand rested on his arm, where he had put it. He had so very clearly made a choice, although he wasn't quite sure what that choice was. He just couldn't leave her behind. He only hoped Dray had been right about Philip and that he had returned to the Near Folk. They might be able to find him later.

She moved in her sleep. Her hand slipped from its loose hold on his arm and fell across his lap. Ed took it in his and then looked up at the raised eyebrow and slight smile on Dray's face. He sighed. The soldier nodded once, and then the carriage jerked to a stop. Belle sat up with a sharp intake of breath and pulled her hand from his, her face reddening as though she might have done it in her sleep.

The door swung open and Captain Barlow stood in the doorway. "We shall stretch our legs."

There was a general murmur, and several girls moved forward to step down. The soldier cleared his throat, looking at Ed directly. Silence fell over the carriage as they turned to look at him.

"I think the ladies are in more need than I," Ed said, indicating the door. He followed them out and then waited to offer Belle a hand as she appeared in the doorway. Dray grinned in the dim light behind her.

She stepped down and then stopped, her hand still in his, and he turned his gaze to more soldiers than he'd realised had accompanied them.

"Your Majesty?" a soldier asked, stepping forward.

Ed nodded once, although the man didn't take to the knee as the others had.

"Your uncle has been looking for you," he said.

"Has he indeed?" Ed asked.

"Did you run away?" the soldier asked.

"I apologise that I don't know you by name," Ed said, well aware of the large man standing beside him. He wondered if Dray would pull a sword on his own men if required to save him. "I have not had my uncle's luxury of spending time with soldiers."

"Major Field," the man said with the smallest bow of his head.

"Major," Ed returned without a bow of his own. This man clearly belonged to his uncle. He glanced around at the women standing by the side of the road, then looked back at the trees not so far away. They had waited until they'd left the trees, and Ed hoped it would be enough to keep them safe.

He looked for the olive-skinned sister of the lord, and she gave him a small smile and bow of her head when their eyes met. The major looked at her and then back.

"Do you want tribute?" he asked.

"I thought them mine already," Ed said, suddenly aware of Belle's hand in his. "Are they not the kingdom's to give to prove their loyalty to the crown?"

"The crown," the man said.

"Is it not mine?" Ed asked.

"Did you run?" the man asked again, his voice flat and unfriendly.

"You forget yourself, Major," Dray said.

"As do you, Captain. I understood you had run from duty, after a girl."

"Barely," Dray whispered. Ed wondered what exactly he meant. That he hadn't run from duty, or that she wasn't just a girl. "I am true in my duty as a captain of the King's Men," he said clearly. "I protect my king."

"Mmm," was all the man said.

"Did you think the tribute would need more protection?" Dray asked. "We have seen some strange sights in the Near Forest."

"I think they can handle ten women," the man said, looking around. Then his gaze rested on Belle, his eyes lingering on her face and then her hand in Ed's. "Although there appears to be an extra."

"My companion," Ed said quickly. "A friend the soldiers were kind enough to make room for."

The man said nothing, but only looked her up and down again. To her credit, Belle stood still beside him, although her hand squeezed his a little tighter.

"How long will we remain here?" Ed asked, looking around for Captain Barlow.

"Not long. We will travel through the night and stop further along the road."

Ed looked out at the sky then, which was just starting to darken. Had they travelled so long already in the carriage? Could he survive bumping through the night?

"Would you rather camp, Your Majesty?" Dray asked him.

"I trust Barlow to know what he is doing."

Belle tugged at his hand.

"What is it?" he asked, leaning down towards her.

"We could use a little… break," she murmured, leaning in towards him.

He nodded, understanding. But in the open fields, he wondered what they could do.

Barlow coughed politely. "We understand, miss." He waved at a couple of the soldiers, who held up a large sheet. He pointed out into the field. "We can assist you."

She nodded, and the girls moved together with the two young men. Ed watched as they directed the men away to watch what might be coming as two of the women stepped up to take the sheet.

Ed turned to the lord's sister by his side. She bowed her head. "Thank you, Your Majesty," she said, then raced off to join the others.

"Go for water," Barlow ordered two others, and they headed in the other direction, where Ed could just see a small river glinting in the distance. They gathered water skins and took off at a run. "Are we to feed your men as well?" he asked the major.

The man scowled. "We have our own tasks to do."

Without a glance in Ed's direction, he turned back for his horse and indicated that the men he travelled with do the same. He looked out over the field and the young women chattering amongst themselves, taking it in turns to hold the sheet up to hide from the soldiers.

The major climbed up onto his mount and, with a sharp whistle, he and his men disappeared quickly down the road. The women paused in their chatter to watch them go.

"My uncle will know now that I'm on my way."

"Unless they plan to ambush us closer to the capital."

"Thanks Dray, that fills me with confidence. Perhaps I should have stayed hidden in the trees."

"Perhaps," Dray murmured. "I'm not sure what allies we have here."

"We are the King's Men," Barlow said sharply, making Ed jump.

"All of you?" Dray asked.

"I give my word for every man present."

"Hmm." Dray sighed, looking down the road after the major.

"I could do with a bath," Belle said, reappearing on the road beside Ed.

"I would love to indulge you, miss, but I fear I haven't the hot water."

Belle laughed easily. She seemed more herself now that they were out of the trees. Although Ed wondered if he knew who she truly was. He had seen her strong and independent, and in the forest something very different and clingy. Had fear changed her? She smiled up at him and took the offered water skin. As the women made their way back to the road, the soldiers handed out dry meat.

"Do you wish to stay in the carriage, Your Majesty?" the soldier asked.

Ed nodded. He hadn't really been on a horse, and he didn't want to fall off in front of all these men and young ladies.

"What do you think?" he asked Dray.

"About the carriage?" Dray returned with a grin.

"Ambush," Ed said quietly.

"I don't trust the major," Dray said, glancing at the retreating form of the captain as the women were assisted back inside the carriages. "I imagine we shall find out soon enough."

"Then what?" Ed asked as he offered Belle a hand back inside.

"We hope you still know how to use your father's sword."

Ed put his hand on the pommel. If only he had been practicing.

Master Forest would be disappointed in his lack of attention to it. Maybe he could have used the soldiers for some work, although he doubted they would be stopping anywhere long enough to ask.

Ana felt the uncertainty surrounding her and was desperate to run again. To hide somewhere they couldn't reach her, although she wasn't sure if that would help her. The whole castle seemed to be in a heightened state of activity and fear. She wanted to talk with the mage, although she was sure he was trying to kill her. And she wanted to scare the regent just because she could, yet she knew doing so would put her companions at more risk.

"What did he say about the body?" she asked, then looked up at the faces surrounding her. "The boy in the hall," she prompted. "The regent?"

"Oh," Master Forest said. "Little. He seemed as shocked as we were. Although…" He glanced at Ende. "He said something about seeing it before."

Ende nodded slowly. "He wouldn't have seen the boy."

"So many boys," Salima murmured. "Was it the same?"

The sword master nodded. "But we never saw the shadows then. Not like now."

"I wonder if they came for something else."

"Then or now?" he asked her.

"Where might the regent have seen it?" Ana asked instead.

"It appeared to confuse him more than it answered any of our questions. Although, I have one."

She looked at him, waiting.

"When will this second shadow creature appear?"

"It has," she said.

"To others, not just their queen," Ende said, his voice vicious.

"Why do you think that is me?"

"The soldier told us what it said. That you want the same

things."

"I don't know what that is," she whispered.

"You don't know what you want, or you don't know what it wants?"

She looked at him, trying to see the old man in the younger one before her. She couldn't connect them. She knew it was Ende, and yet he was something very different. "Why did you hide?" she asked instead.

"From what?" the girl asked on his behalf. As he glanced at her, Ana knew the answer. He had thought them dead, that there was nothing else for him.

"What else do you know of my mother?" Ana asked.

"You think she returned here," Ende said. "If she did, I never saw her. The last we saw of Mariela was when she ran with her soldier."

Ana looked down at her hands. She had asked so many times in the last day, and the answer was always the same. She wondered if anyone else had seen her mother after she had left Sheer Rock, and her longing to talk to the mage returned. She sucked in a deep breath, but before she could move anywhere, the sword master's hand closed around her wrist.

She looked up at him, and he shook his head once.

"Are we to hide away here, hoping that the shadows don't return?" she asked.

He opened his mouth and then closed it, standing instead to move to the window. "I thought you said the maid was lost," he murmured, leaning forward.

Ana joined him at the window and watched the girl race through the streets below them, lost in the crowd by a stall and then back onto the road leading towards the castle. Did she want to be seen?

"She seems to be in a hurry," Salima said, pushing between them at the window. "Perhaps she has some news." She jumped down and raced for the door.

"No," Master Forest called after her.

"I won't get caught," she said, slipping through the doorway. Although Ende took a step towards the door as though to follow, he joined the other man at the window instead.

"She might be seen," Ana said, standing and pulling her cloak around her.

"So might you," Ende said quickly.

"I'm friends with the shadows, and that little maid is far from safe." Ana sighed and then winked out of the room. Ende's disappointment followed her. She wondered if it was aimed at her, or at himself for not seeing what she was. Not that it was any clearer. She pressed her back into the wall of the throne room, lost in the shadows behind the throne. She couldn't see the child, but she could sense her coming. She pulled the hood up around her face to ensure she couldn't be seen, but she knew in her very being that no one knew she was there.

The regent wandered into the room, glanced around and sat on the throne. He was still and rigid, the only person in the room. Ana searched the shadows, fearing the creature had returned this way for a reason. If the maid did not appear here, she would search in the mage's rooms. As the heat moved towards her, she knew the little dragon was not far away.

The maid appeared silently in the room. If Ana had not been watching for it, she would not have seen her. It was almost as though she had winked into existence in the middle of the room. The regent didn't appear to have noticed how she had arrived, and he waved a hand as though waiting for a report.

"What do you want to hear?" she asked, her voice not quite what it had been. The regent sat forward a little.

Ana wondered if he realised what it was he was talking to.

"Is it done?"

There was the smallest pause, and Ana could feel the shadows pressing in on the room.

"No, sire."

"No!" the regent bellowed, pushing up from the throne. He

clenched a fist. Ana could feel the anger flowing from him, but there was something else. Pain. He made to touch one arm with the other and then stopped. He must still be afflicted from where she had grabbed him.

"Has the mage seen my soldiers?"

She tilted her head to the side as though considering the question.

"He has sent you?"

"Who?" she asked.

"The mage," he said, exasperation washing from him as he stepped forward.

She shook her head once.

The regent stared at her, then moved back to sit heavily in the throne. His hand rubbed absently at the arm Ana had grabbed so violently. She had done more than make him nervous, and the idea filled her with a little more confidence than she had felt of late. She refocused on the strange scene within the room. The maid had come, but not at the mage's bidding. She wondered if it would continue to do as he wanted. Yet there was a reason.

"What do you know?" the mage snapped.

"You will learn more soon," the maid said, bowing her head and turning for the door.

"Why are you here, little girl?" he asked unkindly. Ana could feel his hatred for the girl roll from him; or was it jealousy? She was tempted to hold her breath to prevent the feeling from overwhelming her.

"I wanted to see what you would do," the maid said, her voice more like the hiss Ana had experienced in the forest.

She felt the fear of the little dragon flow from her hiding space as she realised the maid was something very different.

"Maybe I should have kept you for myself," the regent growled.

"I serve another," the voice, clearly not that of the maid, growled across the room.

There was a sharp intake of breath in a distant corner of the room, and both maid and regent turned towards the sound. The regent stepped forward, and the maid winked from existence. Ana closed her eyes, wrapped her arms around the girl and then put her hand across her mouth as she dragged her back through the shadows to her father's rooms.

"What is that girl?" Salima blurted as Ana released her hold and stepped back.

"A way to the king," Ana whispered.

"I thought you could keep him safe," the sword master muttered.

"They will know where he is soon enough," Ana said.

"What if the shadows follow him?" the girl asked, panic clear on her face and filling the room around them.

"They won't."

"Can you check on him?" The panic shifted to desperation.

Ana nodded once. But again, the sword master's hand was on her. "It is not safe."

"Ana can keep him safe," Salima said.

Ana looked down, the weight of the girl's expectations heavy on her shoulders. It was a reminder that she was only of use to these people to protect Ed. Even though that was all she had wanted, to find a way to put Ed on the throne. Back where he belonged.

"Could he be on his way?" Salima asked. "If people were to see him, then they would know who he was and the regent couldn't do anything."

The sword master let Ana go.

"He is my only concern," she whispered, looking back to the girl, and then she blew out a soft breath as she searched out Ed.

In the dim carriage, the sounds of sleep competed with the sounds of horses' hooves and wheels travelling at speed over rough road. Girls, young women, curled against each other, having been jostled to sleep by the movement of the carriage. At one end, Ed lay back in a corner, Belle nestled in beside him. His arm wrapped around her, her arm across his chest. She appeared to glow in the dim light. Dray's dark eyes sparkled as the moonlight squeezed through the narrow windows.

"They know," Dray whispered.

Ana nodded once. "They have guessed, and it will be confirmed soon enough."

"I will keep him safe for you," Dray said, and she turned as the knot filled her throat, making it hard to swallow.

26

The regent stood in the middle of the mage's workshop and scowled. Anger burnt in his chest, and he wanted desperately to take it out on someone. Given that the mage had failed him and his little maid had provided nothing but riddles, Thom was fully prepared for that someone to be him. He had gone to all the trouble to drag something from the other side to take the boy out, and that had failed. The regent still wasn't quite sure why that was. But then the beast had started killing people within the capital. At least two that he was aware of. The mark that had been on the boy's arm flashed again before him.

"You had better start explaining, old man," he growled into the dark room. He looked around then, aware at how chilly it was. Was it usually this cool? A single candle burned, but he had carried that in with him. The fire, one of several fireplaces around the odd-shaped room that usually glowed with hot coals, was dark. He crept closer and held out his hand.

He felt suddenly exposed in the dark room, as though whatever the mage had called was lurking somewhere. He was reminded of how strange the little maid had sounded.

"Mage!" he cried into the darkness, allowing his anger and frustration to fill the space. Nothing responded.

How long since Thom had seen him? How many days, and where might he be?

The regent turned and hurried out of the space. The mage knew far more than he had shared, and Thom needed answers. The mark, the certainty that he had seen Mariela, and where the little witch had got to. He was sure now that she had survived.

Ende was here for some reason he didn't understand, and he wanted answers to it all. For all of them led back to the mage and his secrets.

He pushed open the door and climbed the stone steps that led towards the courtyard. A soldier stood at attention not far away. "Have you seen the mage?" he asked, trying to relay his urgency without sounding accusing, but by the way the man jumped he realised he had failed.

"No, Your Highness."

The regent growled out his frustrations. "When was he last seen?"

The man shook his head. Thom saw another man across the courtyard and waved him over. The soldier looked to the regent and bowed his head.

"The regent is seeking the mage. Have you seen him?"

The man nodded quickly. "Several days ago, he took some men and headed out."

"Men?"

"King's Men."

"Do you know where he was going?"

He bowed his head. "Only that he was looking for a girl."

"What girl?" the regent snapped.

"I don't know," he said quickly.

"Let us hope he returns shortly."

The man nodded, but his eyes were on the other soldier.

"Where were you going?" the regent asked.

"The watch," he said, indicating the wall.

"Trouble?" the regent asked, hoping he didn't sound as worried as he felt.

"Not yet, but we are keeping a close eye on the world. Strange things seem to be occurring."

The regent nodded. "I might have a look with you," he said. And after a nervous glance at the soldier still standing in the courtyard, he led the way to the wall.

The regent couldn't remember looking at the world from this part of the wall. He spent much of his time on his balcony looking over something else, the city and the people. This was quite different. The wide river appeared to run along the very wall he stood on, as though it kept the river from the castle. The Near Deep. And he knew it to be fast and deep. There were no bridges nearby that allowed a crossing, but if any enemies were to camp on the other side, they could be easily picked off from the vantage of the wall.

He was surprised to see people moving through the long grasses on the other side of the river. A path tracked along the edge, and when he leaned over the wall, he could see something similar along the bank below him. Where city and people filled the space on the other side of the castle, there was nothing but fields on this side. Although they were not fields farmers filled with crops. They were marshy and soft. He could see the water glinting through the grasses from here, and he wondered at those who moved through it. A man with a pole, children with a net. A woman with a basket.

He had been standing looking out over the world for the good part of an hour, and he had seen no more than four people moving towards, away from or past the river. But no one stopped. No one lingered. There was nothing but grass and water as far as he could see.

"Is there no one out there?" he asked a soldier walking past.

"Fishing villages, further out," the man said. "The sea eventually, only it is not easy to reach across the marshes."

"No, I don't imagine it is," he said. "It would be hard to cross that way to us as well."

"We are well defended, Your Highness."

The regent nodded. There was fighting at various points in their history, but the capital had never been taken and no one had come from across the seas. Now that the provinces proved their loyalty so regularly, he doubted they would be fighting anyone anytime soon.

Their crown was safe. His crown. Almost.

What had Edwin been thinking by running off like that? If he had just stayed where he had been placed, life would have been easier. He could have contracted some disease before the people had started asking too many more questions. The regent sighed and scratched at his beard. Something moved in the grass, something tall and dark. In the midday sun, he was somewhat surprised that it would show itself so openly. And then, just as quickly, it was gone. A soldier appeared beside him, raising a looking glass to his eye and then studying the bank beneath them.

"What was it?" the regent breathed.

"What was what, sire?"

The regent opened and then closed his mouth. Perhaps it was the sun playing tricks on him. He had been staring into the long, pale grass for too long. "There," he said, pointing as it appeared again.

The man beside him shook his head. "Smoke?" he queried, and the regent turned as he lifted the glass again.

When he turned back, the dark shape had gone. Something was playing, and if the mage wasn't around, he wasn't sure how safe he was from what had been unleashed.

Ende watched Ana as she sat forward, her eyes closed, her head cocked a little to the side. She then glanced at the sword master, who also appeared to watch her too closely. He had stopped her running several times before simply by holding her, and then she had disappeared and returned with Salima. The girl had nearly been discovered in her fear of the woman who had come to see the regent, a maid, Forest had said. Ende looked over the girl. If he could spirit the child far away, he would. For he feared she would put herself in danger to save Ed far too easily.

She had initially looked frightened when they had returned, as though she might have seen something else when Ana had done whatever she did to move so quickly between places. But he hadn't had the chance to ask her what that might be.

The sword master reached forward, and for a moment Ende wondered why the man put his hands on Ana as he did. Not just to hold her still—there was something else, some fascination with her that Ende felt should be fear rather than wonder. Did this man feel something else for the girl who no longer appeared to be a girl?

"Ana?" he asked hesitantly.

She looked at him, her green eyes almost glowing in the dim light of the room. "Something is coming," she whispered.

"The creatures you saw before?" the sword master asked, too close to the little mage. Or was she something else? Ende found it difficult to focus on her now. He tried hard to remember her mother, but she had been gone long before he had left the capital. Although he remembered her strength, he didn't feel the same uncertainty he felt around Ana.

"Ende?"

He looked at her then, taking in her rigid stance as she sat up in the chair, her green eyes only focused on him.

"Did you ask something?" he said.

"You said something," she said, raising one eyebrow. He waited for her soft smile to follow, but it didn't. "I didn't call them."

Ende tried to focus on her and her alone. Had he spoken, or was she in his head again? Did he think she called the danger to them? "Do they follow the king?" he asked instead.

She shook her head.

"Can we meet him?" Salima asked, focused more on Ed than whatever else might be happening. He wondered at the pull between them. Was a shared mother enough?

Ana sighed, but Ende wasn't sure if it was the darkness she felt, the confusion at it, or that the child was so focused on Ed. The sword master suddenly grabbed at her, but she was gone by the time he reached the space where she had been, and he turned angry eyes on Ende.

"She does as she will," Ende said in way of defence.

"Do you always have to push?"

"Where could she go?"

"To see what they want," the sword master snapped, pushing himself up off the floor and away from the chair she had occupied.

"You don't want to wait for her?"

"I would rather see if I can determine when our king will return."

Salima opened her mouth and, as he turned a hard look her way, snapped it shut. "No more sneaking," he said firmly. She nodded once and stepped closer to Ende. The sword master sighed and left the room. As Salima made to follow, Ende took her arm and shook his head.

"He is right. It is not safe out there for you."

"Yet is it safe to hide the wit… Ana here. If she is found…"

"She won't be," he said, certain that she could be anywhere she wanted to be, and they had no way to stop her unless she wanted to be found.

The regent was still staring out across the plains when something dark appeared in the field. The man beside him made a strange squeak, and he realised that he wasn't dreaming it. It stood motionless for a time, the wind pulling at it, and he motioned for the man to hand him the looking glass.

It could have been a soldier from the dark cloak, but then the hood fell away and black hair whipped around in the wind. "The witch," he murmured, leaning forward. He was looking at her back as she faced the marsh, but he was certain.

She held her hands in the air, the cloak falling away to reveal long, slender arms in a black material. She dressed as he had hoped then. He had imagined so much more for her than this. And yet, wasn't she what he hoped she would be?

She just didn't appear to be on his side. The idea rubbed, but then he lowered the glass as the man beside him gasped. He thought he saw something dark appear again in the corner of his eye. It almost materialised before her. A shadow that wasn't. And then another, and another, and he wondered what he had done by allowing the mage to bring her here. He had seen the danger. And the boy disappearing hadn't been enough, for the little bastard was causing him just as much trouble.

The shadows closed in around her, suddenly thick. The regent wondered if the mage had managed to find a way to destroy her. But then the shadows were gone, and she was standing in the field with her arms held out to the side. She glanced over her shoulder. He raised the glass as she smirked at him, and then she was gone.

"What was that?" the soldier beside him asked.

"A witch," he said.

"She got rid of them."

"What were they that she got rid of?" the regent asked.

The man shook his head vigorously and held out his hand for the glass. The regent handed it back and then turned from the view. She was something that should have been left at the other end of the kingdom.

27

The inn looked exactly the same as the last time Ed had seen it, but it felt completely different. The fire was out, the tables pushed to the side of the room, or over in some cases. The girls sat in what had been the dining room, either on chairs or on the floor, talking amongst themselves. Ed made his way up the stairs two at a time, Dray only a step behind him. He pushed his way into the room he had stayed in and stopped. Dray almost bowled him over as he tried to stop his momentum following him through the door.

"What the…"

"I stayed here," Ed said weakly, but the room he knew was now splattered with blood. It had sprayed across the walls and the window, and a pool had formed in the middle of the room, which someone had hastily, and apparently half-heartedly, tried to clean up.

"Something very nasty happened here," Dray said.

"I think that creature was hunting me," Ed said. Dray took him by the arm and dragged him back into the hall. "Before it found me," he said, looking into the dark features of the soldier.

Dray sighed and looked back to the stairwell.

"I am not in danger now," Ed murmured.

"You are always in danger," Dray said, then realised he still had hold of Ed's arm and released him.

"Let's find some blankets. If we are to stay here, I suggest we camp in the dining room."

"Agreed," Dray said, striding ahead of him and opening the doors to other rooms. They appeared just the same, sans the blood. Ed pulled at the blanket on the bed of the first room he walked into, although it felt damp. He wondered if there wasn't somewhere else they might have stayed along the way. It had seemed to take so long for him to reach this point. And yet the soldiers assured him it was only a couple of days back to the capital from here.

He sighed. He should have taken a horse. He might have gotten further much quicker.

"Here," Dray called, and Ed found him in a small room with piles of sheets and blankets. He took an armful and carried them back towards the stairs. The women were helping move the tables out of the way, stacking them neatly atop each other. If he'd had a horse, Ed wouldn't have met Phillip, and so not Belle. She smiled up at him then, and he started down the stairs. If they hadn't met, she wouldn't be in this mess. Or she might very well be, as the forest would have handed her over as part of the ten.

He paused to hand her the blankets.

"I found ham and cheese along with some stale bread," a young soldier said, appearing from the kitchens. "And a barrel of apples."

"I would love an apple," Belle said, turning to the young man and ignoring Ed's armful of blankets. The young man tossed it to her, and she caught it easily. She held it to her nose as she turned back to Ed, her grin wide, and then she held it out to him. A hint of disappointment.

"I didn't know you loved apples so," he said, making no move to take it.

"I'd probably eat the stale bread," she said softly, holding the apple back to her nose. "I'm tired of dry meat."

"I could do with a glass of ale," one of the other women said, and Ed laughed.

"That I'm sure they have," he said. "Let's get comfortable and eat, and then we can sleep."

"There are rooms upstairs, Your Majesty," Barlow said.

"And I think I would rather be down here," Ed added quickly.

"Do you know the reason the inn was abandoned?" Dray asked.

The man shook his head. "Some trouble with a tenant, perhaps. You found something?" he said.

"Enough to keep us downstairs." Dray kept his voice low as he glanced over the women. Belle looked up the stairs and then back to Ed.

"It's ok," Ed said. "Let's see where we can sleep. Any chance of a fire, Captain?"

Barlow grumbled something and headed towards the door.

"Are we safe?" Belle asked, looking around the women.

"Yes," Ed said, guiding her to a hard chair. "Now eat your apple, and I'll make up the beds."

"Your Majesty," one of the others said, stepping forward. "I can do that."

"I don't mind," he said. "I don't get to be useful very often."

"You have been of far more use to us than we could ever repay."

"I hope you still think so when my uncle finds you some old man for a husband."

She laughed. "Well, with the king making my bed, I'll be able to claim the best of them. I'll find you some ale," she said, disappearing behind the bar.

"If we take some more supplies from here," Barlow said, joining him as he directed a young soldier to the fire, his arms laden with wood, "we could ride through the next night and be back in the capital early."

"The women may appreciate some time to rest and bathe," Ed said, looking over the group.

"There will be time for that once we are back in the capital. They will be given rooms of their own, new dresses, time and a maid to make them beautiful." Ed opened his mouth to say something about how beautiful they were already, when the man smiled. "They are to be the best the kingdom has to offer."

Ed nodded. He understood, but it was something he had never been a part of, something he didn't remember from his youth. He put the blankets down and then took one out, shook it and laid it on the floor. He then squatted down and folded it over. They weren't going to be too comfortable here. They would have to be grateful for any bed they could get.

He spread another over the top and hoped they had enough to at least try to make them warm. Belle watched, and when he looked up, she crunched into her apple. He laid out another blanket beside the first.

"Do you think Ana is safe?" she asked.

He hadn't thought of Ana, but he nodded and continued laying out the beds.

"Are you worried about her?"

"I'm worried about Salima," he said, looking up at her. "Ana can take care of herself."

Belle looked down at her lap, the apple in her hand. He reached out and took it from her, bit into it, then shuddered at the bitterness of it and handed it back. "Well that wasn't as pleasant as I expected."

She looked at him with open surprise.

"I'm sorry," he said, moving to stand from his position by the makeshift bed.

"Your Majesty," a soft voice said, and he turned to find Dahli holding out a cup.

He took it and gulped from it as she continued to stand before him. "Would you join us?" he asked, indicating a chair beside Belle.

"I could help," she said, reaching for the blankets. But he shook his head, and she sat on the offered chair. "I don't have to worry about my brother, do I?"

"He may try to use you still, but it would have little impact on my uncle."

"You are the king," Belle said, and he looked as she stood beside him. "You keep referring to your uncle."

"He is still regent. It will take more than my appearing in public to change that."

"And will that change what I am?" Belle asked.

He looked at her and tried not to sigh. He wasn't sure what she was. "Tribute," she whispered.

"I thought you were my companion," he said. "My friend," he added, and she smiled up at him. "I won't let my uncle take you."

She nodded, and another woman passing handed her a cup. She gulped at it and then coughed. "Not as pleasant as I expected. Any wine?" she asked.

"It's like vinegar," the girl said as she kept walking. The fire was blazing, and the room was starting to warm. A soldier appeared from the kitchen with a tray of chunks of ham and cheese.

"I should get on with my tasks," Ed said, bowing his head. "Ladies…" He indicated the blankets. "Your beds await."

"Thank you," Dahli said, bowing her head.

He sat the cup down on the edge of a table, picked up his pile of blankets and continued around the room to meet Dray, who was also laying out beds.

"Do you think we should have continued through the night again?" he asked.

"It could be dangerous to remain out here with so many women."

"Someone else might try to steal them?" Ed asked. "How many times might they be stolen away?"

Dray sighed. "Where do you want to sleep?"

"I'm not sure I can," Ed admitted, looking over the group before his eyes fell on the stairs again.

"It is gone," Dray said.

"I hope so." Ed sighed. "What do we do when we arrive back in the capital?"

"I'm not sure of that either. Maybe Ana has made some allies who can assist us."

"Let's hope it is an army of them."

Dray nodded, but Ed noticed he was focused on the stairs and thought he was wondering what they could do when they reached the capital.

Ana sat at the mage's desk and looked over the books. A candle flickered at the corner of the desk. The room was cold and empty, and she stretched out her senses for the old man. She looked around the room again. Nothing. Where had he gone? And why?

She blew out a slow breath that fogged before her and wondered if he was hiding in the very place she wouldn't think to search for him. Her hand rested on one of the heavy tomes before her as she rose from the seat, and something pulled at her. She opened it, tugging at the heavy cover, and the pages flipped over of their own accord. They were blank but for the image of the queen tucked inside. She lifted it from the page and held it out.

The edges were burnt a little where she had tried to use it to reach Ed. She could feel him on the page in the ink, in the love of the woman he had drawn there. She had tried so hard before, but now she felt it all. She wondered if she could reach him like she did Dray, but that was something else. She tried to shake the soldier from her mind.

She had tried so hard to find Ed, and now, with this in her hand, it seemed so easy. She placed it back down on the desk, not in the book. Why had the mage kept this, and why here?

Did she need to hunt him out to discover what she was? For he seemed to have a greater understanding of it. Yet she felt it herself now, the strength within her, the control.

Ende came to mind, his young stern face, the protective hold over the child he had discovered. What would the little dragon do when she learnt just what she was? But Salima's focus was Ed, always Ed. Yet Ende had seen the darkness within Ana's very being. And it had scared him. He might have been right to be scared.

The regent certainly was. She had felt his fear across the fields. They had come to her for a way here. She sat down again. She had felt the pull of their wanting and had gone to see what they were. They called to her because they knew she could help them. Yet she didn't know how to help, or if she wanted to. It would take more than just allowing them passage from beyond. She would have to find them an anchor.

She had denied them, told them to return. But she wondered if that would always be the case. If Ende felt the darkness inside her and she knew it was there, could she call them forth? Would they help her? What did she want, other than Ed to be king?

"But he already is," she whispered.

He comes.

"I know," she answered, "and it is for me to keep him safe."

Can you? Can you give him what he wants and keep him from harm?

"It is what I wanted when I first saw the danger to him. I knew I had to help him."

You must help yourself first.

Ana shook her head. "Ed is my only consideration,"

The voice inside her did not respond. She knew it to be right. She closed her eyes and opened them to the cellar. The hidden door stood like a strange beacon before her, as though she could see the magic glowing from beyond around its edges. But something stopped her moving forward. Something cold touched the edges of her being, and her heart beat too fast. She was afraid. The intense cold of the cells would prevent her from being able to magic herself out again, and it might very well sever the tie to the magic within her. Whether it was the magic or the cold she could remember that made her bones ache, she didn't know, but she couldn't move forward. If the mage was strange enough to choose it as a hiding place, he could stay there forever.

Although she might suggest to Ende that he could look there. She doubted even the frozen walls could dampen his fire. Back within her little room, the one attached to the workshop, she was tempted to light the fire just to stave off the memory of the ice.

The door handle rattled, and she turned to the door. A soldier would not be placed there. She moved to the other side of the wall and waited. The mage would have chosen another way. It was only as she stood by the glass vials and jars and they whispered that she realised she had left the dress on the bed the last time she had visited.

It could only be the regent. What had he seen in the field that would lead him here?

She moved to his rooms—one she had visited before, the balcony, the friendly space, although she imagined a different family here. There was a loud bang on the door, and she stepped back into the shadows, her cloak pulled tight around her.

The door pushed open, and a tall soldier stood in the doorway, one she had seen here before. Another followed. "I told you he was not here. Go to the throne room and I will find him."

"I don't have time for games," the man said.

"They are not games," the other man snapped. "Major," he added, bowing stiffly. "Much has happened."

"Well, more is to come." He pushed past the other man and down the stairs.

What news do you bring? Ana wondered. She reappeared in the room she somehow considered her own. The door was open, the regent's back to her as she pressed into the shadows.

"Major Field has returned," a soldier said hurriedly.

"Does he have news?"

"He has sent men all over the castle to find you."

"Tell him to meet me in the throne room."

"Yes, Your Highness." The soldier bowed and fled.

The regent turned and looked over the small room again. His gaze rested on the dress on the bed. Ana didn't think he had ever been in the room before. Would he realise she had been there? She held her breath, sure that he looked straight at her, and yet he didn't see her. She could hide far better than she had imagined possible. As he left the room, she followed for a few steps, the door left open. It was still very dark. She turned back to the room and blew out the candle.

Then she opened her eyes to the back of the throne. The soldier she had seen in the regent's rooms was pacing before it.

"What is it?" the regent asked, striding through the door. Ana wondered if he had run from her little room all the way here. Or if he knew of secret passages she was yet to find.

The man sighed and bowed low.

"You didn't kill him then?"

"He travels with the tribute. He will be here soon."

The regent slammed a fist down on the armrest and then reached for his forearm. Ana couldn't prevent the smile that spread across her lips. Ed was safe, and people would see him for who he was.

"Do we have anyone in the ranks?"

The man shook his head, and Ana slowly released the breath she had been holding. She had to warn Ed. She wondered who this man was and why he would betray his king, but she could find out more later, once she was sure Ed was safe. Although she had seen him sleeping while Dray kept watch.

Dray came into focus sitting against a wall, the light dim from a fire and several candles. She felt the number of people in the room. She heard the sound of steel being pulled from scabbards, but her focus was on Dray alone as he held up a hand and the swords stayed.

"Ed?" a soft voice whispered, and she turned as Belle shook his arm.

Ana bowed her head. "They know you come," she said.

"We guessed as much," Ed answered, climbing to his feet despite the woman at his side who seemed to want to hold him back.

"Major…" Ana said, the name escaping her.

"Field," Dray said.

She bowed her head to him. "He is the regent's man."

There was a murmur behind her, and she turned to take in the soldiers, some with their swords still at the ready in case she was a threat to their king. She bowed her head to the man closest, the man Dray had held his hand up to. "Do you trust them?" she asked, turning back to Dray. He nodded once.

He looked tired. She knew he would protect Ed. And yet no matter how much she worried for the boy, Dray was what drew her.

"Ana?" Ed asked, stepping forward. She tore her eyes from the soldier on the floor and smiled for him.

"I was worried," she whispered. "He will not forgive you."

"The king has done nothing to be forgiven for," the soldier behind her snapped.

"He has survived. Where is Phillip?" she asked, and Belle looked down at her hands.

"The Near Folk," Dray said.

Ana turned then to take in a dark beautiful woman. "You were not here before."

She stared at Ana, but did not speak.

"Dahli is tribute by choice," Ed said.

"Why?" Ana asked, not wanting to take her eyes from the woman.

"It is a better life," Dahli said.

"Stay with us," Ed pleaded, but Ana turned from the woman to Dray.

"It is not safe for you," she said. "Darkness follows me."

"Follows you?" Belle asked.

Ana studied her. The hint of sunshine she had seen around her in the carriage glowed a little brighter. "Keep him close. Be the light in the darkness."

"I can't protect him like you do," Belle said, looking down again.

Ana felt the shadows pressing in on her before she saw the movement in the corner of her eye. "No," she said, taking a deep breath, then flicked her hand towards the door. As the shadows dissipated, she bowed to Ed and was gone.

Only she hadn't gone very far. The room smelt of stale blood, and she could feel the maid's presence. It had been here. They had been here searching for him, and it appeared they had found something else. But they hadn't taken her, simply fed from her. Ana shivered.

"Captain Sterling," someone called from the other side of the door. Ana pressed against it.

After several minutes and heavy footsteps on the stairs, she sensed him closer. "Barlow," he said by way of greeting, his voice giving nothing away.

"Is there something else you should be telling me?" he asked.

Dray cleared his throat but said nothing.

"That woman," the other man said in a hoarse whisper. "She knew the king."

"She is…" Dray sighed. "She is his protector. Without her, the king would not have survived as he had."

"I thought that was your doing."

"More her doing," Dray said. He sounded disappointed.

"Where did she go?" the man asked.

"Back to the capital would be my guess. She senses when he is in trouble."

"There was something else here," the man continued. "I thought I saw…"

Nothing was said, and she wondered just what the soldier had seen.

"There is something between you," he said instead.

She could hear his footsteps moving away and feel the distance grow between them. Was the connection she was so sure had been there still holding them together? Or had it all been the silly thoughts of a young maid? She had called Dray, after all. She had forced his hand. And he was trying to distance them now. She just wasn't sure why she found it so hard to let him go. He was her friend. He had been her friend. Or had he been a soldier looking after a girl?

She moved into the shadows of the main room as more candles were extinguished and the women snuggled down between blankets. Ed seemed to watch over them, Belle at his side. She hadn't looped her arm through his again, but she had called him by name. Soldiers stood to attention, watching windows, their backs to the women. The dark woman watched Ed across the room. Ana looked up at the landing where Dray stood watching over the room, but his gaze never left her.

Could he see her in the dark, or was he simply hopeful that she would stay? He didn't need her to stay. He was safer with her gone. They were all safer with her gone. When the other soldier said something and he turned away for a moment, she took the opportunity to disappear.

28

In the shadows of the barn, by the dim lantern light, the mage looked at the child before him. A girl of no more than thirteen summers, yet she appeared confident. As the shadows moved around them, she shivered.

"I feel you could be something very great," the mage said to her.

"She is something," hissed the creature. The mage tried not to take a step back as it appeared, and the child turned to it in strange wonder rather than fear.

"Could she be what I am looking for?" the mage asked, untrusting of his abilities in the light of the other girls he had thought might be of use until he had looked into their weak minds.

"You cannot use her for what my queen has deemed unacceptable," the creature hissed, leaning over him.

He grunted. There had to be a way around Ana and her magic. There had to be a way to get Ana to see what he wanted, what the regent needed.

"There is another," the creature hissed.

"I have a twin," the girl said. Her voice wavered a little, but in the face of the creature he was surprised she maintained her confidence.

"Does she feel the world as you do?" the mage asked.

She nodded emphatically. "Sometimes we feel the same;

sometimes one feels something the other doesn't."

"Bring her to me," the mage said. She ran from the barn, leaving him and the creature alone in the straw, certain that the animals watched them.

"She will not return," the creature hissed, stepping closer.

"She will," the mage said. He felt her desperation to be understood, to be wanted. The last child he had found was not what he had hoped. She hadn't even contained the same power as the girls he had used to bring Ana to the castle. He should have left her on her windy islands. "Is it the soldier?" he wondered aloud.

"The connection is strong," the creature hissed as two girls ran into the barn. They were similar in features but not identical, one an inch taller than the other, their hair the same colour, their eyes the same bright golden hue.

The creature beside him licked a forked tongue over its lips, and he tried not to shiver. It stepped forward. Although he didn't want to put himself between them, he said, "I need them."

"As do we," it hissed.

The journey had been harder on Dray's body than he'd expected, being trapped in the carriage for so long. They had stopped several times, but it hadn't been enough for him to stretch out his legs sufficiently. He should have asked for a horse. One of the men could have given one up for him easily enough, but then he had promised to stay by the king.

The blonde hair of Belle never left his side. Every time she caught his eye, Dray thought of Ana and what she had said about Belle being the way to light the dark. She had hidden in the shadows; he had been so sure he saw her. Her green eyes had seemed brighter, but he had been distracted, and when he'd looked back she was gone. He couldn't be sure if she had been there or not.

He pushed the door open and then moved back for the tribute to step out of the carriage. A soldier offered his hand to Belle, and although she looked back at the king, he nodded for her to go. Dray looked into the light next, wanting to be sure they had been delivered somewhere safe. The stables opened up around him, and he looked at the man standing before him with his hand out as though to help another woman from the carriage.

"Avers," he said, raising an eyebrow.

The man snapped to attention and smacked a fist into his chest in salute. "Captain Sterling, I feared you lost."

Dray tried not to sigh as he stepped down from the carriage and the king stepped into the light. "I was distracted by another duty," he said.

The man gaped at the king for a moment and then bowed deeply. The king waved him out of the way, and a murmur went through the soldiers.

"Home again then," the king sighed, looking around the stables and then up to the windows that overlooked them.

"I'm sure they already know you come," Dray said.

The king nodded.

"We are to escort the ladies to their chambers to prepare to meet the regent," Avers said. "Perhaps Your Majesty would like the chance to bathe and change."

The king nodded somewhat absently, then looked at the man before him more seriously. "My guest," he said, indicating Belle, "will require the same, but she is not to be confused with the tribute."

Avers bowed again. "Yes, Your Majesty."

"What if I get lost?" Belle said.

"I will find you. But go with the soldiers for now."

She bowed her head and followed with the other young women. Dray stood and watched them go in different directions, but he was quick to follow after the king.

"I doubt I'll get lost," the king murmured.

"That is not my fear," Dray said, watching as they headed inside and along corridors. He seemed to know where he was going. "Do you think Ana is here?" he asked, then bit down on his lip as the king turned to him, a question on his face that he didn't answer.

He pushed open a door into a small room. A narrow bed sat against the wall, and a large desk filled the space beneath a window, covered in papers and dust. Dray moved over and looked out over the world below. The carriages were still in the stables and several men moved about, but the girls were already gone.

"This is your room," he said, turning as the king opened a cupboard behind the door.

"Where else would a king be found?" he murmured.

"Particularly if you don't want him found," Dray said. He pulled fresh clothes from the cupboard. The jerkin bore the Ilia insignia, and Dray wondered how he had managed to not look like a king for so long. Although the clothes he held were not what he should have been wearing.

He wasn't quite sure how to broach the subject when the door flew open. He drew his sword as something small and red flew through it and wrapped around the king.

"Ed," she sobbed, pressing her face into his chest. The king placed his hands over her head and held her close as he shook his head at Dray.

The sword master's child, he thought, watching her check the king to ensure he was uninjured. The sister, he realised.

"Ende said you had returned."

"Ende?" Dray asked. "He is here?"

She nodded and turned to take him in, although she didn't release her grip on the king at all.

"Salima, I need to change."

"You smell pretty awful," she agreed, finally stepping back. "You are Dray," she said, and Dray bowed to her. "You kept him safe." Dray nodded again. She swung around and slapped Ed hard on the arm.

"Oww," he moaned, grabbing at it. "What was that for?"

"You left without me," she growled. The room rumbled, and Ed looked over her head at Dray.

"It wasn't safe; you were safer with your father."

"I don't know about that. There have been some strange things going on."

"What sort of strange things?" Dray asked as the king opened his mouth.

"Strange shadows, boys killed, the witch and her…" She looked back at the king then and chewed her lip.

"What witch?" he asked slowly.

"Ana," she said, pulling back from him as though he might lash out. "But she's not a witch, we don't think. Ende isn't very sure. Papa is different around her, and the regent wants her dead."

"He hasn't found her?" Dray asked, wondering more about how her father might be altered.

"She is very good at hiding. Even I can't find her anymore."

"When did you last see her?" Dray asked, stepping closer, and the king held up a hand.

"A couple of nights ago. She worries about you," she said, turning back to the king, and Dray felt an overwhelming disappointment.

"We saw her then," the king admitted. "I'm sure she is fine."

"That is what Ende says."

"The old man often knows more than he tells," Dray muttered.

"What old man?" she asked. "Can you come and see Papa before you go to your uncle?"

"I'm not sure," the king said. "You need to be careful. My uncle might be here himself very soon."

"You be careful," she said, reaching up and kissing his cheek. Then she gave Dray a little bow before she disappeared.

"Should you go to your men?" the king asked as Dray closed the door after her.

"Until I am sure you are safe, I don't think I can leave your side."

"You haven't bathed or changed either."

"I'm used to it. Until we know what your uncle will do, I am not leaving your side."

The king nodded and pulled the jerkin over his head. It was only when he stopped moving that Dray realised he was staring at his shoulder where Ana had healed him. He turned his back and allowed the young man to change. Was she a witch?

Two soldiers appeared in the doorway. Two of the men who had travelled with them, and Dray nodded to them both. Despite his reservations he needed to know just what Ana was, and left the king in their care.

29

Ana tried not to sigh as she looked at the damp fields around her. Why she was back in the marsh, she wasn't sure, and she had the strange sensation that the sword master would tell her off for dirtying her dress again. Not that she had seen him in a couple of days. She could change before she returned, but there was something nice in having the man worry over her.

That is not what he does.

No, she thought, he doesn't. He worried what she might do and the danger it might put his daughter in. "Ed will have returned." Showing himself to be king, she thought.

He works against you. Against us.

"The mage will do as he will do. I have destroyed his plans. He cannot bring anything from beyond that could harm the king."

If he were to find something here…

Ana shook her head. He would return to his work room at some stage, and she might be able to learn what he does then. "I have already told you that the king comes first."

When will you show him what you are?

"He knows," she murmured. She had shown herself to a full room. Beautiful women set to be tribute, the soldiers. Dray had seen her, she was sure. Only she wasn't sure she could face him now. He was no longer hers. Or was it just the realisation that he was a man of duty and had never been hers in the first place?

He kept you safe.

He kept me from the mage, she thought. She looked around then, hearing movement in the grass. But it was only a fisherman headed for the river. The shadows had not returned. She could feel them, though, not far away, pulling at her, calling to her, pleading with her to bring them closer. She wondered if she could heal them, heal herself of whatever it was that pulled at her. She thought of the old cleric. He knew her mother, knew what she was, and he had helped her despite Master Forest's concerns.

She sighed and reappeared in their rooms, hoping the child would be able to tell her something, but the sword master stood at the window. A soldier at his side turned slowly as she stepped forward.

"I can try," the sword master was saying. "But the regent will not listen to me, no matter who knows he is king."

"They only need realise he is no longer a boy," Ana said, and the man turned quickly, flinching. She bowed her head. "Forgive me," she whispered.

He surprised her by stepping forward and taking her by the shoulders. "Where have you been?"

"There is more at risk than the king alone," she said. But at his searching eyes, she couldn't say any more. She was thinking only of herself. Dray barely looked at her, turning back for the window.

"You have made another soldier friend," he said, and when she looked up, he was studying the view from the window.

"She made it," the sword master said, as though he wasn't quite sure and yet felt the need to defend her.

"I couldn't get warm," she said as Dray turned and studied the man beside her. "Is he here?"

Dray nodded once. "I wished he looked more like a king. He will attend the throne room when the tribute is shown."

"What would you have me do?"

"Stay out of the way," the sword master said quickly, but she glanced at him. She couldn't. "Is he alone?"

The sword master reached for her as though she might run, but Ed's safety had to come first. When Dray didn't answer, she looked at him. Something sad pushed out from him, and she took a step forward. "What has happened?" she asked. But as she reached for him, he stepped back and bowed.

"There are two soldiers with him. Men I trust."

She nodded slowly. Anger then flowed from him, and she chewed her lip. He didn't trust her. "I will stay away," she murmured, closing her eyes. As she sighed, she felt him reach for her, but she disappeared far from his reach.

She leaned back against the wall, wiping at her face, disappointed that she was so unsure of what she was. That she had only ever wanted to help the king, and now she did more harm than good. The practice hall was empty around her. No one had returned since the death of the boy, and she wondered at what that might mean for the sword master with no pupils to teach.

The door squealed open, and she pressed herself into the wall.

"Your Majesty, I don't think this is a good idea," a soldier said.

Ed was silhouetted in the doorway. Ana understood then what Dray meant. He was dressed as a young man, as any of the young men who would have visited this hall. The regent would be far more lavishly dressed, and she wondered if Ed might disappear into the crowd of the throne room. She doubted his uncle would have provided anything of worth for him to look like the king he was.

"Is someone there?" he called into the space.

She wondered then if the mage knew he had been found. She blinked away from him. She would want to be in the throne room when the tribute was shown, to see what they would say of the boy returned. She stood before the fireplace in the little room. The sword master had not commented on her state of dress, but then he had been distracted. As had she.

Two faces beamed at her, and she took them in. Two girls, clearly sisters, the same and yet so different. They bowed their heads to her and then smiled at each other.

Ana moved away again. What had he done? Had he found a replacement that would do his bidding?

"Ana?" Belle asked, her voice a little shaky as she reappeared in the room she had recuperated in for so long. She turned slowly to take in the woman. Belle appeared to glow even more brightly than when she had seen her at the inn. Her dress was far finer than anything she had worn at the castle in the mountains. More real than anything there, Ana thought.

Belle raced forward and took her hands. "I am so happy to see you," she said, squeezing her hands tight.

"Are you?" Ana asked.

"You look so different," Belle said, her face scrunching a little as her eyes settled on the muddy hem of Ana's dress.

Ana wasn't sure what she could say. She felt different, and yet just the same.

"How did you find me?" Belle asked.

"I wasn't looking," Ana said honestly. "I stayed here for a time myself."

"And now?"

Ana shook her head. She didn't stay anywhere for very long. If she managed to sleep, it was usually under the careful watch of the dragon, in a chair.

"You look tired," Belle whispered, pulling her close.

There was a sharp knock at the door, and a soldier opened it. He bowed and then smiled. "His Majesty has asked if you will meet him in the courtyard. The tribute is to be presented, and he would wish to see his uncle."

Belle nodded and then turned back to Ana, her brow creasing when she couldn't find her in the shadows. She nodded again and lifted the fine dress to follow the soldier out of the room.

Ana appeared in the shadows behind the throne, but she was soon aware that she wasn't alone. The mage, his odour all too pungent, and something else—something Ana had thought gone.

Soldiers filled the doorways, and Ana was tempted to step out of the shadows. Then a soldier stepped forward and bowed low before the regent, and Ana realised they were the only ones in the room.

The regent nodded, and women filed into the room. Beautiful women who were dressed as elegantly as Belle had been, their hair all tied up in a similar fashion, even the dark woman from the trees. They all looked down as they walked and lined up before the throne; and then, as one, they curtsied.

Ana wondered at what training or instructions they might have had. They were all likely farmer's daughters, yet they appeared as though they had lived in the capital their whole lives.

Something shifted in the shadows behind her, and she was tempted to send it away. Would it want to be seen, or did it want something else? They, she realised, although this wasn't the creature she had seen in the trees, the mage's maid. This was a scared boy, wanting something—power, strength? She was distracted trying to determine the feelings she sensed from the shadows when the room hushed and anger washed from the throne.

"Ed," she whispered.

The king moved forward, Belle on his arm. He didn't bow before the regent, although Belle gave a small curtsy. Some of the guards pulled swords; the regent grinned. Dray stepped into the room behind him.

"Captain," a soldier to the side said, the same man who had reported the king. A major. "Do you want to explain this?"

Dray smiled, and Ana felt the warmth of it across the room. "His Majesty, King Edwin of Ilia, returns from his visit of the provinces," he announced.

Ed gave him a quick glance, and Dray returned a nod.

"I thought you ran away with a maid," the major sneered.

"You should not believe all that you are told," Dray replied.

"What was she then?" the major asked.

"Enough," the regent snapped. "How can we be sure this is my nephew? He has been missing for some time."

Ana took a deep breath, closed her eyes and blew it out across the room. Whispering followed, and she opened her eyes to see the king dressed as she thought Dray would expect. Belle's mouth hung open. Dray's eyes darted around the room. He was searching for her, but she wouldn't be seen.

"My queen," a voice hissed in her ear.

"Leave," she replied.

"I have business here."

She turned to the towering beast. Despite being lost in the shadow, she could sense the solidness of it. "Not business I want you to undertake," she said under her breath.

The shadows closed around her, tight and constricting, and then they were gone. She wasn't sure how she had such power over them, but she was grateful for it now.

"Do you have some magic?" the regent hissed.

Ana focused on the group before her. The women had bunched together, Belle holding tighter to Ed's arm. Dray had pulled his sword. Had he not realised it would be her doing?

"This was not your mage?" he asked.

The regent shook his head, standing slowly from the throne. "Where have you been, boy?" he asked. Ana could feel the hatred ebb from him.

"Doing what any king would," Ed said calmly, despite all that was occurring in the room.

"The tribute?"

Ed held out his hand, and the women smoothed over dresses, gently touched hair and reformed into a line. The regent walked towards them, looking each one over. He paused at the dark woman from the trees, but not for long, and then turned back to Ed.

"Who is this?"

"Belle Poales," he said. "My friend."

"Did you steal her from the tribute?"

"Can you not count, uncle?" Ed said. "There are ten, as the

province promised. I met Belle prior to meeting up with the tribute in the forest."

His uncle stared, and Ana wanted to step between them. The soldiers by the door still held their swords, as did Dray.

"Go," the regent said, waving his hand towards them. "I accept payment. They will be presented before the capital tonight."

"You have husbands selected?" Ed asked.

"Some," his uncle said with a sigh. "I have offered one to your sword master; he needs a mother for that child of his."

Ed clenched his jaw. Ana wondered if Ende would let her stay when it came time for him to go, and if he would be present tonight.

The women filed back out the way they had come. The number of soldiers in the room didn't appear to decrease with the tribute.

"Are we not to talk, uncle?" Ed asked.

The man looked over Belle again before he shook his head. "I am busy. Tomorrow."

The shadow moved quickly out of the darkness behind Ed, and yet it reached for Belle. As she flinched and turned, it disappeared. The regent took a step back as Ana took a step forward from the shadows.

"You bring your shadows here, witch!" he cried, stepping out of her reach.

"Your mage brings them. I prevent them," Ana said, stepping closer. He backed up.

The creature moved to her side. And as the mage stepped from the shadows as well, Dray moved forward with his sword.

"I have told you, they are not to be touched," Ana said quietly.

The creature bowed, and the boy inside smiled. He glanced up briefly at the king and then disappeared.

She waited silently as the mage stepped forward to stand beside the regent.

"You control them." The major pointed towards her.

She turned on him then. Her hood had fallen down, and the

room stood still around her. "Do you want to see what I can do?" Her voice was darker than she intended, not her own. "You are darkness itself; you are what they want," she said, and although the man maintained his pose, the confidence and hatred clear on his face, she felt the shadows moving in with the permission she had given them.

"Ana?" Ed said, slowly stepping forward as Dray held a hand across his chest.

"Protect the king," she said, her eyes on Dray. Then she turned back to the major as the shadows moved in around him. She could feel the want, the hunger. "He is yours," she said.

The scream filled the room. Belle pushed her hands over her ears and dropped to her knees. Ed turned away. The regent raised his arms before his face as the mage stared into the shadows, a grin wide on his sharp face.

Soldiers raced forward, except Dray didn't move, his eyes only on Ana. She wasn't quite sure what she could sense from him. Disappointment, perhaps, as the major was pulled away. When the shadows cleared, there was nothing of the major left. She had seen the darkness in him, and despite the cry he had gone willingly.

"Protect the king," she said to Dray and then disappeared herself.

30

Dray shuffled the king towards the door. His feet seemed frozen to the floor. He wondered what exactly Ana had become. "I think we should hide you in Belle's room," he said when he finally had the king out of the throne room. The regent was screaming at the mage and several of the soldiers, but no one seemed quite sure what had happened. Let alone what to do next.

"What…" the king stammered.

"She said to protect you," he snapped, trying to focus the king's attention enough to get them out of the way of the regent. He wouldn't be surprised if the man had the king killed before the whole kingdom and found a way to pin it on someone else. Ana most likely.

She had been something very different, as she had been in the forest. Confident, but not like when he had first met her as she had led him from the castle. This confidence scared him.

"This way," Belle said, leading him through the courtyard towards the walkway that ran along the side of it. They were headed towards the main tower, and he wondered just how close to the royal suite the regent had put them.

She pushed open a door as the king followed, and Dray half expected Ana to be waiting for them. He rushed forward and pulled the curtain open, allowing the light to fill the space and reduce the shadows. Belle was struggling to lock the door when it pushed open and a tall man entered followed by the red-haired girl, who raced straight for Ed. Belle squealed.

"Let me do it," he said, taking the key from her shaking hand. Dray wondered what further madness this was.

The man stopped and looked at Dray, then bowed his head to the king. "You certainly look like a king." His voice was low, but it filled the space.

"Ana," the king stammered. "What is she?" He turned to Dray as though he might hold the answers, but he could only shake his head.

"Still drawn to each other," the tall man muttered.

"Shall I find Papa, Ende?" the girl asked, her grip tight on the king.

The man shook his head and moved to the fireplace. "Ende?" Dray asked.

He turned and bowed his head again, his dark eyes flashing, and then he grinned.

"How?"

"Too much to explain, young man. What happened exactly?"

"She directed the shadows," the king whispered, sitting heavily in a chair.

"Should I fetch the cleric?" the girl asked.

Ende shook his head. "Maybe go to your father."

"The sword master. She is…" Dray whispered.

"No," Ende said, looking at him as though he could see into his soul. "She isn't."

The child looked between them, confused for a moment.

"What did she do?" Belle asked, her voice barely audible.

"What she did in the forest," the king said, "but different."

"She didn't scare it away. She let it take that man."

"What?" Ende growled, stepping forward. He appeared larger in some way, and Dray wondered if he would turn into the dragon he had seen so long ago on the mountainside.

"In the forest," Belle said, "she told the monster that it couldn't have the king or Dray," she added, turning to him. "Today, she told them to go." Ende nodded. "Then she said it could take the soldier."

"Was he a threat to the king?"

Belle nodded slowly and then shook her head. "I thought the shadows were more a threat. What is she?" she asked again.

"Something linking this world and theirs. I fear she is still trying to find her place."

"She knows what she is," the king said slowly. "She told them to go. Her loyalty is to us first."

"Or it appears that way," Dray said.

"You haven't spoken to her," the child snapped. "If you knew her, you would know that Ed is right."

"I have spoken to her," Dray said as calmly as he could.

"Not recently," Belle said. "Not since the forest. You wouldn't talk then."

"Have you met somewhere else?" Ende asked, and Dray looked up at him wondering just what he was asking. What might he know—or had Ana told him?

"You have been here," he said instead to Ende. "What do you know?"

"We don't see her very much," the child answered for him. "We did, but since her magic returned, she hides."

"Where?" the king asked, but she shook her head.

"I saw her here," Belle said, and everyone's attention shifted to her. "When I was preparing to go down to meet the regent. She just appeared. She looked so tired, so frail and yet…"

Dray nodded, although he wasn't sure why. She had done the same when he had met with the sword master. Was she disappearing to this other world? Would she tell him if he asked?

Dray spent the rest of the day searching the castle. At one stage, he stood on the wall overlooking the main gate and wondered if she might be somewhere in the city. There were so many buildings, so many homes; she could have formed a friendship with anyone, and they could be hiding her. Although Salima seemed certain that she was extremely capable of hiding herself.

He remembered the inn, sure he had seen her in the shadows. But there had been nothing, only her eyes focused on him. Would she search him out as she did in his dreams? The last few times he had seen her, he hadn't been asleep.

Belle had thought she looked tired, and she might be avoiding sleep herself. Maybe to keep from meeting him. He wasn't sure how they had come to this. They had been close friends, and despite her calling him, he'd needed to be near her. Now it was almost like he no longer knew who or what she was. He had wanted something very different when she had come to him in the forest, when he'd held her close and her warm hands had worked across his skin.

He shivered at the idea, surprised that he had wanted such a thing and that he could barely bring himself to talk to her now. Maybe it wasn't Ana that wanted something different; maybe whatever linked her to the shadows had been toying with him.

He turned away from the wall. He wasn't going to find her now. No matter how hard he looked. If she didn't want to be found, then she wouldn't be.

The mage had seemed impressed by her despite the regent's fear, and Dray wondered what else the man had seen of her. Maybe the mage had managed to win her over. She had said she wasn't safe. Was her warning a way to keep the king safe?

He sighed and ran his fingers through his hair. He would never know, for he would never find her. Not the girl he could have asked, who would have told him anything. And they would all be expected in the throne room for the official presentation soon enough. He wondered what the regent might have done by the time they returned to the throne room, and if the sword master would accept his gift. Or did the man have other ideas for a mother to his daughter?

Avers stood in the courtyard talking with some other soldiers when Dray came down from the wall. "Captain Sterling, I assume you will stand by the king this evening."

He nodded once and strode towards the barracks.

"Do you have any request?" the man called after him.

"No," Dray called back. "You know how to keep a king safe, I'm sure."

"Not in the current world, but we will try."

Dray was tempted to turn around, but he continued on and then stopped at the practice hall. Something similar to the inn lay beyond. Avers had told him that much already. And instead of heading towards a hot bath and fresh clothes, he entered the halls. The upper windows were smeared with something and had been cleaned a little to allow light in, but he was all too aware of the shadows.

"Why was she so cold?" he wondered out loud.

"The ice cells," a voice called across the space. Dray swung around to face the sword master. "She was kept in the mage's ice cells, and the cold nearly killed her."

"How did you get her out?"

"Salima," he murmured, looking back towards the space still marked by blood.

Dray waited, but the man said no more.

"She would call for you," the man said, swallowing down something that might have been regret. "The cleric was surprised she survived, but it seems her magic is strong."

"I should have protected her from him," Dray said.

"I doubt anyone could have come between them. The mage wanted her, and so here she is."

"But she is not the mage's apprentice?" Dray asked, wondering if that was the right term.

The other man shook his head. "She scares me," he admitted. "Although I think she is more afraid of what she might be."

"She appeared confident enough when I saw her."

"Truly? She still seems like a scared child to me."

"Where is she hiding?" Dray asked.

"I don't know. She will return when she wants to. She might be here already," the sword master said, looking around. "Or she is waiting for this evening in the throne room. Waiting for the king, to ensure he is safe."

"Is he?" Dray asked.

"I don't know. I'm sure the regent has a way to keep him locked away. The clothes?" he asked.

"Ana," Dray murmured. She was always looking out for him, and he had said himself that Ed wasn't dressed as a king.

He was headed back to Belle's room when he met Avers on the way.

"The presentation is delayed," he said.

"Why?" Dray asked.

"The regent is feeling unwell after the events of the day. Tomorrow."

"Hmm," Dray murmured, "that puts his discussion with the king off. And gives him more time to work out what he wants to do. Keep me informed."

"Where is the king?" Avers asked.

"Safe," Dray said. "Have you told the tribute, and the king's friend?"

The man nodded.

"Then I will take the time to wash."

He turned back to the barracks again. Most of the soldiers were out. Only a couple moved through as Dray made his way to his own small space within it. It felt like an age since he had been back in the capital. He reached his room and pulled out fresh clothes before heading to the bathhouse.

Other than the steaming tub, which would have comfortably held at least five men, there was nothing in the large space. He placed his fresh clothes down and looked through the steam. It was one of the few luxuries for soldiers in the capital. They were often gone long days, or weeks, and with the constant hot water, it was easy to become presentable again.

His own clothes were stiff with mud and dirt. He wondered just how long he had been wearing them as he peeled them off and stepped down into the water. He ached far more than he realised, slipping deeper into the cloudy water. Ende had promised to stay with the king and his guest. Dray only hoped they had remained hidden when the guards had gone to announce the change in plan. He shook his head and then submerged it. The king had been looking after himself for long enough; Dray was sure he could survive another night.

And Ende was something very different. He lifted his head above the water and shook it off before running his hands over his hair and his stubbled face. He reached for the soap and one of his knives by the tub, trying not to think of Ana as he dragged it over his skin.

A salt bucket stood on the other side of the bath, and he stood and waded through the water towards it, stepping out to take a handful and rub it over his skin. When a cool breeze blew about his wet skin, he stepped back and sank into the water. The door was still closed behind him, and he couldn't make out anything in the shadows. He was as clean as he could be without soaking for a week. After rinsing the last of the salt from his skin, he climbed out. Taking a clean sheet from the pile, he rubbed vigorously at his skin, before donning the fresh clothes. He dropped the sheet in the basket by the door, pulled his boots on and carried his armour and sword back to his small room.

He set them on the chair and then sat on the narrow cot, leaning his head against the wall with his hair still damp. He felt much cleaner, but still drained. How long since he had slept? He closed his eyes, knowing no one would disturb him unless he was really needed. He wondered for a moment if he should have told the king where he was going.

He was sure he was drifting when the cot moved as someone sat silently beside him. Dray maintained his pose, not giving away that he knew someone was there. There was a soft sigh as a head lay down on his lap. He gulped at the strange feeling in his chest as he rested his hand on her shoulder. It could have been his cloak, the same black, scratchy wool wrapped around her too-thin frame.

"You smell better," she whispered.

He couldn't speak, in fear she would disappear again.

"Dray?"

"Hmm," he ventured.

"What am I?"

"I don't know," he whispered, running his fingers through her hair and pulling it back from her face.

"You won't talk to me," she said.

"I'm talking to you now," he said.

She sighed and closed her eyes again. He wondered how long he could hold on to her.

He woke the next morning to the sound of footsteps running past his door. He stretched, then took in the warm figure curled against him. Her cloak still wrapped tight around her, her face peaceful, her head on his arm. He ran his fingers through her hair, longing to see her green eyes.

"Captain," someone called in the doorway, and he rolled towards them. "The regent is preparing for the presentation."

Dray nodded and rolled back to find the bed beside him empty. He sat up slowly, wondering if that was the last time he would see her. The last time she would sleep against him like the girl he had saved from a fall.

The man stepped in and held up his armour. "I fear for the king."

Dray nodded and allowed the man to help him into the armour, then tied his sword to his belt.

"Did you sleep?" the man asked.

"I'm not sure," he said honestly. "Although I did have a good dream."

31

Ana looked over the people gathering in the room. She felt the chill surround her again. She had slept well for the first time in she wasn't sure how long. She had been safe and warm curled in his arms, but she didn't feel that certainty now. People moved through the room quietly. She could taste their anticipation on the air. They too sensed there was more to the event than the presentation of the tribute.

Ana pulled the hood up around her face, although she knew she couldn't be seen. The shadows were hers alone, other than a little dragon hiding further down the room. Had Salima's father allowed her out? Or maybe she had snuck out before he could keep her at home. Ana longed for her heat. She wondered if the girl would squeal if she plucked her from her hiding spot and moved her to the shadows behind the throne.

Ende and Master Forest stood amongst the crowd, and there still seemed to be too many soldiers in the room. Ana couldn't see Dray, and she wondered if she should have left him. But it would not have helped Ed if a witch had been found with his guard.

The tribute entered and moved gracefully single file down the centre of the room. The watching crowd whispered. Ana closed her eyes and focused on the distant sounds. How beautiful they were, and how much the Near Forest loved the kingdom. Several men jostled amongst themselves, each expecting to be gifted with one of the women and guessing at which of the beauties before them that may be. She heard nothing from the sword master. Would he be gifted one of the women, or had that simply been a threat from the regent?

He sat smugly on the throne, and although Ana was behind him, she could sense his condescending attitude. He glanced around from time to time, but if he was truly worried about her being in the shadows, he would have placed the mage. Perhaps he was busy with his new pets.

She would need to find out what the girls were destined for, but not now. Ed was her first concern. He entered the hall as she thought of him, Belle on his arm and Dray a step behind.

The tribute all turned his way and curtsied. Several members of the crowd bowed their heads, although most simply stood and openly stared.

"Uncle," he said, bowing his head towards the throne.

"I don't know you to claim such a title of endearment," the regent said, pushing up from the throne quickly. "Who do you think you are to appear dressed this way?"

Belle's jaw worked, and Dray drew his sword without hesitation, standing beside the king he had promised to protect. Too many knew who he was for the regent to get away with this.

"Our king is but a boy," the regent continued.

Ed glared at him. "I have been a man long enough now to know what is mine."

The regent scoffed. As soldiers moved silently over the doorways of the throne room, Ana wondered what she could do to help Ed this time.

"How do you explain me then, Uncle?"

"An imposter. You knew our king had fled, and you hoped to claim to be a man the kingdom has not seen. But it will not work, for they know the boy."

"How, when they have not seen me?"

The mage made his way slowly through the silent crowd, his

eyes on the shadows, but Ana doubted he could find her. She wondered if she could ask the shadows to take him far away.

"You have used the powers of the witch," the mage announced, snapping his fingers. The fine clothes returned to the ones he had appeared in the day before.

Ana sighed but remained hidden.

"I have done no such thing," Ed said calmly, and Ana wondered at the young man who had appeared so uncertain when she had met in the mountains.

"That is his father's sword," someone cried out across the room.

"A copy," the mage said, reaching out his hand. Ed drew the sword quicker than she expected—and the mage too, it appeared as he stepped back.

"I am Edwin of Ilia," he said firmly.

"Prove it," the mage whispered. Ed's hair changed to a lighter colour, and his face didn't quite look as it had. "You have been formed," he said, his voice light, although he maintained his distance.

The little dragon growled. As she stepped from her hiding place at the other end of the hall, Ende moved in front of her and Ana was sure she smelt cloth burning. They wouldn't be able to keep that secret for long. She wondered what the little dragon could do when she was unleashed.

Ed pushed Belle behind him as the other women of the tribute whispered amongst themselves.

"You came to steal from us," the regent said, taking a step forward. "Arrest him."

"What would I steal?" Ed asked, something more desperate in his voice.

"The tribute," the regent said as though it answered everything. Belle's face paled as her jaw dropped open.

"She is not part of the tribute," Dray said, taking her by the arm and pulling her further from the regent.

"And you, Captain Sterling, are not what you were. We have

heard of your treachery to the crown."

Ana's heart beat too fast. She wasn't sure what she could do, or what she should do.

"Arrest this imposter," the regent cried, and several men moved forward.

"You are mistaken," Captain Barlow said. "I assure you this is the king."

"I second that," the sword master said, stepping forward. "I have taught him most of his life."

"Are you certain that this man before you is the king?" the regent asked, stepping further into the room and holding out a finger towards Ed.

The soldier stopped, taking in the changes the mage had made. He looked to Dray and then back to Ed.

"Take him!" the regent shouted.

Dray's sword met that of another soldier's as they moved forward. Belle squealed as two others pulled her away.

"You have stolen what is mine," the regent said. "She will be part of the tribute."

"No," Ed pleaded, and Ana could feel his desperation flow across the room.

"Ed!" Belle cried as two men dragged her towards the door.

Ana could save her, but what would that mean for the others? Could she save them all?

"Please," Ed called into the increasing noise of the room. He sounded like the boy Ana knew from the mountains, the orphan. Belle continued to scream as she was dragged from the room.

The mage stepped forward. He held out a hand, his head cocked to the side, then turned to the regent. "I want her." He whispered it, but the sound travelled clearly to Ana's ear.

"Not this one," she whispered, willing the shadows from the depths of the room. "Bring her to me," she whispered.

Someone screamed as darkness enclosed the room.

"Hey!" a soldier called, and Belle screamed again before the candles flickered back to life.

"Where did she go?" Ed asked. Dray shook his head, his sword still held to the neck of the soldier before him.

"Arrest them all!" the regent screamed. Anger and fear flowed over Ana. "Get them from my sight so that I might continue with the formalities of the evening."

The soldiers who had been holding Belle looked at each other and then ran from the room.

Two more soldiers moved in on Ed, taking him by the arms and manhandling him towards the door. Another grabbed at Dray, despite his sword so close to the skin of their fellow soldier. But he swung around, his sword slicing towards the man who approached.

Ana had to act before either of them were hurt. She took a deep breath and appeared in the middle of the room. The world stopped around her.

"I'm sorry," she said to Dray, stepping forward and running her hand over his cheek. "Your Majesty, forgive me," she whispered, turning to Ed and wrapping her arms around him before she pulled him from the room.

"Where are we?" Ed stammered, stepping back from her, a fear she hadn't seen before all too clear on his face. "I can't leave the capital. I need to face him."

"You have," she whispered.

"Ed?" a voice queried in the darkness, and he turned. "Oh Ed," Belle sighed, stepping into his arms and holding him tight. "Thank you," she whispered. Ana nodded her head once.

"This isn't how it was meant to be," he said.

"How was it meant to go?" Ana asked. "Should I have let the mage take her?" She held out her hand to Belle. "Allowed the regent to take you away, lock you up where you couldn't run away? Where he could have you quietly killed?"

The anger was building in her bones, and she wasn't sure why. She had abandoned Dray for this, to keep them safe, and yet she couldn't leave the king to a fate she was all too aware of.

He sighed, his hands clenched, not looking at her. Belle's arms were tight around him.

"Do you want me to take you back?" she asked, her voice soft and kind. "You want to be King, then be King, but don't sacrifice yourself thinking the men in that room would back you."

He turned then and stared openly at her.

"What happened to your face?" Belle asked.

He put a hand to his cheek.

"The mage," Ana said. With a single thought, the clumsy work was undone.

"They will think that you did this, that my uncle is right and you are manipulating a stranger."

"What do you want, Ed?" she asked, her voice dark and scary even to her own ears.

He didn't respond, his glare hateful.

"I can give it to you. A quiet farm? A merchant ship? A crown? You will never find these without me."

He opened and closed his mouth.

"You said he was the king," Belle whispered.

Ana nodded once. "Then let us find your crown." She bowed low, holding out her hand. And at the still-stunned face of the man before her, she disappeared.

Ana pressed her back into the wall of the little room. She blew out a soft breath. She could feel the uncertainty closing in around her. She looked over the narrow cot where not so long ago she had been comfortable, where she had slept a dreamless sleep.

She had promised to protect him, promised to help him be the king he was meant to be, and yet she had failed. Now he trusted her even less than the regent. She stepped forward. She wanted to reappear before him, strike at him while he felt safe, but she knew it wouldn't help her and it wouldn't help Ed. She would have to start again with Ed, earn his trust and find a way to put him back before the people. She closed her eyes and thought of the room she had stolen him from. The women, the tribute, had trusted he was the king, as had many of the soldiers who had travelled with them.

Too many doubted. The mage again had managed to steal the crown from the boy before he had the chance to wear it. Dray. She wiped at the tear.

"Where is he?" she asked.

The shadows called to her, and she followed them through the darkness to the cells beneath the castle. Dark, not light; dry, not frozen. She breathed a sigh of relief as she took the man in, sitting on the edge of the wooden bench that would have served as a bed, the cell not much larger than the one she had been held in.

His armour and sword gone, he was the man who had curled around her during the night. Although when he lifted his dark eyes to her standing on the other side of the bars, it wasn't the same look he had worn when he'd swept her hair back from her face.

With a sigh, she stepped forward and squatted before him, resting her hands on his knees.

"Is he safe?" he asked.

She nodded once.

"Belle?"

She nodded again.

He reached for her and then stopped, pulling his hand away as though she might not really be there.

"I can take you to him," she said.

He shook his head, unable to look away from her.

She dragged in a breath, looking around the small dim space. Shadows moved over the walls, and she nodded. "I can keep you safe," she said, looking back at him. "I would rather do that far from here."

"They will think that you were behind it all."

"The regent would have killed him," Ana said more forcefully.

"I know," Dray said, resting his hand on hers. But as soon as he touched her skin, he lifted his hand away again.

She stood and stepped back, looking at him once more through the bars. "Is this better?" she asked, hoping she didn't sound as hurt as she felt. It was hot and dark, and she only wanted to take him far away. "Do you feel more comfortable with me on this side?"

Something growled within her, within the space around her.

He looked warily around. "Has the mage…"

"They will watch you for me," she said, stepping back and bowing her head. "If he is in danger, you are to bring him to me," she instructed the shadows.

"No," he said, standing quickly and clinging to the bars. "You have to leave me to whatever fate I must face."

"I won't," she said, holding her chin high, feeling the darkness wrap around her. "You are mine, Drayton Sterling." *You are mine.*

32

Ed stood in the doorway of the cottage and looked out over the tall grasses that stretched before him. The light was fading, the sky expansive and pink above him. He pulled at the fancy tunic. In all the changes she had left him looking like a king, but far from it.

"Where in all the hells are we?" he growled at never-ending fields of tall pale grass beyond him.

"It could be the grasslands," Belle whispered. Still dressed in all her finery, she sat in the dust by the door, her legs stretched out and her feet bare as she leaned against the small building and watched the same sky.

"Why did she bring us *here*?" he asked, slamming a fist into the rough wood that surrounded the opening he stood in.

"To keep you safe," Belle's voice was just as quiet, but she didn't look at him.

"I'm sorry," he said, squatting down and reaching out to place his hand on her shoulder. But she was quick to leap to her feet, and she was out of his reach. "I'm somewhat frustrated," he mumbled.

"Really? I would never have guessed that Your Majesty could be annoyed at our current situation."

"Belle," he said more calmly than he felt as he stepped towards her. Despite her sarcastic tone and her arms crossed savagely over her chest, he really just wanted to hold her. Mostly to reassure himself she was real.

She turned her back and looked again at the sky.

"Do you think she will come back?" he asked, unsure if he wanted Ana anywhere near them. She had done what she'd thought was best to save them, although she had left Dray behind. It had been hours since he had seen her, and so she might have returned for him.

"Not after the way you talked to her," Belle snapped.

He nodded slowly. She scared him, far more than he'd ever thought possible. The memory of the darkness that had covered her face when she had allowed the shadows to take the major made him shiver. He was grateful in some ways that the man was gone, yet he wished it wasn't Ana who had created such mayhem.

But her words to him inside the small hut, and the way the darkness clung to her, truly scared him. Belle walked further out into the grasses and then squealed. Ed raced after her, wondering what she was doing as she looked up at him, her skirts held high and her feet sinking into the mud.

He looked down as his own boots squelched, then looked around them at the sea of tall grasses and pushed his way past Belle further into the field. It wasn't a field; it was marshland. He turned slowly, taking in the expanse around them. But there was only grass, although in the distance he thought he could make out another dark hut nestled in the pale stalks.

"What has she done?" he asked.

"Where are we?" Belle asked. "Did she give you the farm she thought you wanted?"

"What do you think she could do?" Ed took Belle by the shoulders.

She shook her head. "I think something slithered over my foot," she whispered.

He scooped her easily into his arms, and she gasped as she wrapped her arms around his neck. He turned back to the hut, or cottage, dark against the pale grass, which had started to turn orange as it reflected the sky. Standing in the doorway, Ana watched them come. The shadows stuck closer to her, clinging as they had before, almost giving the impression that she wasn't quite there, and he wondered if she truly was.

Standing before her, Belle still in his arms, Ed bowed his head at the strange woman he'd thought he had known so well. "What can you do?" he asked.

"Whatever you wish," she said, bowing her head to him, "Your Majesty."

.

ACKNOWLEDGMENTS

The team at Deranged Doctor Designs (DDD) for absolutely brilliant cover design work and all the marketing extras. Thank you for your support and clear emails around what was needed from me to make the magic happen.

TWG members and Melissa for listening and support in all things writing related. Special thanks to Yasmin for taking the time to read my draft and providing ideas to make the story stronger.

Allison E Wright for wonderful editing work to make my sentences smoother and my intentions clearer.

My parents, Francine and Ken Smith. Amazing, supportive people who I don't thank often enough. Thanks for keeping me grounded and being the best grandparents ever.

As always, Temwa for being my biggest supporter.

ABOUT THE AUTHOR

Georgina Makalani survives life as a servant of the public by hiding in her office at lunch time with dragons, witches, a laptop and a little bit of magic.

For more about Georgina and her books visit her website: www.theflowofink.com